THE
MAGICAL
ADVENTURES
OF
PRETTY PEARL

ALSO BY VIRGINIA HAMILTON

Zeely

The House of Dies Drear

The Time-Ago Tales of Jahdu

The Planet of Junior Brown

W.E.B. Du Bois: A Biography

Time-Ago Lost: More Tales of Jahdu

M.C. Higgins, the Great

Paul Robeson:
The Life and Times of a Free Black Man

The Writings of W.E.B. Du Bois

Arilla Sun Down

Justice and Her Brothers

Dustland

The Gathering

Jahdu

Sweet Whispers, Brother Rush

Junius Over Far

A Little Love

Willie Bea & the Time the Martians Landed

The People Could Fly

THE MAGICAL ADVENTURES OF PRETTY PEARL

VIRGINIA HAMILTON

Fic
Ham

A Harper Trophy Book

HARPER & ROW, PUBLISHERS

The Magical Adventures of Pretty Pearl
Copyright © 1983 by Virginia Hamilton Adoff
For information address
Harper & Row, Publishers, Inc., 10 East 53rd Street,
New York, N.Y. 10022. Published simultaneously in
Canada by Fitzhenry & Whiteside Limited, Toronto.

Library of Congress Cataloging in Publication Data
Hamilton, Virginia.
    The magical adventures of Pretty Pearl.

    "A Charlotte Zolotow Book."
    Summary: Pretty Pearl, a spirited young African
god child eager to show off her powers, travels to the
New World where, disguised as a human, she lives among
a band of free blacks who have created their own
separate world deep inside a vast forest.
    [1. Afro-Americans—Fiction] I. Title.
PZ7.HL828Maj 1983   [Fic]   82-48629
ISBN 0-06-022186-0
ISBN 0-06-022187-9 (lib. bdg.)

    (A Harper Trophy book)
ISBN 0-06-440178-2 (pbk.)

            First Harper Trophy Edition, 1986.
                    Designed by Al Cetta

THE
MAGICAL
ADVENTURES
OF
PRETTY PEARL

CAST OF HEROES

Pretty Pearl
A young god child

Mother Pearl
A middle-aged god mother

John de Conquer
The folk hero: the hope of black people
Cast here as the best god
Older brother of Pretty Pearl

John Henry Roustabout
The folk hero: a steel driver on the railroad
Cast here as a god
Oldest brother of Pretty Pearl

Dwahro
A spirit of the gods

Hodag
A folk animal
Cast here as a spirit of the gods

The Fool-la-fafa
A folk fowl: from the African Fula-fafa, or giant woodpecker
Cast here as a spirit of the gods

The Hide-behind
A folk beast
Cast here as a spirit of the gods

Coachwhip
A mythical snake from mountain folklore
Cast here as Virgil Coachwhip

John de Conquer root
A well-known root in black folk medicine
Called the king of the forest
A strong luck charm; its scientific and common names are kept secret

Black Salt
Leader of inside folks

Old Canoe
Leader of Cherokee remnant band

The one hundred fifty and more inside folks

The Cherokee and Shawnee Amerinds

AUTHOR'S NOTE

John de* Conquer and John Henry Roustabout actually exist in American folklore. The creatures Hodag, Fool-la-fafa, Hide-behind and Coachwhip also exist in American folklore. The John de Conquer root is an actual root.

de is pronounced *deh*—eh sound as in red. It stands for *the* throughout the book.

CHAPTER ONE

One long time ago, Pretty Pearl yearned to come down from on high. One clear day it was, she daydreamed of leaving her home on Mount Kenya.

What good it is bein' a god chile, she thought, if I got to hang around up here all de time? What there for me to do when I beat all de god chil'ren at de games, and I learns everythin' so fast?

Great Mount Kenya of Africa was known as Mount Highness by Pretty Pearl and the other gods who lived there. It was a vast and glorious mountain of peaks, valleys, grasslands, forests, bare rock and glaciers. It was also an extinct volcano with a dome almost a hundred miles around. The Kikuyu, Embu and Meru human beings cultivated the lower slopes of the Mount. Some of the lesser gods on high kept a watch over them.

They too many of us gods, Pretty Pearl decided. We too scared to leave de Mount and find out what's goin' on.

I know! she thought all of a sudden. I'll go find my brother, see if he have somethin' for me to do.

Now the most powerful one of the gods who lived on Mount Highness was Pretty Pearl's older brother. He was John de Conquer, and all knew him as the best god.

"Call me 'de Con-*care*,'" John always did say to the lesser gods. And "de Con-*care*" was always the way they called him.

Pretty and de Conquer had an even older brother, also named John, who was the oldest of the three of them. He was John Henry Roustabout. John Henry had left the Mount for way-low ground ages ago.

"I expect John Henry think he 'most human by now," de Conquer had said one day to Pretty. He had frowned his disapproval. "John Henry livin' with ungodly peoples so long. I warn him 'bout that before he left, so."

"Any which way John Henry go, and how far he go, he be trouble for somebody, usually himself," Pretty Pearl had said. She didn't know this to be true. She was only parroting what she had heard lesser gods say.

Can't much remember John Henry, she thought, he been gone so long.

But she had a warm feeling for her oldest brother, and she kept it deep inside. She knew in her god child's heart that he had gone far.

Now she hurried on, searching for her brother John de Conquer.

"You seen John de Conquer?" she asked a lesser god called Nandi.

"He over there in de bamboo grasses," said the god Nandi. "He makin' some him noisy drums for de god chil'ren." Nandi lay on the ground on his back with his legs crossed. He pushed the clouds around by fluttering his eyelashes.

"Humph!" Pretty Pearl said, hurrying away. "Everybody got nothin' to do!"

She entered a forest of bamboo that looked like trees. The bamboo's hollow stems were called culms, and they grew over a hundred feet high.

If these be grasses, Pretty thought as she'd thought before, then they grasses for de giants.

"Grasses for de gods," John de Conquer corrected her, reading her mind.

"Oh!" Pretty exclaimed, jumping back. "John, you scare me! Was I talkin' out loud? I didn't see you lyin' there."

John de Conquer was lying flat, with just his head up against a tall bamboo. His ebony crown was low on his forehead. He had his hands clasped on the nape of his neck. His feet were crossed at his ankles. All around him were unfinished singing drums.

"How you doin', Pretty?" asked the best god, John de Conquer.

"Not too well," answered Pretty Pearl. She sat down beside her brother.

"Not so?" he asked. "Why come—you got fittin' pains agin?"

Occasionally, Pretty complained that she was fitting into god power too fast, worse than most god children, and that she ached all over.

"No fittin' pains," she said. "John, I got nothin' to do with myself."

"Play with de god chil'ren," de Conquer murmured.

"I do," she said. "But I beat all of them. Everybody else be keepin' de place so clean and neat—de forest and de glacier—I can't find nothin' worth even thinkin' about."

"That's somethin'," said de Conquer. "I always have a head full of stuff. Take this here bamboo. De leaves grow directly from de culms. It stand like trees. And it so quiet and peaceful here. Think I'll spend half a whole day here."

"Maybe that de problem," Pearl muttered.

"What's that?" de Conquer asked.

"Been studyin' de god time and de human time," she said. "Half a god day be fifty human years. We all lives too long on de Mount. And got nothin' left to fix."

De Conquer closed his eyes and smiled to himself. He could watch Pearl just as well with his eyes closed. But Pretty didn't know this yet, because she was still so young. There were lots of things she didn't know about de Conquer.

"Gods live forever," de Conquer said. "That be their nature. And they's plenty left to get fixed. What's on you mind, Pretty? What be troublin' you?" he asked softly.

"Oh, John, bro!" she said, excitedly. "I been watchin' and spyin'. Oh, they's things goin' on real strange!"

"Uh-huh," he murmured, like he was about to fall asleep. But John was watching his sister closely. So it begins, he was thinking. She growin' and wishin' for to test her strength.

"John, don't get mad at me!"

"Hmmmm? Why would I ever get mad at my baby sister?" he asked.

"Well," she said, "I notice how you and de other gods don't like to spend too much time off de Mount."

"Why should we?" he asked. "We got all we want right here. We help everythang within our reach. We got our godly minds and our godly thoughts. . . ."

"John, I been spyin' on some of them Embu and Kikuyu. But mostly, spyin' on de way-low ground. Somethin' awful strange goin' on down there."

"You shouldn't ought to go near them kind, Pretty," de Conquer told her. "Best not to interfere with human bein's too much. Course, they in our charge. But most de time, they be work for de lesser gods. Not for you, Pretty. And me, I have no truck with them unless I has to."

"Why not, John?" Pretty asked.

A frown crossed de Conquer's face. "Because they got winnin' ways. They grow on you," he said. "You can't fool around de human bein's too long, else you commence actin' human youself."

[9]

"Is that bad?" she asked.

"That's terrible!" de Conquer said, so loud he caused the bamboo to shake and knock. Pearl jumped back.

"Sorry, Pretty," de Conquer said. "See how just talkin' about them can upset even me?"

"I see," she said. "But John, there be somethin' goin' on."

"You mean with them humans, Kikuyu and Embu and Meru?"

"I means de ones on de way-low ground below Mount Highness. I means de ones who lives at de bottom of things and spread out."

"What about them?" he asked.

"Well, it most strange," she said. "I spy de ones who out gatherin'. Some other ones come grab holt them, hit them and carry them off somewheres. Don't know where. It all seem most strange, though."

Grimly, de Conquer nodded. "You been spyin', all right. You must've strained you god chile's vision to see so far," he said.

"You right about that," Pretty said. "It give me a head-ache, so I only done it twice. But John, I have a longin' to go down there, see for myself. I got de most strong desire to know what happen to de ones that got grabbed up and taken."

"So," de Conquer said. He closed his eyes. What he saw in his visions behind his eyes made him frown again. He could see what was going on right now.

"John?" Pretty said, softly. "You asleep?"

"No'm," he said.

"Well? What must I do?" asked Pretty. "Can I go down there, John? Can I? I feels I has to go down there!" She didn't tell him she was afraid to go alone.

"You askin' or tellin'?" He opened his eyes suddenly and gazed at her.

The look of John de Conquer made Pretty Pearl bow low.

But then John smiled and reached out to gently touch her shoulder. "You my baby sister," he said kindly. "How can I turn down a request from you?"

"Oh, John, do you mean it?" she said, straightening up again.

"Course I do—what I say?" de Conquer said. "But I can't let you go alone."

She was glad of that. " 'Cause way-low ground gone be scary?" she asked him.

"Worse than scary," he said.

"Ooh!" she said. "Best I take one of de lesser gods or some god chil'ren with me."

"I'll go with you, Pretty," he said. "I don't trust anybody but me with you, and all them human bein's spread every whichaway."

So it was that Pretty Pearl got her wish. She and her brother floated down the great mountain. They said a fond farewell to the lesser gods and the god children as they made their way down. For as de Conquer explained to Pretty, they might want to take their time.

"Gone leave a part of you on de mountain, Pretty,"

said de Conquer. "Since you a god chile, you got more than one part. You got a part that is 'most grown up. You won't be needin' it jes' yet." He smiled at his joke. He would leave the grown woman part of Pretty to watch over the mountain. He could do that because he was the best god and power. He could leave the woman part, or summon her.

"Them god chil'ren need a maw woman watch over them." He chuckled. "Gone leave them you, maw woman, name of Mother Pearl!" De Conquer laughed and laughed.

"I don't feel nothin' missin'," said Pretty, smiling. "You sure you taken she maw woman from me?"

"Sure I'm sure," de Conquer said. "You don't need de grown-up yet. So let she stay to home on de Mount!"

"Good!" Pretty said, as they made their way.

At last Pretty Pearl and de Conquer came to great Lake Victoria. The lake was known as Ukerewe by the many human beings from the way-low ground. Pretty Pearl and de Conquer didn't slow down at the shore.

"Take me a swim," she said. And she slipped under the water with the grace of springtime.

John de Conquer didn't care to get his ebony crown wet. He liked floating above the water. Tribes of shore-folk human beings, even animals surrounding the great water, bowed to see the best god glide on the air.

Pretty Pearl swam right along, backstroking and cooling herself. When she was completely refreshed, she and de Conquer headed for the shore.

"Be a mighty sweet swim," she told him. She sat down

while an ibis fanned her dry. Then she and de Conquer headed farther west.

"This way, Pretty," de Conquer told her, taking her hand. "We follow de sun."

Not long, and the two of them came upon a sorrowing crowd moaning through the tall grass. Staying hidden, they witnessed some other ones who forced the crowd along with prodding poles. The crowd wept pitifully. All were shackled—neck, wrists and ankles—with chains. Dirty and tired, they jibbered and jabbered in twenty tongues.

"This what you be talkin' about?" de Conquer asked, gazing sadly at the poor human beings.

"Yes!" cried Pretty. "It what I spy. What do you make of it, John?" She looked on in awe.

"This I make of it," said de Conquer. "What you see be subtraction."

"What?" said Pretty.

"A taking away," de Conquer said, his voice angry. "For de sum of a human or a god be similar. It de life and freedom he born with. But subtract de life, you got no kind of freedom. Subtract de freedom, you got no life."

"I . . . I don't understand," she said.

"De crowd in chains is enslaved," de Conquer explained. "It mean de other ones has taken de crowd's freedom away. Oh, I seen it happen before. In de time of de Israelites. Best not interfere or you be come actin' human, too. Be come either a slaver or de enslaved."

"Think I understand it now," Pretty said.

[13]

"Understand it, learn it and weep," he said.

"Whew! De odor of them moanin' ones is awful!" she said. "But I don't suppose none of it's they own fault. Oh, John, bro! They hurt gets me deep inside!"

John's instinct was to take Pretty Pearl away. Free her from the sight of shackled human beings and their tormentors. But he listened to her hurt and her caring for the peoples. He understood. For every god child must pass the god test if it was to go on to the next godly plane.

Jes' de way a god become a god father, he thought. I still got that last plane to reach, even though I de best god, de Conquer. Maybe this slavery de beginnin' of Pretty Pearl's test for god woman plane. Didn't realize it would come so soon. She fittin' so!

De Conquer sighed deeply, then said, "Let's follow along behind this human crowd, see what comin' down, be all right with you?"

"Be fine with me," said Pretty. "It what I like about you, brother. You be always god willin'."

The shackled crowd walked long and hard. It was given no food at all. A little maggoty water was poured over the people's heads. At last they were pushed and pulled into barracoons at the shore of the ocean. These were confining pens where they were kept until the tall ships came. When the slave ships arrived, the kidnaped victims were forced aboard. They were barricaded in dark, steamy places belowdecks.

Pretty Pearl had become hypnotized by the sounds and

smells, the whips snapping and the cries of human beings enslaved. She followed along and boarded the ship. So compelled was she to help the poor peoples, she took on a look just like one of them.

John de Conquer would not interfere with a caring so great as hers.

Quickly, now, he thought, before they think she human, too.

At once, he changed himself and Pretty into albatrosses. They flew high up to the mainmast.

"Wheeee!" said Pretty Albatross. "This so fun! You some power, John!"

"Up here we can face de wind," de Conquer Albatross told her. He enjoyed showing her his power. "No slave owner of de ship dare come near two albatrosses up so high."

"Good we can't smell de stench of poor, beaten peoples up here, too," said Pretty Albatross. She held tightly to her perch.

"We be birds of ill wind now," said de Conquer Albatross.

"We not gods no more?" she asked.

"Oh, we that, but in a *fowl* sense," he said. "We could be hurt by humans if they could reach us."

"I see," she said.

"But to harm us would be unlucky for seaman, so they think," he told her. "That slave driver down below us fear him most perishing in de ocean. Think him, albatross fly down, pluck out him eyes."

"How you know so, John?" asked Pretty Albatross.

"Saw it in him glance at de sea. We secure, way up here," de Conquer said.

The two albatrosses had a safe voyage, with fresh wind rippling their feathers all the way to the land of new colonies.

Weeks passed, and they landed at Savannah, Georgia, along with one hundred eight half-dead black African human beings. Human prisoners, soon to be slaves.

The albatrosses gazed down from their perches at the height of the main topsail. They could see a far, far way. Closer below them they spied Fort Savannah on the Savannah River. They spied the cotton market over there, the auction block for buying and selling people and the holding pens to keep the people caught until they were sold. They saw fine houses, parks and squares. They studied the live oak trees hung with Spanish moss, for they'd never before seen such a sight.

"Lookin' jes' like a forest city," sang the bird de Conquer. "So much gray-green moss hangin' and swayin'."

"I've looked everywhere," screeched Pretty Albatross, "but I don't see our brother, John Henry Roustabout."

"He nowhere near us now," whistled de Conquer Albatross. "John Henry been here but he gone. He gone, gone John." This made the bird de Conquer cackle.

"Glad he's gone," sang Pretty Bird. "If him stay around here, him might end up like moss hangin' from de oak. 'Fraid for my big brother. Don't remember much. Just feelin's."

"You feels for him 'cause he yours and mine," said de Conquer Bird.

"It seem like I know John Henry and could recognize him if I ever see him," she said.

"I know how much you care for him, so," he murmured. "But don't you believe it. Nothin' and nobody gone moss hang our brother de Roustabout."

"Hope you right," she said, and let thoughts of John Henry go. All around in the air, she was sensing the misery of one kind of folk and the strength of another kind.

Be clear as black and white, she thought.

"Planters be de big mens here," warbled John de Conquer Albatross.

"Is that right?" sang Pretty Pearl Albatross. "Let's get us gone from this sad place, brother, 'til I have rested."

"We gone," whistled de Conquer. And away they flew.

They found the red clay hills of Georgia colony, and they landed among the hot hills. They shed wings and beaks and feathers of albatrosses. They became their godly selves.

"Now, we got to wait some," de Conquer said. He laid himself down deep under the blood-red southern soil.

Pretty Pearl did the same as her brother. "Why we got to wait, John?" she asked when she had rested. "Ain't we goin' to help de shackled crowd?"

"We won't wait long, maybe a couple, three god days. Be like two, three centuries in human time. You can't move too fast with human bein's. You got to figure them out."

"What's to figure?" she said. "You said it just be sum and subtraction."

"Yes, but when you tally it, you don't want no mistake," he said.

Pretty Pearl and John de Conquer waited one hundred years of dark time in which slave ships came and went and the people broke their backs in the fields. The people earned no wages for their labor. It was a hundred years when no one came to free them, in which a very few freed themselves. Most stayed enslaved.

"Shoot!" said Pretty. "A hundred years seem like more than one ole day! Seem like to me it's forever!" She began wondering whether her brother was afraid of the human beings. "John? You figure we'll ever get up from here?"

De Conquer grunted. "Hear them peoples cryin' like wild to be free in Africa again?"

"I hear them," she said. "So why don't you free them and take them back home?"

"I can't do that," he said. "De human life got to unfold and be written."

"John! You mean it's written somewhere when they's to be free?"

"Everythin' be written of de humans, Pretty. But some of it not too clear. I do know this. A long time ago we learn not to interfere with human progress. You got to let de human bein's roll on out and hope they gits better. You try to make them better, and they will twist and turn until they find a worse way to hurt one another." De Conquer shook his head. "I could spend all my time tryin' to stop them. Because they never content. They always lookin' to find a way to be above some other ones of them."

"So you just go on and let them hurt and 'slave some of theyselves," Pretty said. She sounded disgusted.

"De shackled crowd will be freed, most prob'ly, but not jes' yet," said de Conquer. "It will get written. But it got to unfold some more, don't you see."

Pretty Pearl did see. For god's sake! she thought. I don't care for de way de Conquer be runnin' things!

De Conquer smiled to himself. Patience, he thought. For that, too, was part of the god test for Pretty Pearl. She must learn patience.

John de Conquer was older and bigger than Pretty Pearl. He was smarter, of course. But truly, the god book of human life was written as that life rolled along.

Pretty Pearl of the gods was clever, and she had outwitted many a god child in her long kind of time.

Him too used to havin' his way, shoot, she was thinking about de Conquer. He seen too much, maybe. Too much human bad. It spoiled him. But this de first I see of it. And if I had his power, I sure would use it now!

"You figure to get up soon?" Pretty asked de Conquer on the second god day they had been down from Mount Highness. It was the eighteenth century of humans, and very hot out. Pretty's left foot had gone to sleep. The sorrow of the darker peoples had got behind her eyes. It traveled within her. It found a place in the heart of her.

"I'm dreamin' me a mighty fine dream," de Conquer murmured. "Come one more godly day—be a hundred human years—come war. And after war, de peoples is freed."

"But John!" said Pretty, pouting. "This waitin' is drivin' me crazy. Feel like goin' out there and smashing some slaver heads!"

"Can't let you do that, baby sis," he said. "Violence make it no better."

"Then you do something! John, please!"

"All right, tell you what I'm gone do, Sis Pretty," he said.

"What's that?" she asked.

"Gone let loose a couple my best spirits to help de black peoples."

"Are you now!" she cried.

"Absolutely!" he said. "While freedom wait its time."

Right away, John de Conquer's hard and true spirits caused trouble for the owners of the enslaved.

The spirits took on form. One of them was Johnson and the other was Riley. They urged slaves to run, whispering words of wisdom, words of Africa, in captive ears. The slaves were now field hands, who worked in the fields from dawn to dusk. Once the black folks got the word from the de Conquer spirits, they knew who it was in the fields with them. They knew that the African god was behind them. And they carried on.

Some faded away to the north on the Underground they had made. Others hid food and clothing in the cane for those who would run. Some lifted their arms and rose on the air with magic. They remembered how to fill their hearts with the de Conquer power. Old women hid away newborn babes so they wouldn't get sold from the mothers who must stay.

Johnson worked as a shed man. He taught freedom to other shed men. He and Riley never stayed on a plantation longer than it took to start unrest. Others sang of Riley or Johnson, so all those who were afraid would gather courage:

> *Oh, Riley walked de water,*
> *On a long, hot summer's day.*
> *Oh, Riley he is gone, gone,*
> *Oh, Riley he is gone,*
> *On a long, hot summer's day.*

"That's a *good* song, John," said Pretty. And she was made to see what his spirits could do.

Her brother murmured. He had gone back to sleep. Pretty Pearl sighed.

Be clear John not ready yet to leave de red soil.

And there came the time of war a century later.

"Awful. Awful!" whispered Pretty. All she could do was watch. She had little power to do much else, and that made her so unhappy.

After the war, black folks were said to be free, just as John had said they would be. But former slaves had no homes, no food or work and no place to go. They were starving to death.

"That's no kind of way to die," said Pretty, watching it all. "You call that freedom?" She glanced at her brother. Still sleeping, dreaming his dreams.

Pretty peered through blood-soaked soil, and she saw the peoples getting hurt in one way or another. She did not know that her brother watched and saw and knew everything she felt and thought.

"Enough's 'bout all I can take," she said. "Know a little I can do."

And one fine evening she slipped out from under southern soil. She gathered talismans. They were mojo magic charms from African mysteries some of the dead had left behind. Several of the charms Pretty wound around her wrists and ankles. Those that wouldn't fit she wove through the waves of her coal-black hair. They were like memories, human history she would keep close. After a time she was drawn back to sit next to her brother.

"How you restin', John?" she asked sweetly. But she was feeling tired and irritable. It happened to be a white, shrouded evening of mists. She wanted to *do* something more.

"Restin' smooth and easy, thank you, Sis Pretty," John answered her. "Don't worry 'bout me."

"Then let's play us a game, 'cause I'm feelin' blue," she said.

"All right with me," de Conquer said. He felt proud of her patience. And he waited for her to grow strong enough in herself that she would not need him. He didn't know when, exactly, that would happen. He knew only that it would.

Bet it won't be long now, he thought.

"Even though I be still asleep," he said, smiling his de Conquer smile, "I can play any ole card game."

"Humph!" Pretty Pearl said softly. She smiled at him and said no more. But she was thinking, You may play it, but can you beat *me*?

CHAPTER TWO

They played a sleight-of-hand card game that had no end and no winner. It was called Mount Highness Five-Card Deal You Down. It was named long ago and it was a game of gods and mountains. No mortal could understand it.

Three cards appeared in Pretty's hand, dealt to her by the mountain.

"There!" she cried, throwing down three simooms that were violent winds of desert Africa.

The far-off mountain dealt cards to de Conquer. And John countered Pretty with two harmoniums. They were all the cards he had, and they were enough. They sucked in Pretty Pearl's sand-heavy winds and forced them through metal reeds. Suddenly, eerie tones of mystery made an irresistible music. Hearing it, all of Mount Highness's spirits threw their cards down.

Because Pretty Pearl and John de Conquer were fitting power and best power, they came out on the broad side of even. The best god, de Conquer, never tried to win, although his sister did.

"Don't feel like playin' no more," said Pretty Pearl, pouting. She had so hoped to beat her brother this time.

"You'd have more fun if you didn't try so hard," de Conquer told her. "Nobody ever win de Five-Card Deal You Down. Be like me and don't care one way or the other."

"Don't care don't have no never mind," Pretty told him.

"And don't need any," de Conquer said back.

"Don't care don't have no home, neither," she said.

"I got a home," said John. "De land I'm layin' down in is my home for now."

"You always got to have de last say," she said. "Come on, John, let's sing us some tunes." She was itching to have something to do.

The two of them made up songs—that is, Pretty Pearl brought them up most of the time and de Conquer joined in when he felt like it. Right now he started sleeping and dreaming. While Pretty brought up a song, de Conquer hummed it in his sleep, preparing his voice for better times.

The way Pretty brought up a song happened because

she was fitting into power and quick to see what people felt in their hearts. The songs were out of the hearts of folks everywhere. Pretty knew the songs as well as she knew the souls of peoples everywhere:

> There's too much of worriment goes in a bonnet;
> There's too much of ironing goes in a shirt.
> There's nothing that pays for the time you waste on it;
> There's nothing that lasts us but trouble and dirt.

> Oh, life is a toil and love is a trouble,
> And beauty will fade and riches will flee.
> Oh, pleasures they dwindle and prices they double,
> And nothing is as I could wish it to be.

"That's nice," said de Conquer, waking himself. "Where it come from, Pretty?"

"That little tune?" she said.

"Uh-huh," he murmured. "Your soprano voice is such pleasure. How came de song?"

"Come from a diary," she said. "I see it there in a fair woman's book, and she cryin' over it. Her sons killed in de Civil War, and now she workin' so hard. That's how de song be brought up in me. That woman never found a good time."

Pretty and de Conquer fell silent as a period of better time called Reconstruction spread over the land. It was in human time a time to make life easier for some folks. But good times never came. Some of the former slaves were given land to work themselves. The Civil War was done with. Yet there were bad folks who fought the free folks and took away their land and what little else they had.

Another human year Pretty lifted her head, looking all around. She lay in the soil next to her brother. She was bored, sick and tired being so still down beneath the ground.

Think I smell smoke, she thought.

She sat up, shaking off the soil. Sure enough, over there and not far she spied burned-out slave quarters where folks still lived. A charred black shape hung from a limb of a poplar tree beside a smoldering cabin.

"Bet that's no apple hangin' from de branch, neither," Pretty whispered to the bitter night. "And not no pear nor gourd hangin' so still. Be my poor heart hangin' there—yes, it is!"

Next, Pretty spied Hunger coming near, running down a helpless child. She felt the heartbeat of the child and knew at once what sort of beast Hunger was.

Him not quite a shade and not near a spirit, she thought. Be de shape of a thing that has been free in de world since de world begin.

As Hunger ran by, Pretty reached out and grabbed his hind part.

Don't think de Conquer be mad at me if I take care of this one awful shape, she thought.

She dragged Hunger to her and gave him a pounding. Oh, it felt good to take care of something instead of sitting and waiting! she thought.

Pretty loosened one of her wrist charms. She wound

it through Hunger's gray and hairy ear and out his other cold and wrinkled one.

"Get ye gone from here!" Pretty screamed in Hunger's mouth hole.

All at once John de Conquer sat up, laughing. He caught hold of the helpless child Hunger had been chasing and hugged her in his arms. He held her tight a moment to calm her, and he breathed the high, cool places of Mount Kenya in her face.

"Remember me, little Dora," he murmured, for Dora was the child's name. "Keep close de breath of John 'de Con-*care*.' And you always be free."

"I'll remember you, de Con-*care*," the child whispered. She laughed happily. John gave her a gentle toss in the air. She tumbled for two miles to a place where a widow woman lived in a cave. The widow woman needed a child to love.

Dora was out of sight. John de Conquer doubled over in stitches, watching Hunger. Old Hunger had become so terrified of de Conquer's and Pretty's power, he'd fallen into a hole full of 'possum ghosts. De Conquer split his sides to see Hunger leap out of there just as fast, straight up in the path of a screech owl. Hunger thought the 'possum ghosts must be alive, they played dead so well. He believed the owl, invisible in the night, must be some kind of spell trying to get inside of him.

Pretty Pearl laughed so hard, she cried. "Ohh! Ohh!" she cried breathlessly. "Oh, John, I'm so glad we taken care of ole Hunger like that. It so much fun!"

De Conquer nodded in agreement. He was happy to

see that Pretty was coming right along, growing strong in herself. Patience and action had to be balanced.

"If I had me a Gatlin' gun," he said, "I'd give it a crank and blow Hunger full of holes, de way I seen them do a man condemned."

Hunger was there, caught in the de Conquer power. "But I don't have me a gun," said de Conquer. "It wouldn't finish Hunger off no way."

" 'Cause why?" asked Pretty Pearl.

" 'Cause a shape of a thing will always be. All I can do is a little bit of harm to de shape."

"I already pounded him shape," said Pretty. "I shouldn't've, but I did."

"I know that. I was watching, and you was awful provoked," said John. He turned to Hunger, powerfully caught. "I'm a peaceable sort," he said to the beast, "but I'm gone pinch you and pinch you until you think you bein' pinched when I'm not even thinkin' 'bout you to pinch you."

With that John let Hunger go. He and Pretty watched Hunger flee through the night. All the way, Hunger was caught by de Conquer. It surely hurt the shape of him to be caught so. It didn't make him any less of Hunger. But he certainly grew tired of hurting. All of the rest of his empty days and nights, Hunger felt de Conquer. He felt the pinch.

"You see," said de Conquer to Pretty, "when you start something, you must know how to finish it." He lay back down in the soil.

"You finished it," she said.

"You started it," he said.

"But nothin' much changed," she said. "Hunger still in de world."

De Conquer closed his eyes and smiled to himself. She comin' along, he thought. "We do what we can," he said.

Now was a long time and a turning-worse time. And now came a sour and tainted time. Pretty Pearl watched the free folks running and running and no place to go. Hiding themselves in the blood-red hills of Georgia. There were bad folks around, robbers and thieves, trying to take from the free folks what little they had.

It had been a long kind of time of patience for Pretty Pearl. She had an inkling that de Conquer was trying to show her something. So she continued to keep a close watch over the poor people as they went to live deep in the dark, in secret places of the piny lands. They had a few farm animals with them. They had themselves a time keeping the animals in safe places.

Pretty could see fairly far in her vision by now. Suddenly she leaned forward and squinted.

"Uuum-huum!" she murmured. "I know it's got to be high time now. Brother? John?" she called under the ground. "John, bro, hurry up, please, I do think it's just about time."

"Time for what? What time it is?" John de Conquer asked, grinning to himself. He sat up. Red clay soil fell off his nose and his ears and his ebony crown.

"It dark time, lookin' not so good, but maybe could get better soon, time," Pretty Pearl said. "It just about time for us, and right on time, too. Come on, John."

"Not now," said de Conquer. "Not now." He was seeing all the folks hiding out. He could see them as though they were right in front of him. He feigned a yawn. He knew it was just about time for Pretty to free herself.

"I say it's time!" cried Pretty. She was standing, stamping her foot.

"Aw, sis," de Conquer muttered, "de folks over there be doin' all right for themselves. They don't need me at all."

"Who says they don't?" Pretty said. "Yes, they do too. They need somebody like you to lead them and give them courage."

Somebody *like* me, he thought. But Pretty must find this out herself.

"You de hope bringer, John," she said. "Every time folks discover you, they can't help laughing."

"I know that irresistible urge I give peoples to laugh," he said, "but it still ain't de time for me."

"Every time poor folks is havin' some trouble, John, it got to be your time. You de best god."

"I de best god, 'tis true," he said. "But you gettin' me mixed up with you."

John de Conquer waited. He could see on Pretty's face that certain godly knowledge was coming to her.

"When there is *some* trouble," he said gently, "it's your time, Pretty. But when there's a whole heap, never stop, everywhere *real* trouble, then you'll see me comin'. I may not like much truckin' with humans, but I never turns my back on de poor peoples."

"Well, it seem to me there's real trouble all over de

place," she said to her brother.

John didn't say anything. He needn't tell her all the work he had to do.

"I do understand what you mean by *some* trouble, John. You mean I can help out some peoples hidin', that's what you mean."

De Conquer stayed quiet. His eyes were full of love and caring for his sister, fitting in.

"Shoot," she said, softly, "I thought we would stick together a long kind of time."

"No," he said.

"Well, I sure am sure this be my time to move," she said.

"You positive?" de Conquer asked.

"Positive," she said.

"Well, then, glad you ready," he said. "Every god chile be havin' a chance on its own one time." He grinned. "Figure about seventy-five human years from now, if all goes well, you'll see me agin, Sis Pretty," he said, as lightly as he could.

"Really?" she said. "That's not so long." She was feeling grown up. But now was a time of parting, and it made her sad. She braced herself, keeping her voice strong. "John, you remember de time it rain forty days and forty nights? I didn't see you for two hundred years."

"Took me a lot of work to clean up de place after that kind of downpour," he said.

"Was it bad back then, John?" Pretty asked.

"It was awful bad," he said. "Animals at de tops of

trees. Houses upside down. And babalabalas stuck in de ground."

"What in de world are bah . . . bah . . . ?" She couldn't get the word out.

"Never did find out what they was," said John. "Had to leave them stuck in de mud, clean de place up and get back on Mount Highness in de short time I had for that work. I did think to ask them names, though."

"But them things must still be stuck in de mud someplace," Pretty said.

"Maybe they went down de drain with ever'thang else," de Conquer said. "I really couldn't tell you."

"Down de drain! John de Conquer, you makin' it all up to tease me!"

He was making it up to keep her mind off their parting.

"No, I'm not makin' it up," he protested. "I had orders to sweep everythang I could down de drain. Well, I couldn't sweep de babalabalas because them be stuck. Anytime you find somethin' covered with mud and it won't come free, you can be sure right there is a babalabala. But I think most of them went down de drain when him suction got too strong."

"Then where's there a drain?" Pretty asked, eyeing John. She had her hands on her hips.

"I swept everythang didn't get on that ark out into de ocean. Then I pull him plug. Now, would I lie?"

"You would lie, all right, and you lyin' now," she said. She burst out laughing. "John, you can tell more tales!"

"I'm tellin' you true," he said, with all the seriousness

[33]

he could muster. "At de bottom of de Atlantic Ocean, you can see him plug and de chain. But don't pull on de chain. Whatever you do, don't go pullin' him plug out again."

Pretty giggled. "You hopeless, John," she said.

"Who, me?" he said.

"Yeah, you!" she answered.

They fell silent. After a while, Pretty said, "Feel I have to go now, John. Is it all right?"

"You do what you has to," he told her. "It your time."

"You sure you don't want to come with me?"

"Sorry, Sis Pretty. Best you go ahead on. You gettin' to be the right size, fit for travelin'." He laughed. "I can't come jes' yet. Got thoughts to ponder."

"You always were a dreamer," she said fondly. "Have to go by myself, I guess. Never thought that when I come down off de Mount, I'd be doin' somethin' like this."

Pretty sighed and thought about which way to go. De Conquer waited, which was his way. But she already knew exactly where she ought to end up. He didn't have to tell her.

"I'm goin' in de forest to look in on them peoples," she told her brother. "If I lives like they do, maybe I can help them."

"That makes sense," said John. "But be careful. Them human bein's be awful tricky. They has most winnin' ways." De Conquer pondered a moment. "I'd feel better about you bein' around them if you'd take somethin' of mine with you."

"What's that?" she asked.

[34]

"Watch," he said.

John de Conquer began to grow a bush on his chest. It was a small, neat bush at first. But when it reached its full height and width, de Conquer reached down under his rib cage and broke off a large piece of root. Next, he pulled out two long strands of his coarse, kinky hair and wound them and wound them until he had made a strong, wiry hair chain. Then he divined a hole through one end of the root. The hole was the size of a pinhead. John pulled the hair chain through the hole. And carefully, lovingly, he tied the necklace around his sister's neck.

"Why, it's de richest and darkest . . ."

". . . John de Conquer root, you call it," he explained.

". . . I ever did see!" Pretty finished.

Ever after, the dark, full, mojo-mystery, conjure necklace would be known as the John de Conquer root.

"I'll cherish it, John."

"Keep it power secret," he said.

"I surely will," Pretty told him.

"Here de rules about it," said John, as the full-grown bush disappeared inside him.

"Rules?"

"Jes' listen," he said. "De rules be, you wears it de Conquer root and you don't promise it to *nobody*."

"Yeah, all right," she said, in a hurry to be gone.

"Patience! Listen!"

"I'm listenin'!" she said. But half her mind was already on the way.

"You can flake some of it off for folks, but don't take it off for *nobody*," de Conquer warned. "Never scare no humans with it 'less they about to scare and hurt you first. And *never ever* hurt no human chil'ren with it out of spite or anger. Obey my rules, and there be no power in de world gone do you better than my John de Conquer root."

"We'll see," she said shyly. She'd always hoped to be more power than her brother someday.

Don't like de sound of that, thought John. But he kept his peace.

She'll come out of it, he thought. She jes' fittin' herself strong.

"John, how you gone find me agin when I go off now and leaves you here?" asked Pretty. "Don't know how long I'll be one place and another."

"Oh, I got my ways," he said. "You leave, and I'll find you one more time."

"And then you and me will be close again, just like always," she said.

"Like always," he agreed.

Pretty Pearl and John de Conquer put together her belongings. She had those talismans she had picked up from the ground where they lay beside dead heroes. She had her own butterfly weed. This she kept in a silver sachet bag with dried orange flowers and fleshy root, too. Mixed together, these made a medicine that increased perspiration. It made an unsettled stomach come up.

De Conquer shaped the talismans, the magic charms and Pearl's medicine into a bow ribbon of ebony. He made a clasp for it. Pretty watched closely, studying the use of power. John clipped the ribbon in her hair.

"That lookin' real pretty, too," he told her. "Anytime you need extra spells or him medicine, you just rub that ebony ribbon for de spells. You pinch it when you want him medicine. It'll give you de hoodoo hand."

"Thank you, John," she said.

"Welcome," John said. Then, "Sis Pretty, shouldn't you have some other clothes to wear?" Both de Conquer and Pretty wore simple god clothes. "Clothes should be like them ones de human chil'ren wear," he said.

"I suppose so," she said. "But not no more than two clothes, John. Don't want to seem some better than most de chil'ren."

"And maybe two shifts of larger sizes," de Conquer said. "In case you needs to become de maw woman you leaves on de Mount."

"Will I know when I need to, John?" she asked.

"De maw woman will know, if you don't," he said.

"Thought I was goin' out on my own," she said, pouting.

"Well, you are, Pretty," he told her. "But god chil'ren, they don't have no fathers or mothers, like human chil'ren. They have they parts that they must fit. Part god woman, part god mother, et cetera. Some don't never make de changeover. But you can call on de parts and rearrange de parts, too. Like a god woman mother. De mawmaw woman."

"I see," said Pretty.

"Everybody respect de maw woman. The humans is use to de womens that take care of de baby chil'ren. They

[37]

won't see no difference in you maw woman from theirs."

"Then make de shifts of larger sizes," Pretty told her brother. "I always did like baby watching."

"Be glad to," he said. In a blinking of his dark, steady eyes, de Conquer formed up two small-sized garments first. They had neck holes and arm holes, but hardly any shape to them. He made them out of gunnysacks of hemp. He made them worn and soiled. "So you won't look too good," he told Pretty.

Next, he made two larger garments with sleeves. They were both a dull gray color and they had wide, white aprons to be worn over them at the waist and tied in back in bows.

The larger shifts reached to the ground.

"I do loves to see you 'power' things," said Pretty. "But can't you add some flowers in a pattern, at least down de front of them? Them sure are some sad-sack dresses."

"Nothin' doin'," said de Conquer. "You want be lookin' like any mawmaw woman, or de chil'ren who been runnin' in their clothes. And sleepin' and eatin; and livin' de whole time in them. Only time you able to clean you clothes be when you wash them in a river or stream, and dry them in de sun. Nope. No flowers allowed."

Pearl sighed. "All right, John." But when I learn how he does some power like that, I'm gone dress fancy!

That made John smile to himself. His sister had spunk. But she wouldn't learn the power, nor fit it, all at once. He would have Mother Pearl to keep a watch over the child.

[38]

Kindly now, John de Conquer said, "I'll give you some of my spirits for you very own. Would you like that, Pretty? They's good company."

"Oh! Oh, John! Do you mean it? I'd like that fine!" she said.

"You can let them take on form and size anytime you want them to," he said. "Jes' as long as you keep control. You got de power for that."

"I do?" she said. "I didn't know that."

"How could you know? You ain't got de spirits yet," de Conquer said. "Anyway, don't be lettin' them challenge you too hard. All you have to do is call on you de Conquer root to bring them spirits in or string them out. See, they held in de spirit world of de root. They lined up in there like little ornaments on a string."

"Gracious!" exclaimed Pretty. "Do I have to give them back to you when I'm finished with them?" she asked. Her eyes were wide with wonder.

"No siree," he said. "I been only they keeper, that's all."

"So now I has power over *them*," she said, beaming at her brother.

"That's right. And use it wisely," he said. "De knowledge of what power is, how to find it and fathom it, how to use it, will come. It will come from you, Pretty, for it inside you already."

"Oh, John!" she exclaimed. "Everything is gettin' so excitin'! And can I have my favorite of de spirits? You really gone give them to me?"

"Sure, Sis Pretty. What I say?"

"Then I pick Dwahro and de Fool-la-fafa!" cried Pretty.

"You mean that African *fula*-fa-fa," said John. "He just de woodpecker."

"Whatever he be, him de *fool*," said Pretty, "and always talkin' fowl. And when I call him out to stand beside me, I wants him six feet tall with a hammer beak half that size."

"You got it," said de Conquer. "*Fool*-la-fafa it is!"

"And gimme de Hodag for a work horse," she said. "And de Hide-behind, too."

"Now, I can see that Hodag," said John, "for it has a sharp, curved tail can cut down trees or a field of corn or wheat. But what you want that Hide-behind for?"

"Just for fun," she said primly. "So it can follow some bad folks or some enemies." She giggled. "In de woods, they feel its presence. But when they whirl around to see, there's nothin' there! De Hide-behind done jumped behind a tree!"

"But it can't do nothin' else, jes' hide behind things and scare bad folks and enemies to death," said John.

"Yes!" she said. "I wants it. It might come in handy."

"You got it," said John.

"That's all of them I want," Pretty told him. "And Dwahro, who can look so silly. He simple in de head, sometimes, act like."

"Dwahro know de ins and outs of them old slave streets," said de Conquer. "He fool around with some of them folks when we leave Fort Savannah. I didn't mind. I let him for a while, but he back with me now." De

Conquer chuckled. "Dwahro can *feel* and tell and know better than most. You can always trust him to carry out you commands."

"Good," Pretty said. "That's them, then, de Fool-la-fafa, de Hodag, de Hide-behind and Dwahro. Just four."

"Four, and they are yours," said de Conquer. He gave over the spirits to Pretty for her to keep in the de Conquer root. Black shades were seen to flow from John de Conquer into the necklace he had placed around his sister's neck. The root itself seemed to grow darker.

"You keep that de Conquer root safe, girl," John told her. "Best you wear it outside, so you can grab it quick if you need to."

"All right, brother," Pretty Pearl said. She whispered to the root, "Spirits, get ready! We fixin' to go!"

John de Conquer folded his sister tightly to him. "You take care now, you hear?" he told her kindly. "Be careful."

"I will, John. Ooh, I hates to leave you, but I'll be seein' you, bro, by 'n' by." She hugged her brother as hard as she could, and gave him a big kiss. "So long, brother."

"Bye-bye, Sis Pretty!" His voice shook with the sadness of parting. "Know I love you!"

"Know I love you back!" she said. She forced back the tears.

De Conquer released her. Pretty Pearl turned on her heel and headed on her way.

CHAPTER THREE

John de Conquer waved and settled down in the southern soil to dream his dreams. In some dreams he conquered the land and he conquered the ocean. Suddenly he was out of the ground, hurrying. He carried with him a side drum called a hypocrite. That hypocrite had more tones than anybody ever heard of. It was a singing drum. Wherever there was real trouble and the work was hardest and life most cruel, people would hear that old hypocrite *boom-boom*ing. It made them laugh. "Ol' hypocrite on de road again!" the people would shout. "John de Conquer out of de ground again!" Word had got around about de Conquer by that time. He was out of the ground for sure. Whenever and wherever.

High John de Con-*care*. Making get-up out of lie-down. And worth out of worthless. Making drumbeats of the soul. Making spirits grow.

Pretty Pearl never knew that de Conquer would rise in a dream and go to Alabama and Arkansas, wherever he knew folks were really hurting and in real trouble. De Conquer stayed away from her for months of human time, giving his little sister room to fill up and fit inside herself.

§   §

Pretty Pearl had started on her way. She wore a gunny-sack shift and carried the rest of her clothing, some corn pone and pork cracklings in a bundle slung over her shoulder. She was walking at a good clip, no shoes, but she had fashioned sandals out of wild grapevine. She had conjured the vine, causing it to twist itself into the shapes she needed for her feet.

She looked like any lost child, orphaned by war, prey to robbers and devils, hurrying to find a place to hide.

"What's my name?" she asked herself. "Let's see. Pretty's all right. But Pretty what? Nobody gone care. Call me Pretty Perry. Say there were Perry slaves once. Then that's who I am. Pretty Pearl Perry. Shoot, I can use any name I wish. Who's to know?"

She cut through rolling hills, heading for the deepest forest. It was a dusky shadow off a ways before her, stretching as far as her eyes could see.

"Oh, that's a hiding place," she told herself, "better

than a rock or a cave. Who gone wander around in there? Robbers on the edge of it, I bet. But deep inside, I'll find me a find!''

Pretty slowed and touched the de Conquer root around her neck. She strung out the spirit Dwahro to see how to handle him on her own.

Dwahro took on the form of a young man looking as sharp as a tack. He wore an off-white muslin suit printed with a design of blue stars and moons.

"Hello, Dwahro. Where'd you get an outfit like that!" Pretty said.

"Got it in one of de better shops," said Dwahro. "How you doin'?"

"I'm doin' fine, but you'd best come look the part we playin'. Who gone believe anythin' with you dressed up like a carpetbagger?" she said.

"Who, me?" said Dwahro, sassy to Pretty. "No, me. Mess up this fine suit o' clothes? Who gone tell me everythin' on de street if I'm lookin' like a yard dog? Who look up to Dwahro, me, dressed like a field hand? Nuh-uh, no, me—see my shoes? Got to keep de dust off."

Dwahro's shoes were the finest, softest patent leather.

"Mr. Pay-No-Nevermind passed away last summer," Pretty Perry said, her hands on her hips. Dwahro saw the look in her eyes and began backing away from her.

She touched the bone-ebony bow in her hair. She rubbed it, saying, in a voice of magic mystery:

>*"Tongue hung in a empty head,*
>   *Roll around and rattle.*

> *Dwahro's tongue, I must confess*
> *Is just like him, be one big mess!"*

With that, red-clay Georgia soil was seen to rise in a fine mist around Dwahro. When it settled again, his shoes were covered with red. His once-white cuffs, his lapels, his shoulder pads, were streaked with dirt and red dust.

"Don't that dirt seep into everythin'!" Pretty said. "Hee! You lookin' like you bleedin' from de feet! Now you look like you suppose to look."

Dwahro looked sick when he saw what a mess he'd become. And Pretty had made it so he couldn't speak for five minutes. When the time finally passed, he said, "Did you have to go . . . ?" He didn't finish. He knew for certain that he must never question the wisdom of Pretty Pearl.

"Don't you even think about gettin' away from me, you hear? Backin' away from me like that, fixin' to run—de idea!" she said.

"Don't hurt to think," Dwahro said.

> *"Don't think before breakfast,"* she chanted,
> *"Don't think while you eat,*
> *Or you'll cry out at midnight,*
> *You'll die in your sleep!"*

Dwahro shivered and shook at the thought. "You can't kill me—I'm a spirit," he said, his voice quivering. He knew he ought not to argue with Pearl.

[45]

"As long as you're walkin' around like an overgrown dandy, I can make you scream and feel pain!" she said.

"You just a spoiled little girl, too," said Dwahro bravely. "Your brother sure never treated me bad de way you is. Oh, where is him now! This child ain't nothin' but a baby, and him, de Conquer, given her, Pearl, all so much power!"

"You shut up!" Pearl cried. "I'm not either spoiled. . . . Well, it's not easy bein' on your own. I get mean when I'm scared."

"Well, I wish you'd quit bein' scared," said Dwahro.

"You just be quiet and do as I tell you, and everythin' will be all right," she said. But it sobered her to have Dwahro longing for de Conquer. She was longing for him, too.

Can't you come back just a little while? she thought to de Conquer. I don't think I've got de hang of things yet. Don't be actin' right. Already has Dwahro mad at me.

But no answer came inside her from anywhere. No sharp pain in her right foot, which would tell her de Conquer was fixing to think about her.

Pearl did not know that de Conquer wasn't in the soil. He was playing on his hypocrite on his way to the Texas Brazos. Had a lead on his brother, John Henry Roustabout, and he had to track it down.

Pearl had to keep going it alone. She strung Dwahro out and he walked a few feet in front of her. His fine patent leather shoes were soon cracked and ripped from the heat.

"Sorry," whispered Pretty Pearl. But Dwahro said

nothing. They trudged on in silence. The forest loomed closer. It was immense and darkly still.

§   §

They walked over wide and long stretches of land, closer to where they wanted to be. The forest ahead was like a black night rolling over upland.

"It look like de whole world is one great woods," Pearl said, softly.

They had walked through dead plantations where the ruin of soil and buildings was slowly being taken over. Saplings of chestnut, oak and loblolly pine grew through broken-down steps and once-graceful verandas.

There were black folks secretly living in some of the smaller plantation buildings. Some had taken the logs from slave cabins and added rooms to sheds and cookhouses. When Pearl and Dwahro came near, passing along the overgrown slave street of old times, the free folks drifted from their hiding places. Few would have known where to look for the slave street of sorrow times as Pearl did.

"I'm goin' down that long, lonesome road," Pearl sang,
"I'm goin' where those chilly winds don't blow.
Oh, won't you come along, come along, Rachel,
Come along, Joe,
Come along, come along with me."

Some of the free ones hiding began to hum. Someone commenced to sing:

*"Please don't drive me
'Cause I so far behind.
Oh, I b'lieve I will make it
If'n I takes my time,
Takes my ti-ime."*

Theirs was a wistful melody. Another began singing it, repeating it:

*"Oh, I b'lieve I will make it
If'n I takes my time,
Takes my time, ta-akes my time."*

Pearl nodded. "Yes, ma'am! You all soundin' all right with yourselves."

For a moment she was about to say more. Then she remembered she was dressed as a young girl. Dwahro appeared to be her older brother or her uncle.

"This my brother, Toby," Pearl piped up, skipping around. "My name be—" A sudden inspiration came to her: "Bimbe m'Kimbe, that's my name." Pearl laughed— she couldn't help herself. Dwahro looked surprised. The name came to her from ancient places of Africa.

"Bimbe m'Kimbe!" said one of the free ones.

"Pleased to meet yall," Dwahro said, taking their minds off Pretty Pearl. "How far you expect it be to de forest yonder?"

"Be far," said one mawmaw woman, eyeing Pearl. The woman had a baby nestled in sleep in the crook of her arm. Wound around her shoulder was a black snake.

Pearl whispered under her breath, "Ho! Vodu, sister!" Dwahro and Pearl knew right away that the mawmaw was a vodu, serpent worshiper.

"You very much small be wanderin'," the mawmaw said. She reached for Pearl, but Pearl moved quickly out of her reach.

"We only be passin' by," Dwahro said. "Yall do seem comfort here. But ain't you scared of them bad ones ridin' through with their hangin' ropes?"

"We de outside folks," said the witchy vodu.

"But won't you be safer in them big woods with all them dark trees to hide in?" asked Dwahro.

"They de *inside* folks, there," said the mawmaw. "We like it *outside*. We can see what's comin'. We am no afraid of de gray shirts and de white hoods. We no ways scared of nobody." She paused, staring at Pretty Pearl. "What that chile wearin' about her neck?"

"It my John de Conquer root," Pearl piped up.

"Let me take a look at it," said the mawmaw, coming closer. Clearly, she was the leader of the group. The men and younger women all hung back. There were fifteen grown-ups in all and seven children who had come up out of hiding.

"Haven't I heard tell about some 'de Con-*care*' man goin' around fixin' things up and workin' things out?" asked the mawmaw.

"That's my brother!" Pearl exclaimed, surprised to learn de Conquer had finally moved himself.

"You mean, you talkin' 'bout this one here name of Toby?" asked the mother woman.

"Oh, no ma'am," Pearl said, quickly. "I'm talkin' 'bout another brother be named John de Conquer."

"He be dreamin' him some real dreams, too," added Dwahro.

"Well," said the mawmaw, sidling closer to Pretty Pearl.

"And I got another brother, too, be named John Henry; only I don't know nothin' about his whereabouts these days, nor do my brother John de Conquer, too." Pearl managed to say all this in one breath.

"That so?" said the mawmaw woman. "You got some amount o' brothers. John de Conquer, and Toby here, and John Henry. John Henry, is it? Seems like I heard 'bout some John Henry most presently."

"You did!" said Pearl. "What about him?"

"Oh, he a steel-drivin' man, so they say," said the mother woman. "But say he gittin' his head handed to him, too."

"John Henry Roustabout may now be workin' like a steel-drivin' man," said Pearl slyly, "but there's nobody in this world gone hand him his head. Nuh-uh!"

"Well, well, that's somethin'," the witchy woman said. She lunged for Pearl's de Conquer root. She got her hand on it once and burned her fingers for her trouble. There was the sickening smell of burning flesh. But Dwahro healed her palm for her. And in a motion impossible to see, he took her snake and tied her hands behind her back with it. Dwahro then took the baby the mawmaw had been holding and patted its little bottom.

[50]

"Wha—? What you done? Stop it!" cried the maw-maw. "Yall stop it now!" She struggled, but she couldn't get loose from her own snake tied around her wrists.

"It's what you get," Pearl said, "tryin' to take some-thin' that's all mine. Nobody ever to touch my John de Conquer but me, unless I say so, understand?"

Everybody nodded and looked very solemn. Even the mawmaw nodded. "Lemme go, please?" she said. "I won't bother yall no more."

"You sure enough won't," said Dwahro. "That there snake won't be comin' loose until we miles from here. You can try to come loose sooner and get bit, too."

"You be *conjue!*" cried the mawmaw. "You done laid de trick. I got to kill that Conquer root!"

"Oh, hush now," said Pretty Pearl. "We didn't conjure you—don't get so riled. Here." She flaked a flake of the de Conquer root. The tiny, almost invisible flake floated to the ground. Where it landed, a small, neat John de Conquer bush sprang up inches from the ground. Then it stopped growing. "Now that's just a small, baby plant won't be growin' no bigger," Pearl told all of them. "You can take up de bitty roots and break pieces off, or even bigger pieces, and make some de Conquer charms. They make you feel like a sunny day."

"Feel like laughin'," added Dwahro.

"Feel like heaven come over me," said Pearl.

"Feel like you just been born," finished Dwahro.

"Put a string through them tiny roots and wear them," said Pearl. "Remember, any time before de twenty-first day of September, you may pick a clean de Conquer root. Remember Bimbe m'Kimbe!" Pearl turned on her heel and started on her way.

Dwahro handed over the baby to the nearest grown child. He bowed to all, even the vodu, witchy mawmaw. And he left.

No one made to follow Pearl and Dwahro. But the women and children, the men and the baby, the vodu and the snake rearing his head around the woman's back watched Pearl and Dwahro out of sight.

"What they doin' now?" Pretty Pearl asked when they were a good ways off. She was shaking all over. Never before had she used power like that. She looked around behind her, but the outside folks were plainly out of sight.

Dwahro stirred the leaves along the ground where they walked. He let the leaves rustle and jump a moment; then he read them. "De outside folks bendin' down around him de Conquer bush. That mawmaw's hands be free again. She got de snake in her hair. Folks whisperin' and talkin'. Sayin', 'It truly grow, that bush.' Sayin', 'Is she who she say she is?' 'From Africa,' some sayin'. Callin' Bimbe m'Kimbe a true god."

"Well, well," said Pearl.

"Sayin', 'Let us take this Conquer root like she say,'" Dwahro continued. "And de bravest break him bush and pull up him roots and touch roots and not get burned. They all sayin', 'Ah, ah,' like that, too scared. But they each now takin' a piece of root, even that mawmaw. And they takin' one for she babe and one for it snake. And right there in de place that was de slave street that is so overgrown, nobody suspect folks livin' there. They make them necklaces just like Bimbe m'Kimbe tell them. And they put de necklaces on and even it snake wearin' its necklace, and she babe and all de chil'ren."

"Yes!" said Pretty Pearl. "De first real black folks to wear him de Conquer. And if they think about it, they even can plant a tiny root they have and start a new bush sometime, but it's hard to do. Oh, make them safe!"

"Now they safe," said Dwahro. "Well, for true, they in and out of safety. Bein' on de outside, they got to face some stuff soon be comin' down."

"I know," said Pearl, "but that's de price they pay on de outside and bein' black folks."

"Don't I know," said Dwahro.

They did some walking that was fast walking to get where they wanted to be while the sun was still high in the sky. It was about half past three when Pearl and Dwahro got to where they wanted to be.

"You know, it's half past three o'clock in this afternoon," said Pretty Pearl, watching the sun and sky.

"Know it is," agreed Dwahro. "We right on time."

Pearl looked all around. "Never knew a forest could be so much like this," she said.

Dwahro didn't speak. He nodded. He walked, slow and easy, in front and to one side of Pearl. He peered at everything as they came upon the forest.

When they were right with it, no longer did they think how far and how wide and how high it spread.

"You think about only what you seein'," whispered

Pearl to herself. She noticed that a few leaves had fallen to the ground, but not too many as yet. She felt the silence around her; noticed the shade, growing wider all the time.

"Feel like de whole world listenin' to what's comin'."

They walked within. Here is the way it was.

Forest trees had much the same appearance. They were tall pines. Their bark looked black—it seemed as if it had been scorched. The tall trees were spaced apart. Dwahro and Pearl had no trouble walking among them. They were soon deep in a place of twilight. The stillness made Pearl grow quiet and peaceful within.

"This is de place, this is where I wants to stay," she told Dwahro.

Dwahro nodded, said nothing.

"You listenin' at somethin', man?" Pearl asked him. When he still would not speak, she knew he was being watchful for her. He was sensing near them to protect her. De Conquer had said how well Dwahro could feel.

Every other moment, Dwahro would stretch his arm across Pearl as they walked, guarding and shielding her. His gaze fell on all sides. He seemed to listen with his eyes. He smiled up at the magnificent forest trees. High up in the pine boughs, the light of day pressed down and broke through.

Light was a mist filtering down in muted colors. Was as wispy as smoke, but it did not reach the ground. It played odd patterns on pine limbs and bark. The forest sparkled and was magical, as in a serene dawning. But the time was not dawn; it was forest afternoon.

The forest was pleasantly dim. High in itself, it moaned and echoed with nature's whisperings. Pearl felt no wind. She understood that the forest was not only alive, living, it knew no hard times. It knew no wrong, no war. But it recognized the sound and frenzy of kinds, human, good and bad. It kept the symbol of them in its sighing.

The forest was. Once it had been all of Georgia, she realized.

"And men come and cut places in it for themselves," she said out loud.

"Cut places in what?" Dwahro asked. At once, he knew. "In de forest," he answered himself.

"Yea," said Pearl. She went on about it in her mind. Dwahro was going on about it, too. For both had looked and seen what it was.

Men carved huge lands in the forest. They brought in black Africans to suffer the hardships of laboring from dawn to dusk, while they rose higher in self-esteem and grew rich.

The forest was still there when the splendid plantations fell on hard times of too much cotton, too many black slaves and, finally, war.

The forest was, even after war had passed and the reconstruction of life into a new order of living had begun. Some said times would be better for the darker peoples. This did not happen at once. Yet the forest was, still.

"Was once," said Pearl, softly now. Her feet were moving quickly over the forest floor. The forest climbed over the rolling land.

"Was, is once agin, and always was," replied Dwahro. He kept pace with Pearl, a step ahead of her. He made a path for her through the underbrush. The way was growing harder. They had crossed the fall line that separated the coastal plain of Georgia from the upland plateau.

"You know, Dwahro," said Pearl, "things come to me but they leave me. I can't seem to hold on to what I know. One time I understands so much! Then it's gone. I can't seem to hold on to nothin'."

" 'Cause you only a child," Dwahro told her.

"But won't I still be Pretty Pearl of Mount Highness?"

"Sure, you Pearl," he said, "but not no Pearl of de mountain where gods do live. 'Cause you somewhere else, as somethin' else. You be Pearl, little girl. Wearin' Pearl little girl's shift. You Pearl, happily skipping along. And Dwahro guard you, me. See you come to no harm, me." He said this with all of the confidence he could muster.

"But won't I be power no more?" she asked anxiously. She was losing faith in herself.

"You power, girl," Dwahro said, warming to the subject. "You still *come* from de Mount, and de Conquer have given you him de Conquer root. But you small and weak. You can't think to use much de Conquer, and how much power has a little girl?"

"I'm not so little. And I did think to use my power on

that mawmaw woman vodu back there," cried Pearl.

"That wasn't much to do," Dwahro said. He didn't look at Pearl. He appeared confident and wise. "Back there at de old plantation, you did what a human child would think to do. All sassy and fussy to a grown-up, like you haven't had no raisin' up. Better watch out, girl. Burnin' that woman hand! What if that woman been a conjure doctor, what would you a done then?"

"What is that?" asked Pearl, wide-eyed. "A conjure doctor?"

Dwahro still wouldn't look at her. For he believed it was a sin to look a person in the eye and lie to her.

"Conjure queen woman doctor can walk on water and charm de snakes," said Dwahro. "Can make snakes sing and dance. They crawls out of they skins for her. She can doomsay anybody and anybody be doomed. She can rise like him sun and she moon out of water. And she can curse you, me. She can move de winds—east, west, north and south. Conjure queen woman is power and more power, and she take a chile and burn it or waste it away, whatever she want. She god speaks."

"Then that woman back there wasn't no strong con-jure, even havin' a snake with her?" asked Pearl in a tiny voice.

"She wasn't no strong as me and my gris-gris and my mojo-workin' magic," said Dwahro. "That snake de mawmaw had wasn't no python god."

"Thought maybe it was," said Pearl, "come from Africa by way of Haiti."

"Shoot," said Dwahro. "I myself am pure spirit power.

I myself am more best than a woman witchy with some old snake around she neck."

"Thought we was talkin' 'bout *me*!" shouted Pearl. She was getting cranky from walking so long, and confused by Dwahro's many words.

Dwahro shut up a moment. He'd forgotten himself. He had almost let Pearl know about his craving wish to be a free spirit turned into a free, walking man on earth, just the way he appeared to be now. He had never once wanted to be a god. But he wasn't free, he was tied to Pearl. And he didn't want to be a poor, dirty, walking Dwahro.

Wants to be de finest sportin' life on de street, he thought, in de best white linen suit I can beg, borrow or steal.

A day job or any job wasn't worth a nickel to Dwahro, who could talk any fool out of a dime. Once and for all time, he planned to win his way, or steal his way out from under running with Pearl. It all had come to him, right after she strung him out. He was going to break that string that tied him deep in her de Conquer root.

Even if I walks like a man, I ain't. I is still a danglin' man, he thought.

I'm gone break loose that dangle one time. Once I get that root from de god chile's neck, gone break away! Grab it—when? thought Dwahro. Grab it—now! Now! Be careful. Slow down, take your time. She don't know nothin'.

Suddenly Pearl had an urgent, gripping pain in her

[58]

right foot. It came so brutally, with such cruel sharpness, it took her breath. She knew in a second why it had come.

What it is! De Conquer? It's your way of callin' me. John, you tryin' to tell me somethin' ? Tryin' to warn me?

There was a sharp hit of pain, telling Pearl, *Yes!*

You warn me somethin' . . . next to me? thought Pearl.

Yes, came the cruel pain.

Dwahro? Warnin' me, him?

Yes! Yes! The two hits were an awful cramp under her toes.

Watch out, Pearl, she thought.

Just then Dwahro turned on her. He whirled around with such force, he knocked her off her feet. But Pearl was small and quick. She rolled onto her stomach, clutching the de Conquer root in both fists.

Dwahro said not a word. He planted his knee in Pearl's back. Pressed down hard and grabbed her neck. He tried to break the necklace made from strands of John de Conquer's hair.

Pearl held on to the root for dear life. The pain of Dwahro's knee in her back made her weak. She couldn't even scream. Desperately, she searched the forest floor for something to defend herself with. What she spied was a dark hole in the ground. She nearly sobbed with happiness.

Oh, my! she thought through her pain. She was choking. Dwahro was twisting the necklace, trying to break it.

Pearl managed to whisper, chanting toward the hole:

"Long snake, wake snake!
Come along, whip along, help along!
Any way you want along!"

She could no longer speak or breathe. She was about to faint when the greatest, longest snake slithered from the hole. It climbed over Pearl in a ripply run. Then it wrapped itself around Dwahro's knee. Dwahro screamed, kicking his leg, trying to get the snake off. But the come along, any way you want along snake had Dwahro, who would hurt Pearl. Had him, as sure as bees have hives.

CHAPTER FOUR

It was called a coachwhip snake. It was six feet long and two inches around. It was black with a deep-green glint, and it called itself Virgil.

"I'm Virgil, I'm Virgil," it hissed.

Dwahro was yelling his head off. Hopping around, he had one hand gripping the snake's neck and was pulling, stretching the snake away from his leg. Dwahro didn't have time to tell the snake his own name or pass the time of day. But Pretty Pearl did.

She sat up, rubbing the small of her back and the nape of her neck where Dwahro had hurt her so badly. "Hi, there, Virgil Coachwhip," she said finally. "I'm so glad you were home. I'm known as sister of de Conquer, Pretty Pearl. How you doin'?"

"How do, Pretty?" hissed the snake. "I'm doin' all right, but I'm workin' mighty hard just now."

"So I see," said Pearl, amused. The coachwhip had a time getting its neck loose from Dwahro's frantic grip. But it did, at last.

That Virgil got its surname, Coachwhip, because of its tail. It had quite a strong tail that was different from all other snakes' tails. The coachwhip's tail was braided so tightly and so firmly and so neatly, it looked just like one of the black whips that coachmen use to flail their horses. It was as good as a coachman's leather whip. The long, handsome snake had feet for grasping.

Right now the coachwhip, Virgil, was busy, tight as it was around Dwahro's knee.

"Oooch! Oooch!" Dwahro had been screaming for some time. "Lemme go! Lemme go! Get away from me, snake!"

The coachwhip wouldn't let go. It snapped its tail like a whip cracking. It whipped Dwahro hard on his bottom. In minutes Dwahro's pants were slashed to ribbons.

"Stop it! Please, stop it!" yelled the sporting-life-to-be, running around in circles. "Pearl, get this thing to stop beating me to death!"

Virgil had Dwahro running and leaping in circles while it beat and whipped the sporting-life-to-be on the backs of his legs. Dwahro was about to drop from exhaustion. In no time at all, Pearl realized, he would be finished.

She stood up, raising her hands before her. The forest

trees on all sides sighed darkly with knowing.

"Hush!" Pearl commanded, piping in her child's voice. All of the forest place did grow still. Sound from Dwahro stopped abruptly, although he still jumped about and appeared to scream at the top of his lungs as Virgil continued the beating. Dwahro's lips moved, but no sound came out. Virgil's braided tail was in motion, flailing away at Dwahro, but it, too, made no sound.

"You, Dwahro! You promise never to knee my back again, nor try to steal my necklace?" called Pearl.

Dwahro couldn't get any words out, but he nodded as hard as he could. He shivered in terror. The feel of the coachwhip on his leg was more than he could stand.

"The very idea!" Pearl went on. "Tryin' to say I got no power. Tryin' to make me believe I'm too young and don't know nothin', shoot! Don't ever try to fool me again, you hear? You almost had me believin' it."

Dwahro folded his hands in a gesture of pleading.

"Swear you won't bother me no more, you won't try to steal what's mine," said Pretty.

Dwahro crossed his heart and hoped to die. He licked his finger and pointed straight up to the heavens. Pretty squinted up. There was a patch of afternoon sky, bright and blue, above the trees. She waited, for she suspected the gods might well strike Dwahro down. But sky remained sky. Pearl guessed Dwahro was telling the truth this one time. He had sworn never to bother her again.

"Well, all right, then," said Pearl. In her sweet child's voice, she commanded the snake, "Yea, Virgil Coachwhip, crawl along now."

[63]

At once Virgil hissed and flicked its forked tongue. It loosened itself from around Dwahro's knee. Slithering down over Dwahro's foot, Virgil crawled off among the tender green ferns of the forest floor. It slid and it slid sideways until it arrived at Pearl's shoes. There, it flipped over on its back and raised its feet. Virgil had the pinkest three-toed feet Pearl ever did see.

She leaned down and patted each and every little foot. There were four pink feet for every twelve inches of snake, and there were twenty-four tired little feet in all.

"Bless 'em!" Pearl spoke kindly, massaging the flat, pink feet for just a moment.

"Hissss-ah," sighed Virgil Coachwhip. "Pearl, pretty, you are a good chile, my friend."

"Don't I know it," Pearl said. "And you, you a nice friend to have between a rock and a hard place. You may go now, Virgil. Get yourself some good rest. Remember me, in case I ever come back this way."

"I most ways will remember you," whispered Virgil Coachwhip. "Good-bye-hiss, Pretty Pearl."

" 'Bye, Virgil Coachwhip," said Pearl. The long, dark snake slithered down its snake hole on tiny, flat, pink, worn-out feet.

"Well, well, well," said Pearl. "My, my." She smoothed out her shift, which had become more wrinkled from her sitting. There were weeds and sticks stuck on the fabric. "Guess we be on our way again." She did not look at Dwahro.

Dwahro was on his back, resting. His arms covered his eyes. But he was watchful of Pearl, afraid of her as he could be. He didn't know what had possessed him to attempt theft and escape. He was fooled by the way Pearl looked like an ordinary ten- or twelve-year-old girl. Her disguise was the best job he'd ever come across, next to his own. He thought his muslin suit of stars and moons and his patent leather shoes were the very best costume. That is, before Pearl went and spoiled them with red Georgia clay.

Dwahro pouted. He tried to ignore the dirty mess he'd become. He rubbed his knee, which ached like rheumatism where the horrible reptile had wrapped itself around it.

Pearl got up, went to Dwahro and sat beside him. "Turn on over to your stomach," she said. This time he did not even ask what for. He did as he was told without a word.

"Look at that," Pearl said.

"Huh?" said Dwahro. "Look at what?"

"Never you mind. I can fix it," she said confidently.

Dwahro didn't know what she was talking about. He felt an awful pain in his backside where that Virgil had whipped him, and the ache in his knee where the snake had wrapped itself around it.

Only Pearl could see that the seat of Dwahro's pants was a raggedy ruin. She took up a pine leaf and broke off several strands of her coarse, dark hair. She swirled the hairs together until she had a single, stout thread. Then she fashioned a hole throught the pine-leaf needle and threaded it. "There," said Pearl, and began sewing up the seat of Dwahro's pants.

"That feel better?" she asked him when she had finished.

"It a lot less drafty back there," Dwahro murmured. He had almost fallen asleep, so exhausted was he from his struggle with the snake.

"Well, get up now," Pearl said. "We got to be on our way."

"You not even mad at me?" asked Dwahro. He acted almost ashamed of himself.

"What's to be mad about?" Pearl said. "You, Dwahro, given over to me by my brother John de Conquer. You are spirit given in my charge. I expect you to look out for me like you suppose to, and not be tryin' to trick me and such. Least not more than once a day!" She grinned at him, and she didn't seem much like a human child now.

"Yes, ma'am," Dwahro said. He stood up and tried to look decent. "I'm gone behave myself because I'm tired of bein' bad, yes I am. I'm gone behave because I wants to get on to where we s'pose to be gettin' on to—where we goin' now, Pretty Pearl?"

"We goin' where de chilly winds don't get behind my back and under my skirts," said Pearl. "We goin' where de secret is secret and will stay secret. The peoples is had enough of plantations and bosses and chains!"

Pearl quietly walked behind a tall pine tree. Dwahro heard rustling back there. He thought for a minute that the chilly wind had indeed started up. But it was only Pearl, although her other self. Pretty Pearl had gone behind the tree to *change* her dress. When she came out she was all grown. It was Mother Pearl. She had felt the need to help out Pretty Pearl.

Mother Pearl wore a long shift with an apron covering it from the waist down. She had a sky-blue kerchief decorating her head in a broad, twisted band. She was wide and handsome. She was old enough that every babe anywhere would run to her and hold out its arms to her. She'd carry the babes and love them and feed them, and make them safe. Tell them mighty tall tales, too. And she looked to be a human mawmaw woman, although she was the godly one, part of Pretty. She was much older than Dwahro.

"Mother Pearl!" Dwahro exclaimed. He recognized her right away. "How come you come?"

"Because little Pretty gettin' all too tired out. She need a rest," said Mother Pearl. "How you doin', Dwahro, bro?" Mother Pearl had good manners.

"Doin' all right," Dwahro answered. "But where Pearl keep you when she wearin' her little dress? Where you be bein' then?"

"Nothin' to talk about," said Mother Pearl. "I be gone then, is all, on de Mount, or thinkin' about nothin'. But come on, son, we got to walk some walk. You up to walkin'?" she asked him kindly.

"I'm doin' almost pretty good," said Dwahro. "I got my comeuppance with it snake."

"Well, I dreamed about that, ain't that somethin'?" She laughed a husky, friendly laugh. "It ain't nothin' to get upset over. It just Virgil. She call it and it do de job!" Mother Pearl laughed again, while Dwahro dug his patent leather toe in the ground. "Let's walk some," Mother

[67]

said. They did walk. They climbed up and over the rolling hills.

They came to oak and pine woods and chestnut-pine ridges. They discovered tremendous shagbark hickory trees in rich coves. Mother Pearl and Dwahro picked some of the hickory nuts. The nuts were sweet to the taste. Mother Pearl put some in an apron pocket marked "Pretty."

"I'll leave them for her later, when I change my dress," Mother explained.

"That's nice," Dwahro said, trying to be pleasant.

Mother gave him a sharp look; then she smiled. "Least you workin' at it. You tryin'."

Dwahro said nothing. He limped at Mother's side. Ancient trees shaded them, drawing them closer together. They were climbing higher grades and it wasn't easy. Mother Pearl was soon perspiring. "Workin' hard," she said, panting. "I don't mind. Heart beatin' true." Being in human form was not always easy. "How's that knee holdin' up?" she asked Dwahro. "Seen you limpin'."

"It all right, I guess," he said. "It achin' like de dickens just this minute. Don't know what that snake done do to it."

"Dug its toes under de skin, most probably," Mother said. "Stop a minute—lemme look at it."

They stopped. Dwahro rolled up his pants leg. Mother examined his bony knee. Sure enough, she found tiny nail marks where Virgil's very small toenails had dug right in.

"Ouch! That hurts!" said Dwahro. Mother Pearl was

feeling the soreness lightly with her fingers.

"Nobody tole Virgil to do somethin' this worst," she said. "You could get a bad infection. Some snakes just have to go too far."

"Yes'm," agreed Dwahro. "Can't you do somethin' so's I don't get sick out here in de wilderness?"

"Can do," said Mother, "You might catch a human chill at that. You just stand still a mite minute." She went off hunting. She hunted beneath the pines until she found what she was looking for, and came back with a pokeweed, roots and all. "Now, you got to help me," she told Dwahro. "We'll scrape these roots as thin as we can. Then we grind them with a rock." They did this, sitting on the ground. Dwahro found a rock and ground the pokeroots right there on the forest floor. When he had something like a paste, Mother Pearl put it into a small handkerchief she had. She twisted the hanky of paste over Dwahro's knee. Then she pressed the cloth directly on the nail wounds made by Virgil Coachwhip.

"Oh, yes!" hollered Dwahro. "I can feel it!"

"Just feel that pain a-drawin' right out," Mother Pearl told him.

"Right out!" shouted Dwahro. "And another pain, too. Wherever it be, pain, in my back, wherever, it drawin' right out de knee!"

"Now don't overdo it, son," said Mother. "I know you enthusiastic, but don't go puttin' it on too thick." She had to laugh at him.

"But I'm not," he said. "It just feelin' so good to have my knee straighten out where that snake try to choke it."

"All right, settle down," Mother said. "We got to get a move on. You all right yet?"

"I'm feelin' more than all right. I'm feelin' strong!" said Dwahro.

"Good enough. Now just don't touch that knee and then put you hands in you mouth," said Mother Pearl.

"Why not?" asked Dwahro.

" 'Cause pokeroot is poison as it can be, and I don't wants to have go cure you stomach 'cause you went and stuck you thumb in you mouth."

"I don't suck my thumb! I never did!" cried Dwahro, outraged.

"Whoo-ee!" said Mother. "You can get upset quicker than a jaybird seein' a stalkin' cat. Goodness! Now roll down your pants leg. Get on up from there."

Dwahro did as he was told. "Why come you didn't just heal my knee with you own hand?" asked Dwahro. "You de mother power."

"Why use a sledgehammer when a feather will do?" Mother replied. "Now, hush up. Lemme straighten out them clothes you feel so strong about and best be wearin' for a good, long time."

Dwahro stood before her. "You . . . you mean . . . ?" he stammered.

"Yes, I do mean," she said, reading him. "I won't make this here suit of yours absolutely fit and clean. For de folks would surely comment you be some kind of boogeyman." She paused, raised one hand to Dwahro's lapel and then slid that hand all over his jacket. She smacked Dwahro's palms with her own. "You run your own hand over de pants," she told him.

"Like this?" he asked, sweeping his palms over his trousers.

"That's right, that's it. See what it done? Your own hands done it. See that?" Mother said.

"Mercy!" Dwahro whispered. He did see. Dirt and red clay dust had vanished from his wonderful sporting-life suit.

"Not all of it gone," Mother said, "but enough of it so you lookin' more like somebody than anybody."

"Do I really look like somebody?" he asked. "Do I, Mother Pearl?"

"Of course you lookin' like somebody," she said. "I can't have you meetin' folks and lookin' like Scruffy-Ain't-Been-Nowhere, shoot."

"Thank you, Mother Pearl," Dwahro said, humbly. His trousers were only slightly off-color, with no sharp creases. His jacket was a little darker still. But he would look better than any poor folks he would come in contact with in the great forest.

Dwahro held his head high with pride. While other folks might sit in pity's chair, Dwahro's patent leather shoes alone made him look like he was at least sitting there stirring a pot of luck. Mother Pearl had breathed on his shoes and made them shine like new money.

"Folks gone be down in sorrow's kitchen, you wait and see," said Mother Pearl. "We gone have our work and play all laid out in de skillet and already fryin'. De best of it we must do is cherish de poor folks, I do believe."

"Yes'm," said Dwahro. "I'll do my job, like always."

Mother Pearl eyed him narrowly. "You workin' for me and you workin' for *her*," she said.

"Who her?" Dwahro said, innocently.

"You know who. Young Pretty Pearl, that's who. You work for us both," said Mother Pearl.

"And for no pay," said Dwahro angrily. "Just a slave with two masters."

"Dwahro, don't you be makin' like that. Only human bein's once was slaves. You not no human. You and me both know that."

"Wish I was," Dwahro said grimly. "Then I could get myself free like other folks." He couldn't help letting it out.

"So that's it," Mother said. "Listen, Dwahro, you is better than any human. For you is *spirit* of de gods, born out of gods' wantin' and needin'. Nothin' to do with freedom and slavery."

Dwahro held his tongue. He knew this dangerous ground, like quicksand, that could disrupt his thoughts. Now he would not dwell on being a human. But it was his deepest, most solemn wish. To be a man. To be free. Freeman.

CHAPTER FIVE

On and on, Mother Pearl and that worrisome spirit, Dwahro, went walking on through Georgia land. Walking through the rolling upland where the forest became even greater and darker. Under centuries of fallen, rotten leaves, a mast of acorns and chestnuts, hickory nuts and walnuts, husks and shells, covered the hills. There were rotted dried berries, and the entire mast measured a foot thick.

The continually rising grade toward distant mountains was a hard going and a work of strong muscles for Mother Pearl and Dwahro. It was of panting and sweating, and being ripped at by thorny, stinging vines and bushes.

" 'Most like a jungle!" whispered Mother.

They were walking, but it wasn't any kind of stroll. No leisure time in which they might pass gossip or remark about the forest flowers growing in bunches out of the mast.

The creeps suddenly came over Dwahro. The shivering shakes were also in his mind. Either his imagination played tricks on him, or he and Mother Pearl were being watched.

"Did you let that Hide-behind out of your necklace?" Dwahro asked. They wandered into a shadowy, grim stretch of forest shade.

"De Hide-behind still inside my de Conquer root," answered Mother.

"Whew!" she said. The closeness of heat in the forest place took her breath.

"Why'n't you let that brat Pretty Pearl do she work?" said Dwahro. He was much too tired now to be nice all the time.

"Let her be," said Mother. "But what be worryin' you, Dwahro? You actin' some queer, lookin' over you shoulder every other minute."

"Don't know for sure," said Dwahro. "It seem like de Hide-behind be jumpin'. But ever' time I turn around, he must jump behind a tree trunk. I don't see nothin'."

"De Hide-behind's not there, that's why you can't see nothin'," said Mother.

"But I feel somethin' like you feel when death come

[74]

creepin' near." Dwahro shuddered at the thought.

"Interestin'," Mother said. "I don't feel a thing. But Dwahro, you was made to feel before anybody else can. I expect we'd better pay attention."

"Well, I don't know woods too well," Dwahro said. "I'm a street man, don't you know. I'm a sportin' life on my way to being de best time o' life, yeah!"

Dwahro commenced strutting the way only he knew how, to make himself feel better. He moved as if he were making his way down a crowded street among the people. They were on every side watching him and looking and clapping for him. And he waved at them on every side. Just like he was human, too! As if they were right there.

Dwahro stopped. He stood, dumbstruck. He'd strutted twenty feet ahead of Mother Pearl and stumbled through thick undergrowth into a clearing. Dead center of the clearing in a half circle of pines was a yellow poplar tree.

It was not just any tree. Not just any yellow poplar, Dwahro thought. "Is this . . . is this . . . is you . . . *real*?" he said to the tree.

Mother Pearl caught up with him and stood behind Dwahro's back.

"She real," said Mother. "She a woman and yellow, she so old. Hundreds of years old. What be green and white and yellow, Dwahro?"

"Don't know," murmured Dwahro, staring at the tree.

"A poplar when she young, and middle age, and old. Huh! Ain't she somethin'?" said Mother.

Centuries old, the poplar's trunk was more than twenty-five feet around. The side they could see was ten feet across. Dwahro saw how high it was that the branches began, way up and up. At the very top of the tree, which had to be at least a hundred feet up, the trunk swayed in a tight circle, like a pole going around and around.

"Look at that!" Dwahro managed to say.

Mother Pearl went up close to see. " 'Scuse me, olden woman, my friend," she said respectfully. Mother climbed a little way up the tree trunk, for it was like a platform she could stand on. And she gazed up at the high, very top high of the trunk like a pole.

"Goin' around and around, like it can't stop. Yes, it is," said Mother. "Ain't that somethin'?"

"Do you suppose it's de wind up there, making her circle she head so?" Dwahro asked.

"No, sir," said Mother, glancing down at the roots, and up and down again.

"It's de earth doin' it. Slow down, Mama! Ho! You heighth is grand! Don't be breakin' you neck up there."

Mother climbed down and stood straight in front of the grand tree.

"You lookin' real small next to she poplar," said Dwahro.

"Is small," said Mother. "Wish you can draw me so's I always have de picture."

"Can too draw you," said Dwahro, "if I had me somethin' to draw on."

Mother smiled and held out her apron that spread

across the front of her dress. It was ivory colored and almost as long as her shift. She untied the bow strings behind her back. Took off the apron and tossed it to Dwahro.

The apron fairly floated to him. Its long bow strings reached for him like two loving arms. Dwahro caught the strings; smiling, he spread the apron on the mast of the forest floor.

"Need a title for it?" asked Dwahro.

"No title necessary," said Mother. "Just draw me and she poplar. Gather you de dye colors. Now, as I tell you."

"Yesum," said Dwahro.

Under the direction of Mother Pearl, Dwahro gathered the dyes for coloring the apron and drawing Mother and the yellow poplar tree.

"Get some dark-brown color, dig for walnut roots. That will be my skin tone."

"Yesum," said Dwahro. He found a walnut tree close by. He found a root of it and tore it off with his spirit strength. Then he peeled the bark off and laid it on a flat rock.

"Get some black hickory bark for yellow to draw de yellow poplar," Mother commanded. "Beat it off them trees. That bark was made for fine, clear yellows."

"Yesum," Dwahro said. He went for the hickory, found it near and beat off the bark. He brought it back and placed it carefully on the flat rock.

"Now. Green from green oak leaves; you can still find some green—I expects there is one or two still bein' born, or slow," Mother said. Dwahro was moving fast.

"And use maple bark for indigo blue—de inside bark is best. And some purple, maybe," said Mother, "from pokeberry roots, but you don't has to have it, necessarily. Just me and she tree be all." She looked up over her head. "That so nice up there." Above them was a tiny patch of blue sky growing deeper blue with afternoon. "You can put a peek or two of sky in my picture."

"Yesum," Dwahro said. He had what he needed. "I'm ready."

"Then take some power," said Mother. "Add it to you spirit." She scraped the de Conquer root and tossed the scrapings in the air. A fine rain of de Conquer fell in the dimness in front of Dwahro's face. He opened his mouth and breathed in de Conquer. A heavy weight seemed to lift from him. Dwahro's eyes turned all colors at once.

Standing before the tree, Mother Pearl lifted her hands, cupping them as if shaping the air. Dwahro dug up a hump of red clay. He sat by the rock and fashioned a clay bowl to the rhythm of Mother Pearl's hands shaping the air.

When the bowl was shaped, Dwahro looked to Mother. Mother pressed her hands tighter and tighter in the cupped shape of space in her hands. The bowl Dwahro had made got warm. It got hot. It turned darker with heat and it grew hard as it was fired. Dwahro held on to it. His eyes were every color of the rainbow and two or three colors never before seen or heard of. These were the colors: *yennier, glamina* and *uleena.* They were too marvelous to behold. They were seen only by gods and spirits.

Dwahro looked at the bowl and the colors, yennier, glamina and uleena, fell from his eyes. They spread seed shapes of color inside and outside the bowl. The bowl gleamed with their magical hues.

"Done," said Dwahro.

"Begin, then, you," said Mother to him.

Gently, Dwahro placed the bowl next to him as he kneeled before the rock. He took up all the ingredients of dyes he had collected and put them in the bowl. Next he squeezed the rock, mumbling spirit words, *Hovu-haga, somasa,* which were his private, spirit-magic words.

"Hovu-haga, haga, somasa," he murmured.

Water gushed from the rock and poured into the bowl. That done, Dwahro took the bowl and set it on the rock. The rock grew warm, hot; it glowed like a red coal. Both he and Mother were whispering now, a mile a minute.

Dye colors came from sources of nut, leaf and bark. They did not mix together in the water but stayed in separate streams. Dwahro broke off strands of his coarse hair. He tied the strands together with green bark. In this way he made a paintbrush. Mother divined salt as mordant to fix the dyes.

Dwahro began. He looked at Mother Pearl, the poplar, the sky, and dipped his brush in the magical bowl of paint before him. He did paint what he saw on her apron. Almost. Since he was using Mother's apron on which to paint the scene, he must paint in an apron on her clothes in the painting. He would do this, but first he painted the sky a blue indigo. He painted Mother, herself, in dark walnut. He painted her shift, just the way it looked as she stood there by the poplar tree. He painted an apron on the shift, as if he were seeing Mother wearing one. He colored in a great yellow poplar from the apron hem to the waist.

When he had finished the painting on Mother's apron, he painted the scene again on the apron in the painting. And again. And again. When he was finally finished, he had a painting within a painting within a painting in a painting on Mother's apron.

"Done," he said at last. "See? How it look?"

Mother came close to see. She peered at the painting on her apron and the paintings on aprons that got smaller and smaller. "Goodness! I feel like I'm fallin' in there. This be a most fine painting. Dwahro, you an 'ceptional artist," she said.

"I'm a sportin' life lookin' for a high ole time," Dwahro said.

"Oh, no, you not just all that," said Mother. "You a rock-hard painter, and this be de best painting anybody ever make of me—it de onliest one, for true."

"Then that's why you like it," said Dwahro.

"Oh, now," said Mother. She reached for Dwahro and folded him to her. Held him tight for a moment, just like a mother would a troubled son.

"If ever I has me a son of Mount Highness, he gone be just like Dwahro," she said. "I mean it. I don't mind you bein' devilish sometimes. Who wants good all de time in him spirit?"

"Thought they gods was always great and good," said

Dwahro. He didn't mind being hugged by Mother Pearl, just like he was a real son.

"We always great," she was saying, "but I'm not sure about always got to be good, shoot. Is that brother Roustabout John Henry always good? You heard de stories. And be you always good, Dwahro?"

"Nosum," he said quietly.

"Well, then, there you go," she said. "You be not always good 'cause de gods in whose image you made be not always good—we try, though. We do terribly try! And will not stand for deliberate badness."

They relaxed a moment. Mother put her apron back on. It looked wonderful with its fine painting, and paintings within it. Dwahro cleaned the lovely bowl and wore it on his head like a decorated hat. They faced the enormous tree, she poplar.

"Great woman, poplar, you," breathed Mother Pearl. "Sure would like Pretty Pearl to have a look at you, too."

Then they were not alone. Dwahro had been right. Like smoke, three figures drifted out of the pines surrounding the yellow poplar.

Mother Pearl and Dwahro jumped back.

"Ow-ow!" cried Dwahro. "Knew there was somethin'. Run! Run!"

"Shhh," Mother Pearl said soothingly. "Not to worry atall."

"But what . . . what be them?" Dwahro whispered loudly. Mother had to hold on to him to keep him from tearing away.

"They jes' . . . white folks," said Mother Pearl. "They look like de bad sort you sometimes has to run into come day or night."

"White folks?" said Dwahro. "Haven't seen them kind in a long while."

"Well, take a good look," Mother said, quietly. "They aim to bother us for sure."

"What we gone do!" said Dwahro.

"Hunh, watch you don't drop that bowl on you head for a minute."

"Yesum," said Dwahro. He stood as still has he could before the woman, yellow poplar, as three white men came slowly to surround him and Mother Pearl.

"Well, well," one of the men said. He was tall and lean, with a dirty beard and a thin mustache. He held a Colt revolver in his right hand. In his left hand he carried a neatly rolled hanging rope. The man walked around Mother and Dwahro, looking them over. With his gun barrel he lifted the rim of the bowl Dwahro was wearing.

"Some danged funny-lookin' shap-po," he said. "That's French for sombrero." The two other men guffawed. They each carried a plains rifle, and a hanging rope wound around over the shoulder and under the arm.

Dwahro was terrified, for the cold steel of the Colt revolver was pressed to his forehead. It was the sight of a gun that scared him. He had no reason to fear for his life.

"Looks like we found us a buck and a wing, boys," said

the first bandit to the other two. "Now my question is what we best do with them."

"Make 'em dance!" came the fast reply from a short, round fellow. He had his hair tied back on his neck. He pointed his rifle at Dwahro's feet.

"Let's give 'em plenty rope!" said the third bandit. His hands twitched, touching the hanging rope.

Dwahro was wracked with shaking. Mother Pearl reached for him to comfort him. The first bandit knocked her out of the way.

"Who tole you to move, Mammy?" he said. "Now did you hear me tell you to make a move?"

"No," Mother Pearl whispered.

"No?" said the bandit. "No!"

"No, *suh*," Mother said, sweetly. But there were fierce glints of fire and ice deep in her eyes.

"That's better," the bandit said. He grabbed Mother by the hair and glanced at the grand yellow poplar, then back to Mother. "Ah think first thang," he said, "we have us a target shoot."

"Whew! Sakes alive!" shouted the second bandit. "Ah get to go first 'cause Ah's the best shot."

"No you don't. No you don't," said the first bandit. "Ah heard 'em talkin', Ah was the one found 'em here. *Ah* go first. And 'fore Ah hits the bull's-eye"—he pointed at Mother Pearl's nose—"Ah'ma have me the lo-cation of a passel o' black crows."

The second bandit slapped his thigh, threw back his head and shot his rifle straight up in the air. The report from the long gun was deafening. The forest gathered itself in, it seemed. Instantly, a crested flycatcher fell like a stone at the bandit's feet.

"Looka that!" yelled the bandit. "Lordy, got it straight through the heart without even aimin'—ain't that somethin'!"

"It's somethin'," the third bandit said, probing the dead bird with his shoe. "Ole yellabelly, still got flies in ee's mouth." He flipped the bird over and the wings fell open.

The bandits stared down at the bird. Mother Pearl had turned her face away when the bird fell. She hated to see life end so cruelly. The first bandit still had her by the hair. And Mother was gazing on the great woman-tree, poplar.

We be bound, you and me, she thought to the poplar. Sorry you have to see such bandits as these in you forest. But never you mind. Never you ever you mind!

The first bandit remembered what he was about. "What yer doin', a-foolin' around like this!" he hollered at the other two. "Ah said we was havin' a target shoot. We got us some two good targets to start with."

He shoved Dwahro in front of Mother Pearl. "Oh, no, suh, no, suh, don't you harm me," pleaded Dwahro. "I'll work for you. I'll do most anythin'."

Mother Pearl took up the plead. "Oh, please, don't put us up there in front of that tree. Please don't target us, Massa!"

The bandits laughed uproarously. "Ain't they somethin'?" one of them said. "Skeered of they shadows. We gone find us a passel o' crows!"

They marched Dwahro and Mother Pearl to the poplar. The forest listened, brooding—Mother Pearl and Dwahro could feel it.

The two of them knew the forest to be their friend, and magical. Mother Pearl sighed deeply. Dwahro held his spirit in and hoped the end would come quickly for him. Neither he nor Mother would ever tell free folks' secret.

Guess I won't ever become human, he thought. Wouldn't mind even bein' one of them bandits, if I could just live and breathe like they be doin' it.

He knew if he was shot, he wouldn't die. But to be wounded still frightened him. It would be a grave insult to his spirit, and the pain of that would hurt him through and through. He wasn't sure he would be able to stand it.

Mother Pearl knew very well that she could go through the throes of death, being as she was a grown woman form. She knew what it was to feel blood and guts, and soul. She was able to go through the natural process of dying, enter into death and come out the other side to start again. So now she prayed to the mountain where those others of her kind resided. She asked that the proceedings that were about to occur not be too difficult for her to bear.

Mother smoothed out her apron. She bowed her head; her lips moved.

"What you sayin', you old black crow?" said the first bandit. He aimed his gun at Mother. "Cain't hear ya—speak on up."

"Weren't talkin' to *you*," Mother said, as nice as she knew how.

"Why you . . ." The bandit had his aim right on Mother's nose.

The forest waited for the agonizing instant. But the moment came and went, and the bandit did not pull the trigger. Ever so carefully, he lowered his revolver.

"Ezra, what's awrong?" asked the second bandit. But Ezra wouldn't say. He stared before him. The two other bandits came up beside him, looking in his face. They followed his gaze to what he was seeing. And then all three of them had their eyes fixed on something.

Mother Pearl chuckled. "Huh, huh, huh, heh, heh, heh," she went. She said to Dwahro, "Now that's somethin' there. That's a fine piece of work, Dwahro, didn't I already tell you so? You de bestest and de master for true!"

"Shhhh! Shhhh!" Dwahro warned. He stood, trembling from head to foot. "They gone hear you and shoot us down! Oh, me, go ahead, go ahead, shoot us and get it over!"

The bandits continued to stare. The guns dropped lower and lower, and if the bandits had shot, they would have hit their own feet. They stared some more; Dwahro leaned forward to get a better look at them. Then he got up enough courage to take a step closer. And closer.

Until he was staring into their faces. Dwahro flashed his hand in front of their eyes. The bandits didn't blink once.

"Mother Pearl, come on over here," Dwahro whispered.

"No, me," said Mother. "And don't you get in de way of them lookin' at me, either," she warned him. "Yea, you sure done fix 'em good, Dwahro."

Dwahro walked back to the tree and Mother Pearl. "What is happenin'?" he asked. "What in de world happenin' to them white folks?"

"Don't you see?" Mother said. "You done addled they brains! It's that painting on my apron! They look at me and de tree, and take aim on me. Then they see my apron with a painting of a tree and me, and another painting of a tree and me inside it, and still *another* one inside that one. They musta got pulled in—remember, I told you it felt like I was fallin' in de apron picture after you had painted it?"

"I remember," said Dwahro. "But that paintin' don't do nothin' to me." He stood back to look at the apron. "Uh-uhh," he said. "It don't 'fect me atall."

"Well, you him painter," Mother Pearl said. "It can't no ways trick you."

"But it trick them white folks!" he said. "I has mesmerized de bandits!"

"Yes indeed," Mother said. "But we got work to do, Dwahro. I can't do it, because I has to stand here for de bandits. So you has to do it."

"What's that?" he asked.

[87]

"Take they ropes," she said, meaning the bandits' hanging ropes. "Tie each bandit's hands with one end of he rope."

"Yesum," Dwahro said. He went to work tying up the mesmerized bandits. He put each bandit's hands in a praying position in front and tied them tight.

"Now," Mother said, "talk to them. Tell them to walk over to this tree."

"Yesum," said Dwahro. "Now, you listen, white bandits," Dwahro told the men. "We march to that tree. You keep you eyes on Mother's apron, you hear? And don't dare to talk back to Dwahro! Yeah! Yeah!"

Mother had to laugh at him, he was so brave. The three bandits came to the tree and didn't take their eyes off the painting.

"My goodness, it's somethin' I never thought I'd see," said Dwahro.

"Don't never sell de pigs before you get them money," Mother warned.

"Yesum," Dwahro said, sobering. "What we do next?"

"Take some lengths of they ropes," Mother told him. "Wrap they chests around and under they arms. Make a good knot for each, right behind on they backs."

"Yesum," said Dwahro. In a moment he had the bandits kneeling. Next, he tied the ropes as Mother said to do.

"Now, you gone climb she poplar. Between you and my John de Conquer root," Mother said, "we be givin' these bandits a good swang in de forest breeze."

"Mercy!" Dwahro doubled over, laughing. "I can't stand it!"

"Stop it, crazy," Mother said, for he had got her giggling, and she shook all over.

"Yeah. All right," Dwahro said. He got hold of himself. "What must I do now?"

"Hush and listen. Take each rope end in hand and climb up she tree. Power of him most high de Conquer be with us."

"Yesum," said Dwahro in a hushed voice. He didn't hesitate. He walked right up the broad side of the grand yellow poplar. It was the way no human could possibly walk up a tree. Dwahro stuck straight out from the tree trunk. He was like an arrow, or a branch. He was perpendicular.

When Dwahro got up in the tree, he found the Hodag from the John de Conquer root already there. The brown-and-black-spotted Hodag's tail was almost like a sickle, the curved cutting tool with a razor-sharp blade. The Hodag barked and wagged his tail at the sight of his friend Dwahro. His tail whipping around sliced off two poplar branches just above Dwahro's head.

"Watch it, Hodag, 'fore you cut me in two!" cried Dwahro.

The Hodag barked and pranced, having a conniption fit over Dwahro.

The Fool-la-fafa was up there, too, bigger than life. It was the redheaded woodpecker, grown to a nightmarish size. Its wingspan was twenty feet and its head was the size of a fifty-pound gourd.

"How you doin', Fool?" hollered Dwahro. "Sure didn't 'spect to see you here, my friend."

"Doin' all right," said the Fool-la-fafa in fowl birdcall. "Just peckin' my way."

"Hurry up there," called Mother Pearl.

They went about their work. The Hodag cleared away branches that would interfere with the free swinging back and forth of the bandits. One slash of his tail cut away the lengths of three branches, leaving suitable stubs just the right size.

The Fool-la-fafa used his chisel beak to break a hole through each stub. Then Dwahro tied the ropes through the holes. With the help of the Hodag's clutching teeth and the Fool's vise-strong beak, they hauled up the bandits and let them swing. Hands tied in front of them, and the rope snug under their arms, they swung gently back and forth and around, back and forth and around. "Whee!" said Mother.

The three spirits of John de Conquer came down the tree. Mother rubbed the de Conquer root. The Hodag and the Fool-la-fafa became shades streaming back into the dark root. In a twinkling they were out of sight on that invisible string.

"Dwahro, yall did a good job," Mother Pearl said. She eyed the bandits, who were stunned mindless. She yawned, "Mercy me, I'm tired. Must be gettin' old or somethin'."

She and Dwahro stared up at the great woman poplar for a moment.

"Well, yellow woman," Mother Pearl spoke kindly, "we sure hated to shave and chisel some of she branches. We hope you understand why we had to."

The grand poplar breezed and her boughs sighed.

"You got some Thanksgivin' decoration there, and some Christmas, too," said Mother, "and not long 'fore them holidays come."

The forest was heard to moan as the poplar rustled and swayed.

"Let all who pass this way see what become of bandits," Mother Pearl spoke strong. "Three long months may they swang! Let de birds feed them; let rain wash them and sunshine dry them." She laughed. "Let this here demonstration be a warnin' to all bandits."

Mother Pearl rolled her hands in her painted apron. She stumbled around to the back of the poplar. For a moment human tiredness got the better of her.

"Mother? Where you goin'?" called Dwahro. But she made no reply.

Out from behind the tree came small and sweet Pretty Pearl. She was dressed in a small-sized shift. That's how Dwahro knew it was her. She had her thumb in her mouth, just for a second before she took it out.

"Too old for thumb suckin'," said Dwahro, under his breath. Again, he forgot Pretty wasn't human.

Pearl rubbed one eye with a fist.

"Hi, you, Dwahro," she said, softly. "Have I been asleep?"

CHAPTER SIX

"Not just been asleep," said Dwahro. "You done been *changed.* And all this time me and Mother Pearl has to git us in an' out of *bad* scrapes!"

Pearl stared at him. "That bowl on your head—did it really happen?" she asked. Her eyes were bright and alert, now. No signs of sleep anywhere.

"Did what really happen?" said Dwahro impatiently. "What we standin' around here for? We got to get goin'!"

"But I dreamed somethin' awful," said Pearl. "I . . ." She whirled around and stumbled backward at the sight of the great poplar.

"That was in my dream!" she said, pointing at the tree. And when she saw the roped men swinging from up high, she exclaimed, "They were there in my dream, too. Did I do that? Way up there?"

"Save me from dumb bunnies!" Dwahro said. "Did you do that in de dream—huh?" he said. "Huh, did you, li'l dummy?"

"Don't be callin' me no names, Dwahro," Pearl said.

"Yeah? Yeah?" said Dwahro irritably. "Who you think it was that climb up there and hang them mens, huh? Not you! It was me and Fool and Hodag, that's who. You weren't no place to be seen when the trouble starts. You do some disappearin' act. Left us to work it out ourselves, and them white folks 'bout to shoot us . . ."

Dwahro didn't get the chance to finish. Pearl held the de Conquer root in her right hand. Suddenly Dwahro's shade lay stretched out on the air, heading for the de Conquer root. His brightly colored bowl crashed to the ground and smashed. Dwahro himself was nowhere to be seen. Just that shade of him streaming toward the necklace, and the sound of his voice:

"No! No! Please, Pretty Pearl, don't put me back in to dangle on that string again. Please, Pretty, I am sorry I loses my temper so. Give me one more chance. I'll make it up to you, I swear!"

Pearl relented. She let go of the root. The shade of Dwahro streamed away from her to the spot where Dwahro had been standing when he had made Pearl angry. His suit reappeared and filled up with him.

"Oh! Oh!" Dwahro moaned, touching his arms and

face to make sure he wasn't a shade again. "Am I still is? Oh, I am. I be is. Thank goodness! Oh, thank you, Pretty."

"Say you sorry," said Pearl, watching him, rocking back and forth on her heels and toes, arms folded.

"I'm most certainly sorry. I don't know what gets into me, either," said Dwahro, shaking his head.

"I do," said Pearl. "You just some meanspirited when you want to be."

"I am!" said Dwahro. "I am just awful when I want to be." He shook his head forlornly.

"Well, you just better stop it and look after me de way you s'pose to, or I'll put you back and let de Hodag and de Hide-behind walk along with me."

"Please, Pearl," Dwahro said earnestly, "I wants to be right with you. Give me de chance to prove myself."

For a moment Pearl regarded him. She cocked her head to one side and the other. She did love having Dwahro along with her, and she wondered if she should tell him. Let him know that in the short time that they'd been together, she had grown quite fond of him.

Course, he can't take de place of my own John de Conquer, but he 'most like a brother that I has right here and now. But don't tell him nothin', she thought, else he'll turn right around and use it against you one time. He is so most strange like that, she thought. Jes' about as human as he can get without bein'.

Slowly, Pretty Pearl smiled at him. In a second Dwahro was grinning from ear to ear and practically crying, he was so genuinely grateful.

"All right," Pearl told him. "We gone forget everythin' you said bad this one time. Done forgot it."

"Let's go, Pretty," Dwahro said, quickly. "Let's get away from de awful stuff here."

"Yeah!" piped Pearl in her child's voice. "Let's get away from all de awful stuff. Humph! Humph! Humph! Fiffle!" She sniffed her nose at the men slowly swinging around and around up in the great poplar. The three men had observed the magic of Mother Pearl, of Dwahro and the Hodag and the Fool; and now that of Pearl when she made Dwahro into a shade. They simply stared.

They looked as if they had stumbled upon a world that couldn't possibly exist. But it did. They were captured on it, and no such thing could ever happen to them. But it had. Any minute, their stares seemed to say, they would awaken from this nightmare. But they didn't.

"Bye-bye!" Pretty Pearl called to them sweetly. "Come, Dwahro! We gone!"

Pearl skipped away from the clearing, going out under the grand woman poplar tree branches.

" 'Bye, she woman," called Pearl, as she waved back at the tree.

The poplar breezed and swayed, which made Pearl giggle. It frightened Dwahro. "She gone fall over doin' that," he said.

"Oh, be quiet, scaredy-cat!" Pearl said lightly. She skipped along. She had her bundle of clothes and a little food. She had her charms, her de Conquer root, sandals on her feet, and Dwahro for company. She skipped and twirled along.

[95]

Dwahro skipped right along with her. Then, instead of skipping or twirling, he commenced dancing or, better, hopping and slapping a ham bone, a half-spoken song.

"Ham bone, ham bone, where's you been?"

Dwahro started the song. He pressed his suit jacket tight about himself and placed his right foot on the other leg below the knee. With his right hand he beat out a difficult rhythm, smacking from his chest to his rump.

"Been to Georgia and back agin!"

shouted Pearl. She clapped her hands with delight, skipping in rhythm with Dwahro's hopping and smacking. The song came to her out of old slave times. She could add her own words to it.

"Ham bone, ham bone, where you stay?"

sang Dwahro, smacking front and back.

"Stayed in de forest most of de way,"

answered Pearl.

"Ham bone, ham bone, what'd you do?"

asked Dwahro.

> *"I caught a bird and fairly flew!"*

answered Pearl, giggling her head off.

On and on they went with the patter, Dwahro hopping and smacking himself in the fast ham-bone rhythm, and Pearl skipping and jumping, and clapping her hands in excitement. They made so much noise, they did not notice for a long time that the forest had grown very still.

> *"Ham bone, ham bone, what'd ya see?"*

asked Dwahro.

> *"Saw a forest come over me,"*

whispered Pearl all at once. She stopped skipping and was very quiet.

"Naw, that's no good," said Dwahro. "See, it has to make sense. How can 'a forest come over me' make sense?"

"It does," answered Pearl. "It just now come over me. Feel it?" she said.

Dwahro looked at her like he thought she was crazy. But then he felt it, too. "What's that?" he asked. "What's goin' on?"

"De quiet," said Pearl.

"Did you make it quiet?" asked Dwahro.

"No," said Pearl. "De forest did."

"How come it do that, Pearl?" asked Dwahro.

"You s'pose to know things first, Dwahro!" Pearl said angrily.

Dwahro was silent. He looked sheepish.

"What it was?" she asked.

"It was tellin' me," Dwahro said, "I got no business actin' up when we on our way in a strange place and don't know where we goin' or what we might stumble into. It my fault," he said. "Sorry, Pearl. I was too busy singin'."

"My fault, too," she said. "I was 'joyin' myself just as much as you."

"All right," Dwahro said. "We gone take care now."

"Yes," Pearl said.

"Let's walk and be quiet for a spell," Dwahro said.

They walked and were quiet. Dwahro had his arm protectively around Pearl.

The forest loomed around them. It was exciting to Pearl the way the trees could be all loblolly pine in a clump; then a whole grove of chestnut trees, spreading wide and handsome.

"They all kinds of trees in de forest, you know, Dwahro?" Pearl said. "Just as many, many kinds as you can think of."

"Know it," Dwahro said softly. He wasn't going to make the mistake of being loud again. "You know all what kinds?" Dwahro asked her.

"This a testing?" she asked him.

"Yesum, somethin' to pass de time, and somethin' to learn."

"Well, there's pines of all kinds," said Pearl.

"Loblolly, longleaf and slash!" whispered Dwahro. "Them kinds of pines."

"Them kinds of pines!" repeated Pearl, enjoying the rhythm of it. "And more trees are black birch and sourwood and sassafras and dogwood."

"Make me a fine cane of sourwood as soon as I can," said Dwahro.

"There's black gum and oak, white ash and cherry, maple and poplar, and walnut and locust."

"Make my cane knob of maple," said Dwahro. "And cherry bark for cough syrup."

"Ain't that somethin'?" said Pearl. "Don't forget them chestnut and hickory."

"If him be cold," spoke Dwahro, "burn him de best fire of hickory. But if him freeze to death, season de chestnut and build him de casket from it."

"Whew!" said Pearl. "Dwahro, you turnin' to sorrow."

"No, me," said Dwahro. "Just tellin' you true. And somethin' else. Mother Pearl be leavin' you some hickory nuts in de pocket of her apron."

"Dreamed about that and found 'em, too," said Pearl. "Have 'em later, if I feel like eatin' somethin'." Pearl being as she was, she ate only when she felt like it.

"But that's all them trees," said Pearl. "I don't guess I seen any more different trees than them ones I name, on the way to where we goin'."

"They enough and 'bout all of them, too," said Dwahro. "Now, you learn somethin'."

"Them names of lots of trees wasn't knowin' I had in my thoughts."

"Well, names be part of it, but not near all of it," said Dwahro.

"Not?" said Pearl.

"What you learnin' is why all kinds of peoples come find de forest so perfect a place to live."

"Yes, but why come they think it so?" asked Pearl.

"Because them trees and all them bitty plants give to de kinds of peoples all they need for life of self-sufficiency." Dwahro looked proud of himself and his many words.

"Really?" said Pearl. "How trees do all that?"

"Wheels," said Dwahro, "barrels, buckets, chairs, posts, shingles, tools, toys for de babes, floorin', beds, spoons, bowls, drawers, knobs, rollin' pins, toothbrushes, brooms, mallets, doors, sheds, fires and caskets, all from trees."

"Goodness!" said Pearl. "They can live practically offn them trees!"

"Practically," said Dwahro, "plus weeds and plants, like milkweed and cresses, greens such as mustard, and all them bushes, too, that grows wild."

"My!" exclaimed Pearl.

"And plus what they plants themselves. Corn and potatoes and onion, carrots, and vines o' melon," said Dwahro. "They got meat, too, maybe livestock; and wildness, what they catch by hunting and trapping.

"They get a thousand more things from trees and plants, which I don't feel like namin' o' them names," Dwahro said.

"You mean, you done feel all this about this forest?"

asked Pearl, awestruck by his knowledge.

I WANT TO BE FREE! I WANT TO BE HUMAN! Dwahro screamed inside. The desire for life rose in him. He wanted more than just the form and the costume. Then the wish fell away as abruptly as it had come.

"I know what I know about them kinds of peoples," he said seriously, as if he had never been a silly, foolish Dwahro.

"Dwahro, what you mean by them *kinds* of people?" asked Pearl. "They only one kind of folks here, I bet, and they them black inside folks."

Dwahro had stopped a moment. He looked straight ahead, as though he was examining the air with all of his spirit's senses. He slid his arm from around Pearl's shoulder and clasped her hand in both his hands. Then he started out again, moving ever so slowly. Pearl was slightly behind him, her hand tightly held in his.

"What is it, Dwahro? What you feelin' so, now?" she asked.

Dwahro's face appeared to darken with its wisdom. He smiled a smile of knowing. "Kind," he said, softly. "Blood, him all around. Hear him?"

"What?" said Pearl. "Hear what? Stop so I can hear. I can't hear nothin' when we movin'."

They stopped, but Pearl still couldn't hear anything unusual. "Nothin'," she told Dwahro. "Just nothin'. You makin' him up. And what is 'blood' you talkin' about?"

"Full bloods," he said quietly. "They calls themselves *Ani-Yun'Wiya.* Them 'Real People.' Most know them by *Cherokee.* Be easier to say. And come from Choctaw language, *Chillaki,* mean 'cave dweller.'

"Look around," Dwahro said. He looked serenely in front of him. "They all around us. See for yourself."

"What?" whispered Pearl. Swiftly, she turned from one side to the other. What she saw made her cling to Dwahro. All around them were men, ever so still. Strange men, each one with his hand up next to his shoulder. For each held the bridle of the horse he led. There were twelve men with twelve riding ponies and several pack animals. The men were fairly tall and light in complexion. They wore buckskin shirts, sashed around the middle, leggings and moccasins with porcupine-quill ornaments. Each wore a turban, the headdress the Cherokee had adopted.

The manner of these Cherokees was very grave. They had come upon Pearl and Dwahro unexpectedly and had had no chance to hide themselves before Dwahro had felt their presence.

"They see us," Dwahro said quietly.

"Well, of course they see us," Pearl said. "We standin' right here in plain sight."

"No," Dwahro said. "See how they don't move? Like statues. See, they never taken they eyes from de ground. Why? Because they see us is why."

"I *know* they see us," Pearl said, exasperated. "They *lookin'* like they pretendin' they can't see us."

"Shhhh!" Dwahro said. "These de ones escape in these mountains long ago when they remove all them Indian tribes in Georgia to west of de Mississippi River. Some were babies then or ain't even born then. Them's people here, de remnant band, hid out. They still hidin', and still will hide for a long, long time."

Pearl watched the solemn Cherokees, and by watching had an inkling of the great suffering of these Real People.

"Don't matter we wear clothes like we black folks. Talk like it, act like it," said Dwahro. "I think they see us for true."

"I think so too," Pearl whispered.

"They know spirits when they see them, for they see them all de time. Live every day with spirits of de woods, de sky and they own people gone over de way."

"Will they tell anybody about us?" Pearl asked.

"Don't believe they will," said Dwahro. "They figure it not their business too much. They don't know what we doin' here, but they suspect we goin' where they goin'. But they won't be movin' on 'til we make a move."

"Why come?" asked Pearl.

"Never get in de way of spirits," Dwahro said. "You show all of best respect for de spirits."

"I see," said Pearl. "Should we talk to them, you think?"

"No," said Dwahro. He was silent a moment, as though listening. "They de 'sang' men," he said, finally. "They de traders to de inside folks."

"Well, I'll be!" said Pearl.

"All of it so secret here," Dwahro said. "They come for miles through mountains. Take goods from inside folks to de ships to trade. All this done in hidin'. When they get near de coast, still hidin', they transfer all de goods to white friends who take it rest de way."

"No!" said Pearl. "They trust them whites to not steal what they give them?"

"All de whites not so terrible, Pearl. Remember there was whites helped runaway slaves get to de north," Dwahro said.

"Oh, that's right!" said Pearl. "It so hard to remember how these humans be. Dwahro—do you think these mens can understand us talkin'?"

She regarded the Real People, who had not moved a muscle and could stand still for hours—and would, right now, unless she and Dwahro went on their way.

"They waitin' for us to make a move," said Dwahro. "Best we move on."

"All right," said Pearl. "Hold my hand." She felt like a child, all wary in the woods.

Dwahro smiled. "Don't worry about de Cherokee, Pearl. They our friends."

So it was that Pearl and Dwahro made their way on through the forest. The Real People were with them. And not even their horses made a sound.

Pearl glanced around at the sang men once, and then quickly back. The men had their eyes cast down at the ground.

The forest was thicker now, and darker. Dwahro had his arm out in front of them to keep low branches and high undergrowth out of their faces.

"Why they called de sang men?" Pearl thought to ask, as quietly as she could. Still, the sound of her voice seemed to whisper an echo in the utter stillness.

Dwahro seemed to gaze inward for the answer. "Because," he said, "they come, carry off de olden root."

"What? A root?" said Pearl.

"The inside folks grow de best root crop in this world. De olden crop. De most valuable crop."

"What crop is that, and what it have to do with what those Real People be called, sang men?"

" 'Cause the crop is de herb ginseng. It called sang by all who know it. And sang men are dealers in it, and sang hunters come from inside folks, who supply it to dealers. Sang grow in China first; couldn't grow enough. Then it found over here, just as good, too. And sang from here go to China, where it be thought a cure-all, 'specially of old folks' ills of old age. Pay large money all de way down de line for sang. And Real People, them best dealers in sang, and inside folks, them best suppliers of wild sang."

"I don't know," said Pearl, quietly. "It all be soundin' most strange."

"Is strange, if you don't know nothin' 'bout the market," Dwahro said smugly.

"Oh, you know everything!" Pearl whispered irritably.

"I know what I feel I knows," said Dwahro, finishing the conversation. For in front of them there was some slight movement among the deep-shaded trees.

Somethin' be there! thought Pearl. She clutched Dwahro's hand tighter. What gone happen to us now?

What happened was the most natural thing to happen. But it occurred without warning. One moment they were in the depths of forest gloom. If Pretty Pearl had been alone, she would have known she was lost. But when she thought about it, she realized that some knowledge of fugitives and dark secrets had led them to this lonely, forbidding place.

What had appeared to be a thick wall of brambles and wild grape vines fell away in a soft rustling. It was like the gentlest, most delicate door opening, Pearl thought.

And before them lay the lane, like a street, only better than the slave street of old times. It was a lane of grasses with hard live oak trees up and down its sides. There were children running among the trees. They had not noticed the delicate door opening. There were some hands near, where the soft rustling revealed the location of the inside folks. There was much movement off the lane, where there were dwelling places. At the far end of the lane was a huge, black cooking pot with a smoldering hot fire under it. The fire was banked hot, with no flames or much smoke that might reveal this secret hiding place. Seeing the fire, Pretty Pearl dashed behind one of the oaks down the row. Just like a child, she loved cook fires.

"Pearl!" Dwahro whispered loudly.

The Real People came up slowly and cautiously around Dwahro, not looking at him. They pulled their horses by and into the lane of freedom. Freedom Lane. They moved the horses, themselves and the pack animals across the lane and into the area where there were dwellings. Soon some of the inside folks came and helped the Real People unload goods and supplies. All this was done efficiently, and mostly in silence.

"Oh, me, that Pearl!" whispered Dwahro. "Where you be to, what you up to now!"

He looked down the lane and saw no trace of Pretty.

He looked up the lane and saw an eyeful. He saw Mother Pearl, big as life. She was stirring the great pot right there in Freedom Lane. At her feet sat a nice bunch of young children. The human, maw woman part of her loved feeding the children. And among the boys and girls sat that devilish Pretty Pearl herself.

"Mother!" hollered Dwahro before he thought. "How yall both be at once?"

Suddenly one of the inside men who had been working with the Real People came swiftly up to Dwahro and gave him a hard smack on the ear. Dwahro jumped sky high, higher than he needed to, anyway. But any chance Dwahro got, he had to perform.

"Hush you mouth!" said the inside man. "You got a place to live here, don't go spoil it."

"Yessuh," Dwahro mumbled. "Where is we, any-ways?"

"You with us," the inside man told him. "Be a place called Promise."

"Promise," said Dwahro. "I like that."

"So do we," said the inside man. "So keep you voice low."

"Yessuh," said Dwahro. "You gone put me to work for no pay, too?"

The inside man was tall and lean. Wise through the light of his dark eyes. He gave Dwahro a good looking over.

"What you mean, too?" asked the inside man. "And how you gone work in that getup and play-pretty outfit? What you do, sing?"

[107]

"I can do that," said Dwahro. "I can dance, too. I'm a right smart entertainer."

"Is you now?" said the inside man. "Well."

Dwahro stood as straight as he could. The inside man looked to be in his forties.

'Bout forty-eight exactly, thought Dwahro. Old enough to be my father!

He liked the inside man. Liked the true light out of his eyes and his tall, straight stance.

"You gone just let me walk in like this, and no questions, nothin'?" asked Dwahro.

"What questions you want me to ask?" said the inside man. His face held little expression, but he watched Dwahro closely. Dwahro could see two of the Real People behind the inside man's back. They couldn't believe that the inside man was actually talking to something they knew to be a spirit.

Inside man, you just done grown about a foot taller in they eyes, Dwahro thought. Then he realized the inside man was waiting for him to answer.

"Uh, no, me, I just wonder about you bein' so open, lettin' us in, them Indians, and like that."

"Ani-Yun'Wiya be survivors," the inside man said, about the Cherokees. "These we trust better than ourselves. They are as ourselves. Don't you ever forget it."

Dwahro hung his head. "Yessuh." He spoke softly. The inside man turned on his heel, then turned back and said, "They come with you?" He looked to Mother Pearl and Pretty Pearl.

"Yessuh," Dwahro said.

"Then the three of you will find your way here as we all have found our way," said the inside man.

"Yeah, but where we gone go, how will we sleep, no bedding?"

"You go to de earth," said the inside man solemnly, "and lay youself on de mast of de forest. Someone will share with you. There are blankets, from trade with Ani-Yun'Wiya."

"But what about food, how we gone get that?" Dwahro asked.

"You work for it, like everybody else," said the inside man. "We all share food and we all work in one way or another."

"Yessuh," said Dwahro. "But what they be callin' you?"

"What they be callin' *you*?" asked the inside man.

"Callin' me Toby," said Dwahro.

"You don't look like no Toby to me," said the inside man, not unkindly.

Dwahro was drawn to this man, who must be like a father. "Not no Toby," said Dwahro, afraid, but trusting just the same.

"Then who?" asked the man.

"I am de spirit Dwahro," said Dwahro. He smiled, almost sheepishly.

The inside man threw back his head and laughed. "Yeah, you be! Yeah!" he said. "Well all right, Dwahro, if that's what you want. Better than Toby." And he laughed again. "By de way," he added, "I am Selah, but all here call me Black Salt." The inside man grinned, friendly enough, and left Dwahro.

Dwahro stood there in the lane. To his left side were all of the brambles and vines, in place again, hiding the opening that had led to the inside. A few people walked by on the far path of the lane. Everyone seemed to be busy. The children had gathered around Mother Pearl and Pretty.

Now what I'm gone do with two Pearls to handle at de same time? Dwahro wondered anxiously. Reluctantly, he strolled toward the far walk of Freedom Lane. He could smell what was in the black cooking pot. It smelled mighty fine, even to him.

But how'd they *do* that? he wondered, about Pretty Pearl and Mother. How'd they *divide* in two like that!

CHAPTER SEVEN

Mother Pearl had the children of Freedom Lane in the palm of her hand. She had become the mawmaw woman mother. She was the caretaker of all children whose folks had to toil for a better time of Promise. Promise was the secret place where they lived freely. A better time would come when they need not hide but could walk and live in the open, side by side with other peoples.

There had been no mawmaw woman in this place of Promise since the last mawmaw had grown ill and had not been able to handle the children. The women who were young and strong had to work in gardens or hunt sang with the men, or help with shed chores, or sew or

weave cloth. Mother Pearl's sudden appearance was
looked on as a wonderful surprise by those who knew she
had arrived—mainly the children.

They bunched around her, the group of them growing
as word spread through Promise. Mother Pearl stood
until one of the children thought to bring her a stool. She
sat, then, stirring the huge pot of okra kinggombo soup
that was thickened with young okra pods.

"Heh, heh, heh," Mother laughed. Her eyes shone at
the children. She smiled and nodded at them until they
were quieted and she had their full attention. Then she
began a patter:

"Hear me, chil'ren, you, granmaws and granpaws, if
you be listenin', an' sleep-a-babes, too!"

"Yes, ma'am!" answered the children in chorus. "We
hear you." They had caught Mother Pearl's excitement.
She had broken the monotony of their days and years in
hiding.

"Hear me, long, tall Dwahro, you!" Mother Pearl
greeted Dwahro as he came to stand on the side. All the
children looked at him. Their eyes grew big at the sight
of his fabulous suit of stars and moons.

"Oooh, yes, ma'am!" they said.

"I may spit fire when de kettle-cook bubbles and biles
over in de street."

"And don't we sorrow to see it spill!" answered the
children softly.

"I may cuff de ears of he chile when footprint him de
lane dust I sweep smooth," chanted Mother in a sing-
song, not too loud.

"And cannot stop he chile him hollering," sang the children.

"I may sic my Fool-la-fafa on boys and girls when they worry pest they granmaws."

"Oh, best woman," cried the children, "don't sic what-it-is on us in de lane. We sure will be good!"

"Sure about that?" sang out Mother Pearl.

"Oooh, yes, *ma'am*!" sang the children.

"Well, I do love my chil'ren," sang Mother, "for it's a nature you to footprint and holler and worry pest, too."

"We cain't help it, though we try," chanted the children.

"I do love me gombo, bubbling up be smooth and thick," sang Mother Pearl. "Gombo be odor rich to bile."

"Sure do taste like it, too," softly sang the children.

"But better you know who I be and what can I do!" cried Mother in a strong, low voice.

"And never miss knowin', she mawmaw," softly chanted the children.

"Knooows you I got him de Conquer root," sang Mother in a pure, untroubled contralto voice. She touched her necklace so the children would understand.

"See what-it-is hangin' there?" sang the children. "Big root necklace! It scare us so!"

"Scaredy-cats!" whispered Mother, and the children covered their mouths to hear her voice. "Him de Conquer root won't bother head you if close mouths you and listen me hard."

"Yes, ma'am," sang the children. "We gone listen a hard ground."

"Listen, John de Conquer root workin' true. I'm Mother Pearl. I may tell you all kinds of tales. But trust me! I double never ever never lie to my chil'ren!"

Mother Pearl finished her patter. The children smiled happily and jumped up and down in appreciation. Then Mother raised her hand. The children sat down and calmed themselves in order to listen. Their eyes were bright and watchful. They waited with enthusiasm.

"Good evenin', chil'ren," Mother Pearl said kindly. It was nearly the end of dayclean and fast traveling to sundown.

The children nodded. One of them could contain herself no longer. "But what it is, de Conquer? And where's yall come from? You and him, what-he-name, and she, too!" The child pointed right at Pretty Pearl. All this time Pretty had been sitting with the children. She had become one of them completely, so it appeared.

"Heh, heh, heh," said Mother, laughing gently. "All right, now. Here it is." She beckoned to Pearl and Dwahro. They came up to stand beside her.

"Be callin' me Mother Pearl Perry," said Mother. "That be my soul name. But you don't be callin' me Mother Perry, be callin' Mother Pearl—yes? It soundin' more frien'ly."

"Yes, ma'am, it do," the children agreed.

"Well, then, this be my chile, Pretty Pearl. Callin' her Pretty or Pearl," said Mother.

"Pretty," one child said.

Another said, "Pearl, Pretty," as though thinking about the name.

And then a strapping youth spoke up: "Be *very* Pretty Pearl!" All of the children laughed and giggled. Pearl commenced to blush and cover her mouth. The boy grinned, but he wouldn't stop looking at Pearl.

"Um-hmm," said Mother. "What you name, son?" asked Mother Pearl.

"Who, me?" said the youth, pointing to himself.

"Who but you?" answered Mother.

"Be name of Josias, son of Black Salt," said the youth.

"Ahm!" escaped from Dwahro's lips like a sighing.

"What it is?" asked Mother Pearl.

"Be talkin' to his father, Black Salt, back there," Dwahro answered. I could be second son of Black Salt, he thought wistfully.

"Well," said Mother. "So be Josias, son of Black Salt. Be Pretty Pearl, too." She smiled. "And last, be not least, name of Toby Perry, my nephew," she told the children.

"No, now!" whispered Dwahro to Mother Pearl. "Done changed all that. Be Dwahro from here and now."

"Say it is!" Mother whispered back. And told the children. "Toby be him slave name, and him don't want it in de land o' Promise. So let him be name of Dwahro to all everywhere."

"Dwahro!" the children said. "Evenin', Dwahro." The named rolled around them in a soft pattering for a moment.

Dwahro bowed to all of them. He did a high step that spun him clear around in a fancy circle.

The children laughed and clapped.

"Dwahro can do lots of dance and sings," Mother explained. "Heh, heh.

"Now," she said. Mother Pearl touched the large root around her neck. She held it out for all to see. Then she took a tiny, red-satin sachet bag from her bodice. It had gold pull cords across the top. She covered the de Conquer root with the sachet bag and pulled the cords tight.

"See?" she said, and showed all the children that Pretty Pearl had a John de Conquer root necklace as well. Pearl's was somewhat smaller. The strand of de Conquer hair that held it safely was almost invisible. It was a thin hairline around her neck. Pearl wore her de Conquer in the open with no sachet bag.

"Now," Mother said, "tell yall a story."

"Oooh!" said the children. "It a scary story?" one of them asked.

"It a true story?" another asked.

"Tell you true," said Mother. "It be not scary. Now here come John de Conquer. Come down from Mount Kenya in Africa. Come down and ride a slave ship from de coast to this land."

"Ohhh!" said the children. "Him a slave come from Africa!"

"No," said Mother, "him come here free from Africa. Come to help de black folks, and de white folks never hear him come. For he come as a great bird with strong wings. Called bird albatross."

"No!" whispered the children.

"Yes!" said Mother. "And John de Conquer brings

hope. And he come to southern soil of Georgia two hundred years before de terrible war."

"Two hundred years!" said the children.

"Even more than two hundred years, and he predict freedom for black folks. Said de war be fought only to mess up de white folks' minds."

"No!" said the children.

"Oh, yes," said Mother Pearl. "And long before that Great Surrender, John de Conquer lay down in southern soil. Nobody seen him for a long kind of time. But he grow a bush name of John de Conquer. And this root be from that first bush ever grow somewhere." Mother Pearl shook her sachet bag. "And Pretty Pearl's root came off from my root, so she has de John de Conquer, too."

"Meanin' to ask you," Dwahro whispered to Mother Pearl, "how come both you and Pearl be here at once? How be it you both have de Conquer, too?"

"Be tellin' you all about it later," Mother whispered back.

"Remember," she told the children, "they's somebody out there just for you chil'ren. Be de Conquer who call de freedom long before it come. Come again when us need him powerful enough. But for now, he be givin' us him de Conquer root."

"Lemme see it?" the children asked.

"Each one come and touch it, gently now," said Mother. The children came up to examine both Pearl's and Mother Pearl's de Conquer. The roots didn't burn them.

"Where can we get de Conquer?" asked a child.

"What you name, chile?" said Mother. "Been forgot my manners. Did not ask what you names."

"Name of Bessie Freedom," said the child, about Pretty Pearl's age. "My daddy be born free in de Choctaw nation, Indian Territory. But he be stolen and sold to slavery down in Luziana."

"Yes, chile," said Mother Pearl, gently. "Be so proud to meet you." She hugged the child.

"Proud, Bessie," said Pretty Pearl, and hugged her, too.

Dwahro bowed and shook Bessie Freedom's hand.

"Name of Jabbho," spoke up a small boy of about ten years. "Come here with my grandpaw from somewheres. Don't know no pappy and no mammy. Grandpaw born a slave in Georgia. He decide to run when my peoples sold to Miss'sippi."

"Yes! Jabbho, bless you, son. Pleased to know you!" said Mother.

"Yesum," Jabbho said. Mother Pearl hugged him, and he could barely hold back the tears as he buried his face in her shoulder.

The naming of their names and the calling out of their histories continued, until all of them were named and their records given.

"Name of Choska," told a child. "Mammy was called a native. Born in de old Creek nation somewheres and her massa was a Creek Indian."

"Name of Willis. I come along, follow the others, slippin' through de forest. Don't know where I comes from.

Don't know where I am at, only it be forest and home."

"Name of Poor Tree. My pa live in Georgia after Surrender, make all kinds of baskets and brooms. De white folks love him baskets but don't wants to pay for them. The Ku Kluck didn't like him, so they ties him to a horse. They shoot him and kill de horse, too. I run to here, follow de Real Mens. They feedin' me."

"Mercy!" said Mother Pearl. Sadness filled her eyes. She sat on the stool with a heavy heart as the children related their sorrow stories. She never ceased stirring the kinggombo. And she listened to every story. That kerchief was soaking wet when at last she laid it beside her to dry it.

"Well, now, chil'ren," she said. "We all together. Nothin' bad gone happen as long as we together." A terrible shame, she thought, that one kind of human hurt de other kind!

Then Mother Pearl fell silent. The long wood spoon she used to stir the soup went around very slowly. Her eyes were distant, deep with dark dreams. And her face closed her inside herself.

The children had many more questions, but they could see that Mother Pearl had shut up tight. Children of freemen knew when to be silent, when to make noise and when to ask questions. When Mother closed herself in, they looked to Pretty Pearl. Pearl moved away from Mother Pearl and Dwahro, and the children bunched in around her.

Pretty Pearl wasn't used to so much attention, having so many young human beings so close around.

What you s'pose to say to them? thought Pearl. But it soon was easy. The children asked questions and she answered.

"Where's you comes from?" asked one child.

"Come from all de place of Georgia," said Pearl promptly. She found that telling the truth was easy. "Got away from Savannah over there and come up and up. Could see de forest a long way."

"Did yall work some places, for to keep mind and body together?" asked Josias, son of Black Salt.

Pearl told the truth, the best she knew how. "We live off de land. We run into some outside folks livin' by a plantation ruin, but they don't wants to leave."

"Heard tell they's lots of outside folks," said Josias. "And bad folks ketch them. So why they stay on de outside, 'stead of hidin'?"

"Think they figure come a long time, and they be stronger for stayin' in de heart of battle. Be made fit for it," Pearl said.

The children stared at Pearl as though she knew everything. She smiled proudly, for she did seem to be able to figure out a great deal in human terms. But when they asked her more questions about the de Conquer root necklace, she grew quiet. The children were fascinated by the de Conquer story and the root. But Pearl wouldn't say.

"Best we put that by for another day," she said softly. "We got most plenty time when we go in de woods and pick us flowers."

"Oh, we don't go in de woods," said a child called

Flossy. "We stay here behind de bramble blind. Nobody ever s'pose to see us and know we's here."

"But if they comes this close, they surely hear you in here," Pearl said.

"Did you hear anythin' when you come up?" asked Josias. He had taken a place on Pearl's right side. It appeared he meant to stay there as close and as long as he could. Pearl didn't mind him.

"Don't 'member hearin' somethin'," said Pearl. "Don't guess I did, then."

" 'Cause long afore you gets here, we knows what's comin'," Josias said.

"How is that?" asked Pearl.

"This be de very edge, de natu'al divide," Josias told her. "You done seen but just a slight bit of what we holdin'."

"Holdin'?" said Pearl. "What, holdin', and how you know who's comin'?"

"We got us see-alls," he said. All the children nodded and murmured.

When Pearl looked inquiringly at him, not understanding, he said, "It be clearer to you much more when dayclean come again. Now is time for evenin'. My father give a *render* soon. He give it ever' time new folks comes."

"That so?" said Pearl. The children smiled, friendly enough. Josias stayed at her side. At first his presence made Pearl shy. But when she realized he felt comfortable beside her, she did not mind him. There were times when she forgot about him, and then she would remember he was there right by her. She and the children sat there in the lane near the simmering pot that Mother Pearl slowly stirred to done-be-supper.

§ §

Dayclean was over. Pearl knew that the sun must have set, although she could not see it. What she saw was a fine orange-and-red light that glinted and shone everywhere along the street and live oaks of Freedom Lane. It reflected in the eyes of the children around her. It seemed to fill the air above her. She looked up and saw no blue sky. She saw that orange-red light on a mist where the sky should have been. And smelled a stifling odor, like the odor when the bandit in the forest shot off his gun, but more suffocating. Then there was a crack of thunder, and a cool, misty rain began.

"Only last a minute," said Josias. "Never does last this time o' year. But it warnin', wettin' things down for what's to come."

"What be that?" asked Pearl.

"Winter," he said. "This be north mountain high. They be weather here that can get most cold when it wants."

"Yay-ah," the rest of the children agreed.

"Do it now!" said Pearl, for she had not come across cold weather since she had been in this new-found land. The misty rain ceased abruptly.

"But first we gone have a little fall, come up yet, afore that," Josias said.

For the first time, Pretty Pearl was able to look Josias, son of Black Salt, straight in his face without giggling like a silly child.

What am I now, if not some silly chile! she thought. What am I, Pearl Perry, first from Mount Highness, now from de forest? One moment she would feel the feelings of the Mount; the next she would know her heart as a runaway heart finding safety inside a great, continuing darkness of trees.

Pearl sighed. Who want to be of a lonely Mount Highness? Be a happy inside Pearl. She looked into Josias' eyes. They were gray with flecks of gold. His skin was oak brown. "How came you so white?" she said. He turned away. And she was sorry she had asked a question before she thought.

The children stared at her, watchful of her all of a sudden, fearing she might hurt them somehow. Had she hurt Josias? She thought and thought about it, about him, so white. And then she knew, and she was so sorry. Knew that some master had had his child by a slave woman. He had not married her. She knew that Josias was the result of such a union.

"Be what happens in slavery," she said softly.

"They be all colors, inside folks. Ain't pay no never-mind," Josias said.

"Josias, I never mean nothin' by sayin' question. Don't matter no skin to me. You, Josias, be my best frien'?"

Josias smiled, and was delighted. "Happy to be you best frien', Pretty Pearl. You be mine, too."

"Good!" Pearl said.

"Good!" said the children in unison. Then they all laughed.

It was eveningtime and suppertime. The inside folks were drifting in from their work. Pearl could clearly see them coming in from somewhere. Some came from one direction, pushing carts. They had hoes over their shoulders. Picks and axes. Some of them had tools she did not recognize. Others carried baskets of food that they took to sheds, or into the cabins. Pearl saw people seem to rise out of bushes a ways off, in back of the cabins that bordered Freedom Lane. Saw women rise up with baskets on their heads. They rose out of bushes, heads, necks, shoulders, chests, waists, all the way to their feet. Saw women with shovels rise up. And men rising, brown and black shapes, up from undergrowth.

"How they do that?" Pearl asked. "Come up from de earth that way?"

"Huh?" said the children. They looked where Pearl was looking. Then, softly, they laughed. Never did they forget to keep as quiet as possible, even when laughing. But they did laugh and grin and giggle, cupping palms over their mouths. Children rocked and swayed, giggling softly.

"Well, what's so funny, you chil'ren!" said Pearl, growing angry. "Don't go makin' me mad, no tellin' what I might do. Ask Dwahro, you don't believe me." She thought of saying, *I got de Conquer, don't you forget!* but decided not to.

"Listen, they don't mean nothin'," said Josias. "You

[124]

wait 'til marnin', we show you what you seein' over there. Come dayclean, I shows you all they is to see here."

"Well, all right," said Pearl. "Just ain't used to havin' somebody laugh at me. Makin' me mad, too."

"They ain't laughin' at you," Josias explained. "They's laughin' with you."

"Didn't know I was laughin'," Pearl said.

"It just a way of sayin'," he said.

Now Pearl could see that all the peoples of inside were coming in toward the cabins. The dayclean was over, and they were home from wherever they had been. Buckets were brought out from the cabins. They were carried off a ways and brought back, filled with water. Buckets were set over holes in the ground where there were red-hot coals. The water was warmed and then poured into gourd containers. Some of the men took up the gourds and emptied them over their heads. They sputtered and sneezed and rubbed the water into their faces, necks and hands. Then they dried themselves on pieces of well-worn cloth. The men and women took up gourds and washed. A bucket of cold spring water was set on the ground. Folks came up with small gourds and drank long and deep from the cold water. All the buckets were put aside in a row, with one left over the hole of hot coals.

Washed from the day's work, with their thirsts quenched, the inside folks turned toward Freedom Lane. They spoke softly to one another. They appeared tired from hard labor, but they seemed satisfied with the accomplishment of working for themselves.

One by one the children got up to greet those they

belonged to. Even those who were orphaned, like Bessie Freedom, young Willis and Poor Tree, lived with somebody.

"Don't you go greet you pappy?" asked Pearl of Josias.

"No'm," he said. "He already on de Lane. He comin' thisaway right now."

Black Salt had taken care of the Real People and their animals. Clearly he was one of the leaders of the inside folks, if not *the* leader. Now he came over to where Pearl and Josias sat.

He stood over Josias and placed his hand firmly on Josias' head. He tilted his son's head upward. Black Salt looked into his son's face. Riveted his son with his eyes and read him. He seemed satisfied with what he saw.

" 'Lo, Pappy," Josias said, simply.

" 'Lo, son." Black Salt had a quiet, low voice. It was not loud; it was firm and clear.

"Be callin' her Pretty Pearl," said Josias, looking at Pearl. "She come from clear Savannah with she, over there. Name of Mother Pearl," nodding to Mother Pearl, who stirred and seasoned the kinggombo, "and him, over there, be . . ."

"Know him, met him comin' in," said Black Salt.

He gave a long, appraising look at Mother Pearl. Mother Pearl saw him and nodded carefully, respectfully at him. There was a pause before he nodded back. Something passed between them. Some knowledge. Pretty Pearl intercepted part of the quiet assurance of it.

He turned to Pretty Pearl. Did not quite smile. But his eyes seemed warm and pleasant looking at her, she felt.

" 'Lo, young Pearl," he said, gently. "Be welcome with us."

"Be named Black Salt, my pappy," said Josias, proudly.

"Evenin', suh," Pearl said, remembering her manners. "Be most proud to meet yall. Glad to be here, some-place!" She laughed. "Never thought we find a home, and bandits in there, they try to caught us."

"How you get away from them?" Black Salt wanted to know.

Pearl thought quickly.

"Mammy have a pocket o' pepper just in case some big animal. Only they white folks and gone hurt us. But she throw de pepper. Strong, red pepper, and we have time get away from them and hide good in de thickets."

"Well," said Black Salt, "yall had a time. You be all right here."

He turned back to Mother. "Glad to have us a maw-maw agin," he said. "That's a new kind o' apron she wearin'."

"No, suh," said Pearl. "That my cousin do, Dwahro. He paintin' de apron when she tired and we stop to rest some. She tell him colors to get from de barks and things. And him get de colors and him paintin' on de apron to please she Aunt Pearl."

"I see," said Black Salt. "So he her nephew, and paint man."

"Yessuh," said Pearl. "He ain't got no fambly but us."

Black Salt looked at Pearl sharply. It took all her strength not to hang her head for lying to him.

But you see, she thought, if I be tellin' you true, you won't believe it and think we are some bad peoples or somethin'. How you ever gone believe in de gods on high? So we wait and see. Wait and see. Forgive us, if you knew.

Pearl smiled innocently at Black Salt. Finally, he smiled kindly back.

Then he turned and walked toward the supper pot.

All of the inside folks came forward into Freedom Lane. Strolled along the walk of a street in the cool of the evening. It was not dark yet, but it was twilight. Dim and pleasantly warm in that most secret of places, in that period just after sunset and before dark.

Behind the inside folks came the Real People, who had brought in the supplies.

"Didn't know they was still here," Pearl said.

"They stay the night. Leave at dawn," Josias said. "Anyway, it better, they be here when my father gone render."

"He gone what?" said Pearl.

"Shhhh," Josias warned.

Suddenly Pearl was aware of the stillness. The inside folks had settled down before the supper pot. They held their children in their laps or hugged them tightly to them. Mother Pearl sat behind that huge pot. Her hands were on the stir spoon but she did not move them, stirring. Black Salt came to stand on the left of Mother and the pot. Dwahro had seated himself at the right of the pot. Finally, the Real People, those dozen men, settled themselves silently at the feet of Black Salt. They did not look around. They knew the powers of black folks were there, stirring the pot and sitting there and over there. They made no mention of it. The inside folks never knew there were godly creatures and a spirit so near. But they knew that something good had hold of their luck. As Black Salt, the leader of them, prepared himself to pass strengthful words to them, and history, ways to live and with promise, they knew that the light of truth was theirs.

"Welcome to de new folks from the outside. Pretty Pearl," Black Salt said. He had her stand. The folks smiled and greeted her. Shyly, Pretty smiled back and bowed slightly.

"Mother Pearl," Black Salt said, introducing her.

"Heh, heh, heh," laughed Mother Pearl, so pleased to be the mawmaw among them.

"Dwahro, who can paint de pictures," said Black Salt. They all oohed over Mother Pearl's apron as she stood in the light to show it off. Someone stoked the fire so that it grew and all could see. They turned to Dwahro, nodding with respect.

"I got lots to show you," Dwahro told all of them. "Glad to be here." And he was. He was as happy as he could be. Hadn't thought about showing off, either.

Just the same as them! he thought.

The Real People looked at Black Salt. They felt the presence of ones who were more than humankind. They would respect all those inside. But they would not look at three of them.

CHAPTER EIGHT

Black Salt raised his hand, his arm outstretched above them. "Praise be!" he said with enthusiasm, but softly. Simultaneously there was movement on the side of Freedom Lane where there were cabins. There was movement from the cabins into the lane. For the first time, Pretty Pearl saw older people. Grandmaws and grandpaws came silently around them and handed out wood bowls and wood spoons. The bowls were made of oak and worn smooth.

"How came these?" whispered Pearl to Josias.

"They be bowls made by woodmen," Josias told her.

"And them old folks," said Pearl, "where they been?"

"Some them de see-alls. Shhhh," Josias whispered back. "Tomorra marnin'."

"You got a right," Black Salt began with ceremony, "I got a right." His voice was low but clear. "We all got a right to de tree of life."

"Yes! Yes!" whispered the old ones. The old folks moved silently among the inside folks, handing out the bowls and spoons. Now and then one of them would pat the head of a child. Another one straightened up at Black Salt's words and answered in song:

> *"Ever' time I thought I was los',*
> *De dungeon shuck an' de chain fell off."*

> *"You got a right,"*

Black Salt sang softly,

> *"I got a right.*
> *We all got a right to de tree of life."*

"Yes! Yes!" spoke Mother Pearl. Now the bowls were passed forward. Old folks handed the bowls to Mother to be filled. Next, the bowls of kinggombo were passed back through the seated crowd, and the song went on and on in the firelight:

> *"You got a right, I got a right.*
> *We all got a right to de tree of life!"*

until all were served. The Real People were served, the old folks had filled their bowls. Dwahro, who had remained at Mother's side, and Mother Pearl, too, had their bowls.

Black Salt had just a gourd from which he supped, shunning a spoon. He stood, eating. And all did eat. Silence, in which they enjoyed the kinggombo.

" 'Tis good," someone commented.

"Mother Pearl make de best gombo," said Dwahro proudly.

"That so?" said another.

"Be glad she come to stay, mawmaw," one woman said. "Not be eatin' so fine before."

Many laughed, saying, "Uh-uh, no we din't, too!"

They ate and enjoyed until the great, black supper pot was nearly empty and taken off the heat.

The folks gathered themselves on all sides around the fire. The Real People were still present and stayed near Black Salt, who now occupied the stool by the glowing embers. Someone else had got Mother and Dwahro a mat to sit on. The old folks collected all of the bowls and spoons. Took them away.

Black Salt spoke quietly. "We all together here. We all together safe for a good long time. This station been here since 'sixty-seven. I ain't the boss of it. No bosses here! But I is de one that talks de most!"

They all laughed in a low murmuring of agreement.

"You talkin' true now!" someone said.

"Man can talk de pinecone off de pine!"

"Ant off de hill!"

"Man out de moon!"

"All right, yall," Black Salt said, laughing, "you got me covered.

"Now me and de Real People smoke a pipe, de way they likes to always do it before they beds down early so's to leave early in de first light."

The Real People and Black Salt and some of the other inside folks took part in smoking a white clay pipe of tobacco provided by the most solemn, the elder one of the Real People. Others of the inside folks now took out their own individual small pipes, filled them with tobacco and smoked them. Soon the air was scented with a heavy odor.

"Makin' my eyes hurt," whispered Pearl.

"Did me at first, too," Josias said softly. "But you get used to it."

"Don't think so," said Pearl. She coughed drily into her palm. "Seems to me somethin' make you feel all tight in de chest can't be no good."

"It for de grown folks, tobac, not for you," Josias said.

"Does you smoke it?" Pearl wanted to know.

"Not where my paw can ketch me!" he said in her ear.

"We all know de rules here," Black Salt was saying. "But for the new ones among us . . ." He glanced at Mother Pearl and Dwahro and then sought out Pretty Pearl sitting with his son. Many turned around to look at Pretty and Josias; then they whispered and smiled amongst themselves. Pretty covered her grin with her hand. Josias sat up straight—going to be a strong man one day.

". . . gone talk it all again," finished Black Salt. "Any man, woman, with whoever chil'ren, has de right to leave whenever. We tell them which is best way to go, always north across de river. Oh, you is free. You is free! But outside, they gone make you work and slave like you not free, too. So I ask you, why they fought that war? Don't wants to pay you. And if'n they do pays you, they gone make you buy de food from them and take what they pays you almost back.

"They ain't gone let you have no land," continued Black Salt. "Once you get some good bottom land, they see how well you grow de crops and they comes and takes de land and makes you grow de crops for them. I ain't sayin' it wrong to go. Never say that! I ain't sayin' you can't reach north without inc'dent. But you gots to stop and work or barter somewheres. Somebody gots to help you along. We can't give you no money when you leave. For de money go for supplies we can't do our-selves. Wool, for we can't have de sheep. Need sheep dogs for sheep, and we can't trust de dogs not to wander. We don't keep much livestock no more, for its way is to wander. And maybe come back and lead de bandits all de way here. So if they wander away, we find them, we bring them back one time. But when they wanders a second time, we slaughter them, we has to. They won't stay to home.

"But you can leave. Ain't nobody gone stop you goin'. But before you leaves, you got to take de oath. Anyone leave for good, take de sacred oath they won't never ever talk about de Promise land. Never tell nobody where it

[134]

be or what it be so that it will remain our secret and we be them inside folks for all time.

"That's 'bout de only rules," Black Salt said. "Everybody works here and nobody need tell you why you has to. Everybody shares and no need explainin' there. Everybody watch out, keep they eyes and ears open when they workin'. Even we got de see-alls, we still got to take care.

"Nobody wander off 'out tellin' Salt, and chil'ren tell Josias, he tell me. Nobody go outside this compound alone, *never*. You go, you take Josias, for I have taught him this forest. There are three tricks of escape he knows of if de see-alls ever fail us. Most you know them. Josias will tell you if'n he consider you mights need know."

Pearl stared at Josias. Josias sat, stiff as a board; looked straight ahead.

"We de inside folks," said Black Salt. "I hopes we all stays that way. No one of us has left this Promise land since 1869. And he who left us we not heard from. Which is fittin'. He may have made it. If he have, he wouldn't tell nobody on us. If he hain't, he still can't tell. But since that time, I figure it better, nobody leave alone. Anybody wants to leave, have to wait 'til another is ready to go, too, whether be woman or chile, or both. The Real People lead you as far as they can. Send word along your way to friends and peoples, help you if they can. But they be in hidin' as well, so they help may not be comin'."

Black Salt talked a long time. As he talked, one of the Real People, the one who had filled the pipe and had taken the first puff, looked increasingly worried. After a time Black Salt left off, but not before speaking about those known by all as Cherokee.

"These, Ani-Yun'Wiya, a great, knowledge people," said Black Salt.

The Real People stood. One of them, the most solemn one of them, stepped a pace in front of the rest.

"Some hundred thirty years ago, Ani-Yun'Wiya was struck with smallpox. In one year, half of them entire people die. We and Ani-Yun'Wiya are tragically bound," said Black Salt, "for de pox was inc'bated in de holds of slave ships docked at Charlestown harbor. Pox came from heat countries. Ships bring Africans and pox, and spread like wind across this southeast land.

"Yes," said Black Salt. "Some of de Real People kept slaves. Of these kind standin' before us, they did not. Now. Speak, if you will, name of Old Canoe."

The one of the Real People who had stepped a pace forward now faced the people. Black Salt stood at his side so that he could see Old Canoe's face.

When Old Canoe spoke, his language was an almost perfect rendition of the queen's English. He stood with one hand in his sash and the other in a fist pressed on his heart. His face was narrow, with dark brows and hardly a wrinkle.

"Thank you, friend, Black Salt, and his people." The man was old, but his voice was strong, a low rumble, like distant thunder.

"I speak the language of the whites, but I am not white, remember," he said. "I was taught this language by missionaries in our territory. All Real People could speak and write in our own language after the great Sequoyah perfected our alphabet. Some of us knew both languages. But you were not so lucky, O black people, to keep your languages. For you came as slaves with many languages, and all of your languages were forbidden to you.

"You have had a long march from your homeland." Old Canoe's voice was suddenly gentle. He looked at the inside folks with sorrow for their suffering. The orange firelight reflected on their faces, in their black eyes upon him.

"And most of my nation had a long march from here to what the whites call *Indian* Territory, far to the west. You see, some of our people signed a Treaty in 1835 that gave away all our land east of the Mississippi River in exchange for five million in moneys and similar holdings in the Indian Territory. My people were given two years in which to remove. No matter that fifteen thousand of us not signing the Treaty of New Echota did not want to go. In 1838 the government of Andrew Jackson sent in troops. Seven thousand troops to round us up, sneak up on every mountain cabin, surround the cabin before the people knew what was happening. Put us in holding pens, much like stockades you were held in. And they forced us to go. They forced us to march a thousand miles!" Tears sprang into Old Canoe's eyes. One of the Real People with him touched his shoulder. But Old Canoe shrugged away the helping hand. He had spoken to the inside folks before, mostly teaching the forest he knew so well. But never had he spoken so personally.

There was a shuddering and a sound of moaning among the inside folks, who listened in rapt attention.

"They really made us walk!" Old Canoe spoke in a bitter voice. "We were forced to march from here, our eastern homeland, far west. They called that wilderness Indian Territory! And four thousand of us died along the way, one fourth of all of our people. That tragic march my people know as *Nunna-da-ul-tsun-yi*, 'The Place Where They Cried.' You may have heard of it as the Trail of Tears." Old Canoe smiled with overwhelming sadness. "But did you know that many of *your* people were on that Trail?"

There was a sudden gasp from the inside folks.

"Oh, yes," said Old Canoe, "black slaves also tramped that trail. Some of those of my people were rich, the ones who signed away our land, and they had slaves who carried their heavy satchels and nursed their babes. And one hundred seventy-five black slaves perished during Nunna-da-ul-tsun-yi.

"But I did not die," said Old Canoe. "These like me"— he gestured to those of his people with him—"and many like me who ran, who hated slavery as much as did the slaves, escaped to the caves and ledges of the high ridges. We did not die. I was a man at the height of his strength, then called Wohsi, a borrowing of the Christian name Moses. Now, look at me—I am weathered, hard worked by time, like an old *tsiyu*. But still I travel the waters of life. I am here. We are here.

"But we cannot stay here. And you, inside people of

Promise land, cannot stay here. No more is this a hiding place." Old Canoe's dark eyes held fiercely to his audience.

"This forest was once all Ani-Yun'Wiya," he said. "Then our lands were pared away a little at a time. And all they could find of us were removed to make that march, that deadly Trail of Tears. But this hiding place we wished to share with you free people. For no land is owned by any one kind. No man on earth is owned by any other. And no earth is owned by any human. It is earth belonging to none and all, to be used by one and all. We shared for as long as you could stay. But now you are not to stay."

An anxious murmuring swept through the gathering by the fire.

"Friends, you are not safe here," said Old Canoe. "It was said that our land surrounded by whites is like a snowball in the sun. Go! Flee! Our forest is broken!"

There was a wild uproar among the inside folks. Swiftly, Black Salt and the leaders of the men and women and children moved through the crowd, calming individuals who were overcome with fear. It was necessary to cover the mouths of some until they quieted. For noise was their enemy. All knew that Ani-Yun'Wiya would not speak lightly. Who knew better the forest paths than the Real People who had walked them down the ages?

"What be goin' on?" whispered Pearl to Josias. "Why that man have to get folks all upset?"

Josias sighed. "He don't do nothin' but help us, that

Old Canoe," Josias said. "And now he say we got to leave here. Can't be true!" For the first time, Josias looked afraid.

The hiding places of the inside folks and the very secretive Real People were in the depths of the great forest. Once, all of the Georgia region had been forests. But slowly, settlers with the gold fever had penetrated it. Mostly it was the hidden, impossible-to-reach heights and depths that remained. There, in secret, a population of one hundred fifty blacks and some one hundred fifty so-called red people prospered, knowing of one another. There were others, scattered, perhaps eight hundred or more, who had other groups and some knowledge of the others.

When the most disturbed of the inside folks had calmed down, Black Salt said, "You folks most likely stay where you be until I say you has to leave." He smiled, friendly enough, at his brother in secrets, Old Canoe. "What you tellin' us, old one?" He looked as though he thought Old Canoe had indeed grown too old for the pressure of secrecy and extreme caution under which they lived.

"At daybreak you come with me," Old Canoe told him. "We climb the high mountain. You will see the smoke."

"Smoke?" said Black Salt. "A new settlement?"

"No," said old Canoe. "It is what some call the iron horse. It is the railroad."

Black Salt threw back his head and he had to laugh. It was not a loud laugh, but it was one that shook him all over in relief. "Railway ain't be comin' way up here," he said. "Pull these mountains? No suh. And where it gone go to?"

"As far as your Jordan," said Old Canoe, "the Ohio River. And one day, they will learn to lay tracks across great waterways. The railroad buys all the land."

"Never!" said Black Salt. "How far be that river from here?"

"Four hundred miles. Days of riding on horseback," said Old Canoe.

"It never make it 'cross no great water, or that far, too. Can't pull no mountains," Black Salt said.

"As you wish." Old Canoe spoke softly. "But we went through and around the mountains when we could not climb over them, so why can't the railroad?"

"It will take a long, long time," Black Salt said.

The inside folks had to strain to hear the conversation, the two of them spoke so quietly, without rancor, at one another.

"But as a great leader of the people, you should listen to an ancient one who has been a leader longer than you have been alive," Old Canoe said.

Black Salt was silent, looking deeply into his brother's eyes. "I don't mean to take your warning lightly, Old Canoe," he said. "But I just don't believe we have a problem yet for some time."

"Long before the railroad comes," said Old Canoe, "come the surveyors and logmen, and section gangs to lay the steel tracks."

"Least they won't be de Ku Klucks," Black Salt said.

There was a laughing of contempt among the inside folks at these words.

"They will find you here, and if they are friendly, they will simply take all you have. But if they are unfriendly," Old Canoe said, "they will take all you have and make you work for them for little or nothing."

"They can try it," said Black Salt. "They tried it once. But this time I don't mean to hang my arms down and let them take over."

A hushed murmuring broke out among those straining to hear. Arms were raised in salute to Black Salt. "We'll fight back" came the whispered replies from the inside folks. "We'll give them a long row to hoe!"

"I will say no more about it this night," Old Canoe said. He stood, handsome, old and surely wise before the people. He held his fist to his heart and bowed slightly. The other men with him did the same. "But when I come again, I will say again." He smiled. No light shone in his eyes. "You must leave here." He turned to Black Salt, placed a hand on his shoulder. Black Salt placed his hand on Old Canoe's shoulder. A careworn look passed between them, and then it was over. Old Canoe and the others of the sang men, the Real People, headed for one of the cabins where they would spend the night.

The inside folks stayed by the fire, waiting to see if Black Salt had anything further to tell them.

Black Salt stood there without speaking. Finally, he sighed, staring at the inside folks. "Where do we go now?" he said, as if speaking to himself. "If we must go, then where?"

"Do we has to go, Salt?" a young man asked.

Black Salt looked at him hard. "Well, what you think 'bout Old Canoe's talkin'?" he asked.

"Don't know," said the young man. "Don't think de railway gone make it up here, but I don't know for true." He stared anxiously at Black Salt.

"Me neither," someone else said.

"I think we should study," said a woman. "Study what you gone see when you gets to de mountaintop with Old Canoe in de marnin'. Study if they's a way for de railway to git by us through a pass, maybe, and not disturb us."

"Now that sound sensible," spoke up Mother Pearl. It was the first time she had made herself noticed since Black Salt had begun talking. She seemed a typical maw-maw woman who knew best to care for children.

"You makin' sense, Swassi," said Black Salt. They all agreed by their nods that she made good sense.

Swassi smiled happily. Looked around and then, shyly, down at her feet.

"We will study it awhile, like Swassi say," said Black Salt. "When I have seen, and all yall think on it, too, then we figure what we gone do.

"Now," Black Salt said, "it be time to rest you."

"Yay-suh!" some said, with tiredness, with relief.

And then folks began to get up and move away.

"I'll walk with you to your maw," said Josias to Pretty Pearl.

"Huh?" she said, before she thought who her maw could be. "Oh! All right, then. But where we gone sleep the night?"

"I'll get you some blankets." he said, coming up to Mother Pearl. But Mother told him never mind. He smiled, then, at Mother Pearl. "Good night," he said to Pretty Pearl. She saw he was tall; Pretty admired him being so tall. She could barely see his face in the firelight. Yet she could see most anything through the dark if she wanted to. All she needed to do was touch the de Conquer root. She did this now. Saw the friendliness and interest in Josias' face.

"Night, Josias," she said. "Sleep you easy."

"Yay, Pearl, sleep you easy, so," he said, going off.

"Uh, huh, huh!" sighed Mother Pearl, as the area of Freedom Lane near the fire emptied of inside folks. Mother, Dwahro and Pearl settled down around the fire. They watched as, one by one, the cabins winked with soft candlelight. It wasn't long, though, before even that light went out. All was still on Freedom Lane in the land of Promise.

Mother Pearl banked the fire to make the hot coals last until morning.

"Don't suppose nobody mind we sleep right here by de warmth. Even warm night feel chilly when you out amongst de trees and dew."

Pretty Pearl hugged her knees tightly to her and smiled, her eyes sparkling from reflected fireglow.

"Ain't it nice!" she said. "Just carin' for theyselves,

and so nice bein' with de inside folks. Oh, I loves it here, don't you, Mother Pearl?"

"Well, it ain't Mount Highness, but it all right, Pretty," said Mother.

Pretty Pearl pouted at the mention of Mount Highness. Who needed that far-off, long-ago place? she thought. She gazed into the fire a moment, then stretched out on the ground on her back.

"Tell you one thing," Dwahro said. "Don't think much of what kinda folks it is make other folks sleep out on de ground, shoot. That Black Salt! Who he, nohow? Promise land, my big toe! This ain't nothin' but a ragged-tail scraggly of poor folks done quit bein' slaves to bein' starvin' on they own, so!"

"You just mad you ain't the leader, either," Pearl murmured. "You jealous 'cause nobody gone listen to you, so *so.*"

"That ain't it, that ain't it," Dwahro whispered loudly. "It just, who he, tellin' ever'body what they gone do next? Who he, and that Injun, walkin' 'roun', bangin' on he chest, so! Ain't nobody gone tell me what to do, and wheres I can't sleep."

"Dwahro, hush!" Mother Pearl whispered. "Both you! Soundin' as bad as younguns youselves. Remember who you be, for goodness' sake. Dwahro, who you *be*?" Mother asked.

"Huh?" said Dwahro.

Mother took him by the shoulder, looked into his eyes. "I say, who you be, Dwahro, and you better know!"

Dwahro hung his head, and finally he said, "I be spirit, Mother Pearl. I be spirit."

"That's right, and don't you forgit no more!"

"And Pretty," spoke Mother Pearl, in a low sound like rushing wind, "who you be, Pearl?"

Try as she might to pretend sleep and keep her mouth closed, Pretty Pearl found she had to answer Mother Pearl. "Be Pearl," she murmured against her will. "Be god chile of Mount Highness." She covered her face with her hands, shivering. It troubled her now to admit who she was.

"She stuck on that Josias," Dwahro said, sneering.

"Hush, Dwahro," Mother said. "Pearl ain't stuck on nothin' but what she s'pose to. Now. Time we lay down, sleep some, act just like ordinary folks."

"What I wants to know is, what we s'pose to be doin' here and how long we got to stay?" Dwahro said.

"You in some big hurry to get nowhere?" Pearl asked. She kept her eyes shut.

"I said to stop it," said Mother. "We s'pose to help de people—you, me and she, Pretty. We gone see de inside folks through this time o' trial. You hear what Old Canoe tell 'em. De railway is comin' and that may mean trouble for them. We ain't gone nosy. But we best be around, to see what happen."

Mother Pearl eased down on the ground, with Pearl on one side of her and Dwahro on the other. She spread her great big painted apron over the three of them.

"There. Don't that feel nice and warm?" Mother said. "Here, in my apron painting, we have de she poplar back over us." She patted the apron right on the poplar branches. And somewhere in the forest a mighty tree felt the touch.

"Look up, you two," Mother said, nudging Pretty and Dwahro.

"Huh?" said Dwahro.

"Up above you head, silly," Mother said, kindly, chuckling. "Heh, heh, heh. Look there!"

"Oh!" Pearl exclaimed. "All clouds is gone."

"That's right," Mother said. Indeed, all the clouds had disappeared in the night. Above them was a shelter of glimmering stars. "Oh, that truly heavenly!" whispered Mother. "Ain't that somethin'?"

They stared at the stars, too beautiful for words.

Mother Pearl, being as she was, never closed her eyes the whole night. Dwahro, spirit that he was, laid his head on Mother's shoulder. He curled himself up and around, just the way he felt humans must make themselves comfortable for sleep. Soon he was most comfortable.

"Mother Pearl," he said.

"Yes, Dwahro . . . son," Mother said. Even she couldn't help herself from associating him, herself, with what was human about them.

"You said you'd tell me how you and Pearl managed to be here both at once."

That brought her back. "Yes, that's right," Mother said. "Well. Ain't a whole lot to it. You know, it happen right at de moment we enter into Promise. Pretty Pearl dash away from you—remember?"

"I do," Dwahro said.

[147]

"She dash behind de tree, though I don't s'pose she mean to—she just forgot herself. She was headin' for that cookin' pot, around which they always some few chil'ren. Anyways, just as she be behind de tree, she has to take hold of she John de Conquer. And she do that, it rustle me up. I think, if Pearl de chile by de fire, she gone need de maw mother. I gets to thinkin' in Pearl's own thoughts. 'Put on de long dress. Put on de long dress,' I tells her. And she thinkin' in a hurry right back to me, 'I don't wants to, I don't wants to.' And whole time she reach in her git bag and take de long dress out. And whole time she don't want that long dress atall, but I sure do. And we struggle in mind, Put on de long dress. I don't wants to. Put on de long dress. I don't wants to. She holdin' that de Conquer, she can't help it. And holdin' it in one hand and my dress in de other, well it be too much. And, *boom!*" Mother Pearl whispered in Dwahro's ear.

"*Boom?*" he whispered back.

"*Boom*, and *boom* agin," said Mother Pearl. "Her and me needin' and wantin' both so hard at once. Her holdin' my dress and that root both so hard at once. *Boom! Bam!* Split that root right in two. But one bigger two, 'cause I is bigger of the two of us. And once that happen, there I am and there she be. Both of us, big as life. Don't ask me why. But we is gods, though she be just a god chile. She still godly," Mother Pearl finished.

"That is somethin'," said Dwahro. "Guess yall can do what you wants to. You and Pretty is gods. De inside folks and de sang men is human. But what am I?"

"Well, you knows what you is," said Mother Pearl. "You is spirit. You know that." She hugged Dwahro.

"But I'm alone. Neither god nor human," said Dwahro in despair.

"You ain't alone," Mother said. "There's de Hodag like you and de Fool-la-fafa like you."

"A dog and a woodpecker!" Dwahro whispered, feeling his spirit wither.

"Oh, now, son, don't carry on so," said Mother. "You be just as important as anythin'."

"Don't wants to be anythin'," he murmured, and thought, Wants to be a *son!*

After that, Dwahro closed his eyes for a long while, practicing. He could still feel the depths of the forest surrounding them. Could feel movement in the cabins as humans slumbered and dreamed. For a time he practiced dreaming. He had one dream, that was all. He had it over and over again.

Mother Pearl kept her eyes on the sky and the night, ever watchful.

Pretty Pearl had fallen fast asleep just after she had seen and enjoyed the brilliant stars. She did not toss or turn. She did not awaken. Pretty slept deeply, just like a child.

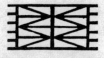

CHAPTER NINE

At dawn the sang men and Black Salt prepared to leave the compound. The Real People had their packhorses loaded with ginseng wrapped tightly in jute bags. The bags were strapped securely to the pack animals. And now the men led their horses and the pack animals out of the compound. At Freedom Lane they stopped to wait for their leader and Black Salt.

Mother Pearl, Dwahro and Pretty knew what was going on. Once in a while Pretty would peek to see. Being as she was, she could gather what was going on among the men. All others in the compound were fast asleep in their cabins. Pretty Pearl listened to Black Salt and the leader of the Real People, Old Canoe.

"You go alone?" spoke Old Canoe. "No one to your back?"

"I need no protection," Black Salt responded. "We'll go to de high ground and I'll be back in no time."

"Still, it is not good that you travel alone," said Old Canoe. "What would happen to your people if you did not come back?"

Black Salt smiled thinly. "I've left this place a thousand times, scoutin' around by myself. I've always come back."

Old Canoe glanced over to the fire where Pretty, Mother Pearl and Dwahro lay ever so still as if in sleep. Over there, the older one had not arrived with him.

"You have much power here," Old Canoe said. "The beings act the same as humans of your kind."

Black Salt did not always understand his old brother in secrets. Now was one of those times. He shrugged by way of answer, and he and Old Canoe moved off from the cabins and out through Freedom Lane. Old Canoe's men followed.

"Dwahro," Mother Pearl said when they were gone, "you follow along behind Black Salt. Make sure he be all right. Don't let them Real People see you."

"Yesum," said Dwahro, yawning like a man. He touched Mother's de Conquer root necklace. It made him invisible, unlike any man.

"Be careful, you, now," Mother told him as, invisible,

[151]

he pranced after Black Salt and Old Canoe.

Pearl was quiet a long while before she said to Mother Pearl, "You know, I really slept. And I can see why folks enjoy it so. Can you sleep, Mother Pearl, the way I can?"

"Oh, now, no, me," said Mother. "Not no, huh-uh. But a child like you play at sleeping, it good for you, you get real good at it too. And I do say, sleeptime is prob'ly one of de best things about being human. But you can only do it when you a chile. Even god chil'ren need so much rest time, don't you know. So you go on ahead. It be all right."

But Pearl didn't feel like sleeping anymore. She was wide awake.

"Mother Pearl," she said, "folks is wakin' up."

Life had begun to stir again inside the cabins.

"It seems so," said Mother. And all at once she was up and had tied her apron neatly around her waist, with a big bow in back. Mother stoked the fire, Pretty found cut wood and put it on the fire. There was a half bucket of clean, cold water off by an oak. Mother Pearl got it and placed it over the fire. When it was nice and warm, she and Pearl washed up. They dried themselves on Mother's apron; they combed one another's hair. Pearl wore her ebony bow.

Then everybody was up and moving about. Folks came quickly from the cabins with buckets. The children grabbed the buckets and ran with them. They were soon back with water. Hot coals were put in the ground holes and the water heated. After all had washed up, as casual and close as a family, the buckets were emptied away from the cabins near the trees. And food was brought out for the morning cooking pot. The huge black pot was carried to the fire by a group of old folks.

"Name of Swassi," Swassi said, coming up to Mother Pearl.

"Name of Simmie," said a small woman with her. They had the unsifted cornmeal that Mother Pearl would use for her porridge.

"Marnin', Swassi, Simmie," said Mother. "Let me take that." She took the sacks of coarse meal and poured them into the cooking pot. Children brought gourds of milk.

"Now pour, chil'ren, pour!" whispered Mother. "Make a porridge inna pot, hot, hot, hot!" She could make a song and a chant out of most anything. The children poured the milk in at Mother's direction. Soon the porridge was hot and thick. Mother stirred it and slipped something into it from the handkerchief she had in her hand. Mother emptied the hanky over the pot when no one was looking. Pretty Pearl saw her. She came up to stand beside Mother as all gathered around to have from the porridge pot.

> *"Walk togedder, chil'ren,"*

Mother Pearl sang softly,

> *"Don't ye gets weary,*
> *Walk togedder, chil'ren,*
> *Don't ye gets weary."*

[153]

They all ate, standing around, dipping their gourds in the pot. Some of the children squatted. All listened to the song. Some of them hummed or sang when they could, when they had finished.

> *"Sing togedder, chil'ren,*
> *Don't ye gets weary,*
> *There's a great camp meetin'*
> *In de Promise land."*

"This is the bestest-tastin' milk-a-porridge I ever did taste!" said Swassi, breaking up the song. "It make me feel like, feel like . . ."

". . . like de good life come over me," someone finished for her. He smiled at Mother Pearl. "Name of Ezekiel," he told her. "Marnin'."

"Marnin'," said Mother and Pretty Pearl at her side.

"That porridge most heavenly," said Simmie. "Make me feel ready to go hoe de row!"

"How you make such strong, sweet corn mush, Mother Pearl?" asked Bessie Freedom.

"Well, good marnin', Bessie," said Mother.

"Marnin', Bessie," said Pretty Pearl. "How you be?"

"Be fine," answered Bessie.

"To answer you, Bessie," Mother Pearl said, "I be de mawmaw for true and I always stirs a little love in my porridge for de chil'ren."

"Ah, a little love," said Ezekiel, laughing softly. "That got to be what tastin' so sweet and cunning."

"Be it, then," they all agreed. "Yeah, it is, a little love

for de chil'ren!" All ate until the pot was empty.

"Now," said Mother Pearl. "Chil'ren, you and me, we gone make a few changes, since I come along here for de mawmaw chores."

"Yes'm," answered the children.

"We olders can work in de veg'ble patches if we wants to," said Bessie.

"And you can work with Mother Pearl, if you wants to, too?" asked Mother.

"Oh, yes'm," said Bessie. "We most free to do what has to be done, like anybody else."

"Well, that's jes' fine," Mother Pearl said. "We gone begin with cleanin' up de cook pot. And de old folks needn't brang it out here no more, 'less they wants to. Me and we can do that from now on. And then we gone make sure they's plenty o' chopped wood for de fire. And then we gone see what is ripped or tore up and we gone sew it. And if we have some wool, we gone see 'bout spinnin' it. And next, we gone gather de acorns and all such that falls from de trees. First we make acorn cakes."

"Acorn cakes?" said the children, mighty surprised.

"And sunflower bread," Mother Pearl said.

"Sunflower *bread*?" the children gasped.

The grown-ups smiled knowingly at Mother Pearl and the children; could see that all the young ones of Promise land were in very good hands. They moved off, then, to do the hard work that had to get done. They did not need Black Salt standing over them to tell them to toil. They toiled for the good of all.

"An' after we make de sunflower bread, we gone fry de

empty sunflower hulls—watch them most carefully so's they don't burn. And grind de browned hulls finely. And bile de water and sweeten it with good bee honey from de mountain chestnut. Oh, yes, that makin' the best sun-flower-seed coffee you ever taste."

"Coffee!" cried the children.

"Shhh!" said Mother Pearl. "Mustn't get loud, you know that."

Just then someone touched Pretty Pearl's hand. She turned to see Josias, son of Black Salt, standing beside her.

"Marnin'," he whispered as Mother Pearl went on about making yellow dye from sunflower petals, and black and purple dyes from the seeds.

"Come with me," whispered Josias. And Pearl slipped away with him, while all the children were enraptured by Mother Pearl's sweet, soft conjuring voice.

"Where we goin'?" asked Pretty.

"Everywhere," said Josias. "It my chore today to show you around."

"Didn't know I was some toil," said Pearl, sniffing her nose in the air.

"Didn't mean it like that," said Josias. "It just that every chile and grown man or woman has to have a dayclean chore. You choose what chore you want each day. And if one won't be enough, then you choose a second. But once it be chosen, you got to stay with it until it done or until dayclean finish."

"Oh, I see," said Pearl. Now she was delighted. For she intended to become a chore that would last a whole dayclean with Josias beside her.

They were beyond the stand of live oaks along Free-dom Lane. And beyond the area of cabins. They were hurrying, weaving in and out among sheds and other outbuildings that were concealed in a grove of trees. Pretty heard cooing from a coop shed.

"Slow down, Josias, or I won't get to see nothing."

"Just de sheds and barns," he said.

"And what's them little houses?" asked Pearl, "those with de half holes?"

"They de outhouses, don't you know that?" said Josias, grinning.

"I do," Pearl said. "I just forgot a minute."

Pearl could now fit herself to know. She was learning how, as de Conquer had known she would. But she realized, suddenly, that she would likely enjoy herself best with humans if she allowed herself to discover and know the way they did. Learning from experience. But now she dove into herself searching for the meaning of the little houses. And, finally, giggled into her palm as she and Josias hurried away.

"Let's look in a shed," Josias said. He opened a shed door. Inside was dark and cool. The shed had a dirt floor swept clean. All sorts of vegetables were stored there. There were gourds and corn hanging from the rafters. There were piles of potatoes in the corners.

"Goodness!" Pearl said. "Such a lot of food."

"That's just some of it. We got root cellars way in de groun' where we keeps lots of stuff for de winter. This in here we use from day to day. Certain folks bring in day food, while others takes most food to de undergroun' storage. Our biggest problem is moles and such. They loves to burrow down to de cellars. Groun' squirrels and chipmunks loves 'em too."

"Well, you should leave a bit o' food out for 'em, and then they won't bother you stores," said Pretty Pearl.

"Oh, we do that," Josias told her. "We shares with de little animals, so. But them likes to take it all."

They stood in the cool shed a moment. They were close and quiet. Pearl didn't remember when she had liked being with someone as well as she liked being with Josias.

'Cept for my brother John de Conquer, Pretty thought. Ho, John, can you see me? You should see me now. I lookin' just like a chile, like we plan. I can even think like one and sleep like one. And Josias, son of Black Salt, is my frien'. Oh, John, I hopes to stay here for a while!

Soon they were out of doors again.

"Now you follow behin' me," Josias told Pretty Pearl. "Don't try to get in front of me because of what might happen."

"What might happen?" asked Pearl.

"You just follow behin'," Josias said again. "I'll take de path and you follow, you hear?"

"Oh, I hear," said Pretty Pearl sweetly. But she did not like following anyone, not even Josias. "I'll do what you say this one time."

Josias said nothing more. He led the way through a bushy thicket. They were soon surrounded by heat.

There were insects buzzing, eating the rotted, drying berries.

"Whew!" whispered Pearl.

"We almost through it," Josias said. "Now. We through it," he said after a time. Gently, he pulled Pearl through the last of the bushes and up beside him.

"How can it be!" Pearl exclaimed. "We up so high!"

"It not so much we up so high," Josias said, "though that be so, but it more that *there* be down so far below."

It was as if they stood on a ledge. Before them was open space. Pearl could see across it to trees, thick and misty on the other side. Below them was a reach of land bathed in sunlight. Hanging above it was a mist shot through with a rainbow. It took Pearl's breath away. Down there were gardens, and small fields of corn. There were tomato patches. Cucumber. Watermelon. And even cotton. Men and women worked through the fields, tending, hoeing and gathering. Pearl saw two-wheeled wood carts. Some parts of the land were being turned up and furrowed, using plow and man-push.

Josias pointed to the far corners of the pie-wedge reach of land where there was shade.

"Over there is where we grow some ginseng we plant ourselves," he said. "But de best ginseng to sell grow wild. And we hunt it by teams of four. We get best price for selling from that wild kind. But this kind bring money, so, the kind we plants and grows. Plant two acres of ginseng will yield one half to pick.

"This be our hidden valley," Josias explained. "It ain't so big. It seem to be just right for to grow all we need."

"It sure seem so," whispered Pearl. "It be so most pretty. Be de best place I ever did see!"

"We name it Abyssinia," Josias said.

Pearl caught her breath. For she knew the African empire, the United States of Abyssinia. Pearl did not tell Josias this.

"Abyssinia," she said, "that be a fine name." In her mind she recalled that high plateau land guarded by towering mountain walls.

"See how them beech trees grow there, on the other side of de valley?"

"Yes," Pearl said, "what of it?"

"And see how de way be a climb and climb, up and up?"

"I see it," Pretty said. "I see stones, there, and pieces o' rock."

"And if you could see behind de beech trees, you'd see de way is going uphill, you'd see de hardwoods of maple and butternut and rock elm. Whenever de timber be changin' from one kind to another, and you find hill and gully, be a sure sign for wild ginseng."

"I wants to see!" Pearl exclaimed.

"Then, so," he said. "Now give-a you warnin.' "

"Yes, Josias?"

"We always move through de place in silence. In silence you can hear, if you knows how to listen."

"I know that," Pearl said, simply.

"Then follow. It ain't too hard gettin' down."

But it was hard for Pretty Pearl. She was not used to the steepness down, which they must now climb to the valley. But the inside folks had helped to make the way easier. They had staked thick hemp ropes to aid in the hardest part.

"Now you turn to de slope," Josias said as they started, and he gently turned her so her back was to the valley. "You grasp de slope with one hand and de rope with de other. I be right behin' you back. Sometime, it be so steep up here, going down, you face most 'gainst de slope. Don't look down, only at placin' you feet. And don't look behin' you."

She did as she was told. The sun was hot all around. She never knew when they were close to the floor of the valley. All she knew was that she was safe; she could sometimes feel Josias behind her—he was often that close to make sure she would not fall. Pearl never slipped once. She stopped often when she would need to fight herself not to think on the de Conquer root to see what was below her. She climbed down as a girl might who was new to the Promise land. Then her feet were flat. She stood on the level ground.

"That weren't so bad, so?" Josias said.

"Weren't so easy, too," said Pearl.

Josias laughed. "Come. We see de ginseng we plant first. Then de wild," he said.

They crossed the valley, walking through rows of tomato and corn. Folks who had been chopping weeds or gathering into bushel baskets straightened as they heard the two young folks come.

"Seen you long way off," one woman said to Josias. "See you brangin' de purty one." She was a tiny, dark woman, with bright black eyes, and no taller than Pearl.

Pearl smiled.

"Name of Miz Molly," explained Josias to Pearl.

"Good dayclean to you, Purty Pearl," said Miz Molly in a husk of a voice.

"Glad to see you, Miz Molly," Pearl said. "A fine day-clean."

And Molly bent back to her tomato-picking work. She wiped the soil off each tomato on a scrap of cloth, then shined the skin on her skirt.

They went on down the rows, pausing here and there to greet others.

"You paw come back yet?" one man wanted to know.

"No, suh," said Josias. "You want me tell you when he come?"

"No, son," said the man. "Be hearin' all he say, by 'n' by."

"Thought you said we has to be most quiet," Pretty Pearl said.

"But folks speak. They knows when they is safe, and they talk to us. All is safe here. But we be always wary, you know, so?"

"I understand," Pearl said. "The rule be, *quiet*, even when you don't has to be."

"That's right," he said. "Now. We walkin' to de planted ginseng."

Pearl tagged along. The mist was above her head now. She could still see the rainbow; but now it looked like it was over there at the height of the land mass they had just climbed down.

Ohhh, she thought, didn't know up there was so high! All around the edge of the valley of Abyssinia, trees were turning.

Leaves some yellow and orange, she thought. It gone be clear to fall any day!

She skipped on down the row. The rows were pole beans and hill beans. Pearl stopped now and then to eat one or two raw bean pods. So did Josias. Silently, they pranced and paused, pranced and paused, eating the delicious beans.

After a time Josias said, "See? We most there. Come thisaway." He led Pearl to a section farthest from the sun. A two-acre piece carved out of the pie at the northeast corner. It was shielded in front by a row of pines.

"See, it farthest from de sun," he said. "In de marnin' sun come up behind forest trees. Afore it high enough to clear 'em, time it slide on over to de southern sky. Then it slide along, slide along all de way 'cross de south. Then it go down, head west and empty out de sky altogether. This corner never do get so much sunlight. Them pines shade and forest shade."

"You mean that ginseng most happy in de shade?" asked Pearl.

"Sang love shade and damp. Not swamp, mind, but damp and dark, and north sides," he said. "Come on in," he added. And they walked within the planted ginseng field.

All at once Pearl felt her necklace stir against her chest. Never had her root stirred at the sight of a plant.

"Look to be a good plant," she said. She watched the

field of sang. The de Conquer root recognized a kinship to the strength in the sang. It came to Pearl that ginseng wasn't as miraculous as de Conquer. But it was quite good for medicines. Mysterious, nearly, in its healing power.

"Some call it Five Finger. See?" said Josias. He bent down near the plants.

Pretty Pearl saw. The plants were less than a foot high. They had long, tapering, thin leaves. At the top of the stem other branches grew that were like prongs. Each of these prongs ended in a five-leaf cluster. From the plants' centers at the top, smaller stems grew straight up. Each plant's center stem ended in a cluster of berries.

Josias pulled at a young plant and showed her a bit of the root. "We dig de older roots each year but we leave most de plants. You can 'most tell how old de plant is by counting de number of prongs. In a couple of years it a two-prong bunch and stay that way three more years. Then it'll grow into three-prong, and so on."

Josias dug up the plant to show Pearl. "When it old," he said, "this here root begin to take shape of humans. Why it valuable, accordin' to de shapes and medicines. China mens values de strange shapes of sang and de great powers."

"I understand," said Pearl. "Can we go now? I wants to walk in de woods."

"You don't walk in de woods," Josias said. "You go out in groups to hunt or to change de post of see-alls. But I guess I can take you out and show you some wild sang. They 'most begins huntin' it soon as Old Canoe

[164]

and his men done taken de last shipment."

But Pearl had her mind on something else. "Who and what are see-alls?" she asked. "You say 'see-alls, see-alls,' but you never quick to explain."

"Hard explainin'," he said simply. "Best you just sees. Come on. Hunt de sang."

"But I thought—" Josias took her hand. Shyly, he turned to grin at her. That was what stopped her from finishing what she had wanted to say.

He led Pearl from the sang field, through the pines, then around the field. They now headed northwest, away from the valley and away from the height from which they had climbed.

Pretty Pearl wanted to ask if sang hunting was dangerous. But then she thought, If walkin' in de woods be dangerous for fear strangers might see, then goin' out to hunt must be just as dangerous.

Now they were climbing again. They walked through lovely stands of birch trees. They walked through gullies. "Not dark enough," Josias whispered.

"What ain't?" Pearl whispered back, but Josias wouldn't say.

Then they were walking on a narrow path, ever going upward. Pearl recognized walnut trees. It seemed almost like they were heading inside someplace. The way became shadier, dimmer, cooler and more humid.

Josias slowed. Pearl was behind him, but every now and again she would peer around him and he would half turn. This time he was grinning. He had stopped on the path.

"What is it?" she whispered.

Josias was laughing silently. "Look around," he said in a low voice.

Pearl looked all around. Trees and bushes were close on the path. She could smell ripening berries in the thickets, or at least she thought she could. Pearl looked and looked. There was lots of sound, swooshing and cooing at the tops of trees. Just birds, plentiful.

"Don't see nothin' like some ginseng," she said.

"Course not." Quietly, he spoke. " 'Cause it not be here. Be the see-alls."

"Josias, if you don't tell me right now what they is, well, I'm goin' on back. And I never gone speak to you no more," Pearl said, pouting.

"So," said Josias. "You gone climb back up that high ground all by youself."

"I'll git one of them field-workin' folks help me," she said.

"Just 'cause they works de fields don't mean you better, or me, so. They works de fields 'cause that what they choose to do," he said. "No slaves."

"Josias! Did I say somethin' 'bout bein' better than other folks? Or slaves?" Pearl asked.

"Well, don't talk 'bout goin' off by yourself," he said.

"You just makin' me upset, talkin' 'bout see-alls again. Where'm I s'pose to see some see-alls?" she asked anxiously. She was tired; nerves jumpy.

"Right here," he said. "Look around."

"How'm I to see what I don't know what some looks like!" she cried.

"Shhhh!" he warned.

Pearl was so upset and so exasperated with Josias, she spun away from him. She folded her arms and stared off into the bushes.

"I ain't movin' 'til he make some sense!" she whispered at the bushes.

"That makin' sense," said the bushes, right back at her.

Pretty Pearl leaped back and fell hard on her bottom. "Oh! Oh!" she said. Frantically, she scooted away.

Josias caught her under the arms and lifted her up.

"Oh, Josias, it talkin', that bush be talkin' straight at me!"

"Yesum, Pearl, it do," he said. And he laughed in her ear.

"It do?" she said. "Bushes can talk around here?"

"Come, Pretty," he said, helping her up. "Let's go back and 'talk' to it."

He helped Pearl up, and they walked back to the bush that had talked. "Now, kneel down agin in front of it," he told her. "Don't be 'fraid. I'm right with you. I'm gone kneel down, too," he said.

Carefully, Pretty Pearl kneeled next to Josias.

"Now look you good," said Josias.

"Look you good, for true," whispered the bush in an ancient voice.

Alarmed, Pearl stared and stared, until finally what she could not see before fairly leaped out at her now. It hadn't moved; and yet she could see it as plain as day.

"I don't believe it," she whispered.

"Howdy, Maw Julanna," Josias said.

"Dayclean," spoke the one who was Julanna. Her voice was like a soft sighing. "Young Purty, Josias, howdy-do!"

Her great black eyes shone like fire in a face lined with wrinkles. She was right there amid the bush.

Maw Julanna was very much alive, and she was most human.

CHAPTER TEN

"Oh, my," said Pretty Pearl. "Didn't see you nowhere comin' by," she said to the woman.

The woman smiled pleasantly, but she did not speak. She looked all around, up at the cooing birds.

"You weren't s'pose to see her," Josias said, "And you wouldn't see her comin' by 'cause she not move for de last hour or so. When she do move in de forest, be like a bunch o' leaves movin' on de branches. All see-alls moves like that. And Maw Julanna de see-all on this path until de sun overhead. She do de seein' for that long. Then Maw Josie come, set herself down and be de see-all 'til end of dayclean."

Pretty Pearl kneeled there on the path and simply stared. Never before had she seen anyone sit down and entangle herself in a bush on purpose. Nor had she ever seen anyone dressed the way Maw Julanna was dressed. The woman was clothed from head to foot in a very light-weight muslin. It was a one-piece suit dyed a deep brown to match the color of the forest bark, bushes and branches in the autumn time of year. Only Maw Julanna's face, and her hands and feet, were left uncovered. They were nearly the same brown as the suit. Sewn to the muslin fabric were cloth leaves shaped to match the leaves of the forest and dyed in fall colors of gold, or- ange, red and purple. There were also some green leaves, as there were some left in the forest. The leaves covered the entire outfit from head to ankle. It was amaz- ing that, once in the bush and underbrush, Maw Julanna became, for all practical purposes, invisible.

"Well." Pretty Pearl spoke at last. " 'Tis something to see, dressed up her. So's can't see her, me. So's you'd never s'pect when walkin' along de path, like me."

"Maw Julanna one of de best see-alls," Josias said.

"But there she be, 'most invisible," said Pearl. "So what makin' her a see-all?"

"We'll give you a showin', then," he said. "Maw Julanna, can we show Pretty some of it so's she know? She most curious."

Maw Julanna grinned her fairly toothless smile. Her arms had been spread over the small branches inside the bush, her hands woven through, and her arms, too. Now she untangled one arm and silently shot it straight up out of the bush. And Josias commenced to explain about her every move.

"Someone come along de path, walk on by Maw Julanna. Soon he is by, she shoot up she hand. You notice, soon as she hand shoot up, de forest be most quiet. No birds callin' atall."

"I notice," said Pretty. For it was so—all of the cooing birds had become still once Maw Julanna lifted her hand. "How she *do* that?"

"Look up," he said.

Pretty looked up and could not believe her eyes. Above them at the tops of trees was a midnight of birds. She could see the mass of darkness rustling and ruffling feathers. And this most unusual darkness up there made no cooing sound.

"You know about all de birds," Josias said. "Black Salt, my daddy, say they more than a million. They once was a billion at least."

Pearl did not know about so many birds, but she never let on to Josias.

"It not so strange to see come over de forest a fifty, hundred-mile long flock of birds," he said. "They come and come, think it will never end, they come so."

"Never ever have seen nothin' like that," she said.

"Well. It be so. And they be nestin' here in de forest for since there be a forest, my paw say. And be findin' out long time ago that some folks be close to de forest kind, animals and birds."

"That so?" said Pearl. She remembered she had always been able to be close with birds and animals of Mount Kenya. But of course, she was different.

" 'Tis so," he said. "There be slaves from Africa bring with them de touch to de animals and birds. And some like Maw Julanna and Maw Josie grow old and know much from de birds."

Maw Julanna's hand was still straight up from the top of the bush.

"So," said Josias. "Maw Julanna."

Ever so slowly, Maw Julanna waved her hand from side to side. Then she whirled it in a circle and again waved it. A long moment, and a bird, pretty as a picture, came down and alighted in the palm of her hand. It hopped to her forefinger, where it waited.

"Don't move," Josias said to Pearl in the quietest voice. "Else it fear and fly away. Now."

Carefully, Maw Julanna plucked a yellow leaf from her sleeve with her other hand. She placed the bird on a branch, and with both hands tied the leaf to the bird's foot. The bird was a wild wood or passenger pigeon, about seventeen inches from tip to tail. Its breast was reddish fawn in color, and it was a lovely gray-blue on its back and wings. It stood on the branch, waiting, a neat and tailored-looking bird.

"If there be a stranger in de forest close by, all de birds know it," said Josias. "They coo and call, coo and call, so's you don't notice no more. You forgits you hear what you hearin'."

"That's so," said Pearl. She remembered the trouble with the bandits and how she had not noticed there were lots of birds. But now, she recalled she had heard them and had not bothered about them.

"Well, de birds be tellin' folks like Maw Julanna what be comin'. Then, when de stranger walk by, she shoot up de hand. De bird come down to she hand. Maw Julanna tie de gold leaf. De bird fly low over Abyssinia for all to see. Fly to Promise, set down de gold leaf in a special place right by Black Salt's cabin. Old Minnie, she be a hundred thirteen year old, sittin' there, always wait. Case de bird come, you know."

"Yes, I see," said Pretty. "And she take de yellow leaf."

"She take de yellow leaf," he said. "And carry it to someone, or call someone. For de yellow leaf mean a stranger be near. Watch out! And that's how we know whoever comin'. One gold leaf, if be only one soul. A red leaf if be more. Purple leaf mean more and trouble. All done by de see-alls, she, Maw Josie and others. They be a few in every direction. We gots lot of old folks can feel things and know de animals and birds. So," Josias finished.

Pretty Pearl got up from the ground. Maw Julanna untied the leaf from the pigeon's foot. Handed the leaf to Pearl as a prize.

"Oh, thank you," Pearl said. "I will keep it, always." And she tied it to the bow in her hair. "There," she said.

The pigeon flew away. Maw Julanna's hand disappeared back down in the bush.

Josias was standing with Pearl. And from their vantage, it was again difficult for them to see Maw Julanna.

" 'Tis a magic," Josias said.

Pearl nodded. " 'Tis, almost," she said.

"We be gone now," he said to the see-all in the bush.

There was a sighing from the bush, but no more. "Come," he said to Pearl.

They went on down the path. The birds had become noisy again as the two of them left. But they grew less so the farther from them Pretty Pearl and Josias went.

They traveled down in hollows in silence, and they climbed a dogwood ridge where there was rich ground. But Pearl saw no ginseng anywhere.

"We gettin' most far away from Promise, Josias, is it?" she said.

"No, not," he answered. "We makin' a wide circle is all. Can't you tell?"

"No," said Pearl.

"We are, though," he said. And quietly, he began talking, telling her.

"You find sang where de sun hardly ever hit it," he said. "Don't see much of it on south ground. It partial to de north and west ground. Never hear of it on east ground. It be friend to some of de dry places. But it most be where ground is damp and shadowy. There it will always grow a bigger stalk."

Now Pearl walked next to Josias, and she liked the sound of his voice so close to her.

It was a long walk. Pretty Pearl's legs were feeling like

they wouldn't hold her up any longer when Josias said, "Now. We here."

Suddenly they were somewhere where, off to the sides, Pretty could make out the forms of a few people digging.

"If they must hunt de sang, how you know they hunt here?" Pearl whispered to Josias.

"Didn't," he answered. "Jes' has to come by, think they might be here. They weren't here last year, so they might be this year."

"You know everything, don't you?" she whispered back.

"No need to whisper. They know we here. Probably heard us comin' away back there."

"Oh," said Pearl.

They walked within a place of twilight. It was a deep cove where the sun never shone. It was a north cove, where there grew poplar and black walnut trees. It was dark and damp in there, a perfect growing place for ginseng.

The hunters carried long sticks with narrow metal blades called sang hoes.

"The Real People have a man works with iron on a forge," said Josias. "We had us a iron man in a cave. Made all kinds of horseshoes and hammerheads, shoot. Only de sound him made echo in these mountains, so. Black Salt had to tell him to quit it. Man didn't like it, too, and he de one leave here and never heard from again."

"That so?" said Pearl.

"For true," he said. "But now Real People make us de blades for sang hunting. They has a deep cave undergroun' for it."

The hunters did not look up as Josias and Pearl walked near. With heads bent to their work, they quietly spoke a greeting. Josias and Pearl spoke a greeting back.

There was something awesome about the twilight cove and the sangers bending to their task. It came over Pearl that she would like to join them. Like to take the sang hoe in hand and carefully dig down under the root and gently bring the root up. The careful and gentle touch of the sangers showed that they honored the sang ground.

"Wouldn't mind bein' a sang hunter," Pretty Pearl thought to say.

Josias looked at her. "It suit you?" he said.

"Think it might," Pearl answered. "How do I go 'bout learnin'?' "

"What you wants to do by labor, you do," he said, simply, and that was all he said about it.

They left then. Pearl felt as though she were leaving a sacred place. She looked back into the long reach of the cove. Saw the sang hunters bend down, as though praying.

" 'Bye," Pearl whispered to them, but none heard or looked up. What did sang hunters think about, she wondered, during their long days of silence and digging?

Digging for gold, she thought. The sang plants, when ripened, were a gold color, a yellow unlike any other in the forest.

"Best go back now," Josias said.

Pearl nodded and prepared to follow.

Josias put his arm around her to help her. "You feelin' all right?"

"Just some tired," she said. "Ain't used to so much walkin' and sleepin' out in de air. Can't I sleep in a cabin tonight?" Being as a human, she wanted human comforts.

"Talk to Salt about it," Josias said. "Be room somewhere for you."

"Thank you," she said.

They went back. Pretty Pearl saw no see-alls, but she knew they were there out of sight where the birds nested high in the trees. She looked up and saw as many as fifty nests in one tree. "Don't ever walk under *them* trees!" Pearl said.

Josias laughed. When they came to the height they must climb out of the valley, Pearl thought maybe she was going to be sick. "I can't make it, I surely can't," she said. "I clean forgot about it, so!"

"You can make it. Just when you think you most tired and can't be no more tired, you find de strength," Josias said.

It was true. Pearl had to climb. And with Josias urging and persuading, she managed to climb and only slipped once or twice.

"It scare me so," she said, once they had reached the top and were resting. "That be 'bout de only thing I can think of that would stop me from sang huntin'."

"If that's all, then I'll show you a way to de valley where you don't have to climb up or down."

"What? Josias!"

He laughed again, fell on his back and folded his arms behind his head.

"We least has four or five ways of coming and going from any one place," he said. "If we didn't, we'd risk a trap one time, if and ever somebody come lookin'."

"I surely understand," Pearl said, pouting. "You just makin' things hard for me."

He sat up. Touched her hand. She grew shy. They both did. He took his hand away, managed to say, "We has to know de strength of folks comin' new here. We has to. Didn't mean nothin' bad by it. But best to know who can be counted on."

"Could've asked me," Pearl said. "I'da told you I was strong enough."

"All right," he said. "I'm most sorry."

"Well," she said. She got up, smoothed out her shift. "Think I best find Mother Pearl, see if she want me to help her with somethin'."

There was an awkward silence between them. It soon passed. Pearl was good-natured and so was Josias. She couldn't stay peeved at him for long. And as soon as she relaxed, he responded with a smile and a touch of his hand.

He always touching somebody, Pearl thought. But it not be wrong. Be nice, to know he be kind to me.

They walked unhurriedly back through the shed area and around the cabins. There were not many folks around that were old enough to be maws and paws. Just the ones like old Minnie, who could do little more than sit and remember and watch.

"That be Minnie by de cabin I shares with Black Salt," said Josias.

There she was, in a comfortable cane chair before the chink of a window in the cabin front. Minnie was chewing something, and Pearl watched her jaw move up and down. Minnie watched everything with small, beady eyes.

"She 'in de mind,' my paw say," Josias explained. "For her, every time, now and yesterday, is all de time."

"I see," Pearl said. "That what bein' real old be like."

" 'Tis so," he said. "Not so bad, to sit and watch and chew all dayclean."

That struck both of them as funny, and they giggled about it.

Mother Pearl was nowhere to be seen. But Dwahro was. He was back now and in charge of the children. Pretty Pearl could hear Mother Pearl talking in one of the cabins.

"Your maw and Salt," Josias said.

Mother Pearl and Black Salt were discussing something on one of the cabins.

Josias and Pretty went to see. They did not interrupt but stood there in the doorway watching and listening.

Black Salt was telling Mother Pearl she needn't work so hard, that she didn't have to clean each and every cabin and do everybody's laundry when folks had been doing all that themselves. But she insisted.

"How they gone feel when they gets back from de labor, havin' to clean cabins and warsh de clothes?" she was saying. "And me with nothin' but de chil'ren. And he, Dwahro, got more games and things to teach 'em. Let him teach 'em de fun. Dwahro nothin' but a chile hisself. Cain't do much but playact. He just some 'musement most de time."

"Did you know he must've followed me?" Black Salt said. "That Dwahro come behind me. I swung around, hearin' somethin'. Thought somethin' bad had me for true, and there be Dwahro, him."

"You mean, you *see* him behind you?" Mother Pearl asked.

"Yes. Comin' back, and how I know he there, I see him there."

"Hmmmm." That was all Mother Pearl would say about it.

That Dwahro! thought Pretty Pearl. He was to stay invisible. It must've worn off or he fought it off. That way, she thought, he make Black Salt think he some smart to track de leader so.

"I'll admit," said Black Salt, "Dwahro some tracker, he got there and back without me or the Real People ever knowin'."

"Well," said Mother Pearl. She gave an angry flash of her eyes in the direction of Freedom Lane, where Dwahro played with the children.

"Let's get away, 'fore they make us work, so!" whispered Josias.

They backed from the doorway, then turned and ran as fast as they could.

Pretty Pearl giggled, gulping air. "Let's hide amongst de chil'ren," she said.

"Be a good idea!" he said. And they ran for the children and Dwahro.

Dwahro could feel any song in the world and he could translate it into words, much the way Pretty Pearl could. But his art was the contagion of his energy and his dancing. Once the children saw Dwahro dance anything, they had to learn it.

Now, he taught them a ring-play song in which all of the participants joined hands in a circle. Both Pretty Pearl and Josias broke into the circle and joined hands just as the song began.

The first verse was sung:

> *"Go round de border, Choska,*
> *Go round de border, Choska,*
> *Go round de border, Choska,*
> *On this long summer day."*

The children swayed and swung to the rhythm. Then the child called Choska broke free of the ring and began to move about on the outside of the circle. And everybody sang, with Dwahro singing softly, too:

> *"Turtledove she started, shoo 'way my little one,*
> *Shoo 'way my little one, shoo 'way, shoo 'way,*
> *Turtledove she started, shoo 'way my little one,*
> *Shoo 'way, shoo 'way, on this long summer day."*

Just as they began to sing the next verse, Dwahro

commenced following Choska, to the delight of the other children. All of the singing and prancing about was done in tones that were no louder than clear whisperings:

> *"Out goes de hornet, shoo 'way my little one,*
> *Shoo 'way my little one, shoo 'way, shoo 'way,*
> *Out goes de hornet, shoo 'way my little one,*
> *Shoo 'way my little one, on this long summer day."*

Suddenly, everyone raised their arms high above their heads, hands still joined, and sang:

> *"Open de cabin doors, shoo 'way my little one,*
> *Shoo 'way my little one, shoo 'way, shoo 'way. . . ."*

Choska weaved in and out of the ring under the arms held high. "Don't miss no doorway!" the children shouted. Then, when that verse was finished, the next one came. It was the final one, and it was always sung when the boy and girl were both on the outside of the circle:

> *"Close up de cabin doors, shoo 'way my little one,*
> *Shoo 'way my little one, shoo 'way, shoo 'way,*
> *Close up de cabin doors, shoo 'way my little one,*
> *Shoo 'way my little one,*
> *On this long summer day."*

And now the chase began. Choska, the turtledove, turned in every direction trying to escape Dwahro, the hornet. But the children were becoming too excited. They would begin to scream and shout at any moment. Swiftly, Dwahro made the capture and swung the turtle-dove up to his shoulder. There she waved down at the children, and the game came to a satisfying end.

"That was good," Dwahro said, setting little Choska down.

"Can we has some more, Dwahro?" asked a child.

"Course," Dwahro said. "Has as many as you wants. But make that circle strong. 'Cause de ring song don't like no weak circle, you hear? Make de circle most strong.

"Now," he said, "set youself on de groun' this time."

All of them did sit down. Pearl sat down, and Josias was right beside her.

Oh, it was just fine, she thought, to be a child and to sing and play all the dayclean!

"Here we go," Dwahro said in a low voice that only the circle could hear. "Join hands again. Hold de hands tight. Here it come." And he began to sing. Only a moment passed, they had the idea of it and responded to his call:

CALL:	"Heaven above."
RESPOND:	"Heaven above."
CALL:	"We not what we oughter be."
RESPOND:	"No, we not, no, we not."
CALL:	"We not what we wants to be."
RESPOND:	"That most true, Dwahro, most true."
CALL:	"But thank de heavens, chil'ren, We not what we was!"
RESPOND:	"Sing it agin! Sing it agin!"

They sang it again and again. When they had finished singing it, Dwahro got up to do a buzzard lope for them. It was a solo dance, like the kind Dwahro had seen done by the lowland people across Africa. There were many such dances that copied the way animals and birds moved about. This one was for the buzzard, Opete, as the Ashanti called him. And he was sacred in all of West Africa.

The children had to learn the buzzard lope. Pretty Pearl had to learn it. And with Josias at her side, laughing at her and at himself, too, she learned it.

Dancing, Dwahro went about in a circle. He bent his body forward from the waist. And he threw back his arms in perfect imitation of the bird. All of them copied him.

On and on while Mother Pearl was busy, Dwahro pranced, and often acted the fool. He taught the ham bone, too. He taught the games and songs to please the children.

Dwahro was as kind as any young man might be who was down on his luck. Caught, trapped and strung out on a short string, Dwahro was as good as he could possibly be. He had forgotten all about his own troubles.

CHAPTER ELEVEN

An hour after the sun was directly over the land of Prom-ise, it rained a good, soaking downpour. The rain brought a cool wind for as long as it lasted. But it did not last long. When it was over and the sun came out again, the heat came down. It spilled over the great forest trees and slid down the leaves. Heat was a suffocating heavi-ness that waited everywhere around bushes and under branches. It pressed in, hot and humid, on all that moved and breathed.

Mother Pearl had reckoned that those who labored in the heat would need nourishment at the halfway point of dayclean.

"Somethin' mos' bettah than they pieces o' conepone they carryin'," she told the children. All of the children and Pretty Pearl and Josias had gathered around her cooking pot again. And the heat was fierce by that fire, although Mother Pearl didn't seem to mind it.

"De idea, so," she said, throwing ingredients in the pot. "They in de fields and not nary but they bread, and onion them dig and 'matoes covered with dust and dirt; eatin' they de raw food right there, settin' in de row. Why, de idea!"

The children watched her. So did Pretty Pearl and Josias. Pretty could see that Mother Pearl had worked herself up over everything that she wanted to make right for Promise. It wouldn't do any good to remind Mother that the field laborers could eat melons, berries, carrots and potatoes anytime they wanted.

An hour ago Mother Pearl had stopped their ring-play songs and dances with Dwahro. She had directed some of the children to sweep the cabin floors. Even the smallest children had to work. They worked in groups separating yarns by colors and winding the yarns neatly around wood sticks. Some children, those who could sew a bit, darned the poor shifts they all had to wear, at Mother's direction. Even the boys wore shifts until they were Josias' age, when knee britches were cut from remnants of cloth or muslin and sewn for them.

Mother Pearl commanded the children to carry small berry buckets of food from her pot to the laborers of the valley and beyond. She had made a whole kettle-boil and steam of lamb's-quarters weed for the field laborers.

Sweet and tender, the wild spinach was seasoned with apple vinegar and smoked slab pork. This last was brought in for the inside folks at their request by the Real People.

Mother Pearl had Pretty Pearl carry a gunnysack of lamb's-quarters-seed bread made into round loaves from ground seeds, cornmeal, wheat flour, honey, salt, fat and leavening. The bread dough had been placed on a large, flat rock, which the boys had heaved into place, surrounded by the fire's red-hot coals. When the rock heated through, the dough was seen to rise and brown.

"It so long way!" Pearl said, softly now. She resented the fact that Mother Pearl had made her carry such a heavy load. Who she to tell me? she thought. She felt put upon, just like a child.

The children sweated. So did she. The coarse shift she wore irritated her shoulders and made her cross.

They were on their way to the valley of Abyssinia, and all of them were tired. They were burning hot and out of sorts with one another.

Josias led them the long way, which didn't take them the steep path down that he and Pearl had made earlier. He hadn't wanted the buckets of food to spill.

Pearl commenced sighing and mumbling as if she were in pain.

"You want to sit down, wait for us to come back?" Josias said quietly. He didn't stop walking. She had to catch up with him to hear.

"Maybe de others need to rest some," she said. She looked around loftily at the others. Shifted her load of bread. The bigger children said nothing. They walked, watching her and Josias.

"We all wants to see de folks git they food while it still hot," Josias said.

"Well, I do too," Pearl said, not to be left out.

" 'Spect we best go on," Josias said. "It hard and long to get there from here."

The children didn't mind going on. It was Pearl who felt like dawdling on the path. Why we have to hurry so in this heat? she thought. The reason she had come to the forest seemed to have drifted far back in her thoughts.

"Do we have to do this every day?" she asked Josias.

He took a long time answering, as if he didn't want to answer such a question. " 'Spect so," he finally said.

"Well, it not very much fun," she told him. Not like the fun it had been when the two of them had climbed down to the valley. And found the sangers in that dark place, ever so quiet.

Oh! she thought. "Josias, who will feed de sang hunters?" she asked. "Can I go take them de food?"

"No'm," he mumbled. He did not turn to look at her. "We call 'em. An' if they's near to hear, they come to de fields."

"I can take it to them," she said confidently.

"You cain't go out alone," he said, frowning, "without me to lead you."

"Why not? I know de way well as you!" Her eyes flashed at him.

Josias wouldn't argue with her. He shook his head.

"Please, quiet, you, so I can hear de woods and know what might be comin', so."

"Wasn't makin' no noise," she said. Her anger at him gathered and smoldered.

I could show you if I wanted to, she thought. Think I don't know nothin', shoot. You don't has no idea who you dealin' with here.

She felt at once a child and, also, superior to these children.

I got real, magical importance, me!

And she had been wanting to show it ever since she came to Promise.

Show them all that Black Salt and his son, and that Old Canoe, weren't so much. Josias think he better than me and de other chil'ren, she thought.

She missed a step on the path, held on to her de Conquer root with her free hand and caught her step again. Touching the root like that gave her pause. She looked at it, and then grinned from ear to ear.

Think I'll let out de Hide-behind. Ho! Show you chil'ren a thing or two, so! It mine to do with as I please, ain't it? she thought.

Pearl strung out the Hide-behind. She saw it leap through the air and land behind a tree. It went off a ways and then began darting closer. All the time it moved, it hid itself behind bush and tree. The Hide-behind was loose. Its power was to scare and terrify.

"Ho-hum!" Pearl said softly. Good thing you chil'ren cain't see what I can see, she thought. If you could, you never walk out here again!

The Hide-behind was the most ugly spirit in the spirit world. It had teeth that hung out of its mouth down to its hairy feet. It had two heads and one red eye in each head. It had purple fingers and sickly blue arms. Oh, it was ugly and fierce to see. Hunched over the way it was, it hurled itself along from one hiding place to the next.

It sure can move fast! Pearl thought admiringly.

The Hide-behind moved fast and closer, for it saw the children. Its scare tactic oozed around them and they began to feel it.

"Somethin'," Josias said, the first to notice.

At once Pearl had a stabbing pain in her big toe. She couldn't stand any longer, it hurt her so. And she sat down hard on the path.

"You feel it too?" Josias asked her.

Pearl couldn't get a word out because of the pain. De Conquer! she thought. For the pain in her foot was the way her brother would call to contact her. You want somethin'? You tryin' to tell me somethin'? There danger?

There was no stab of pain to tell Pearl, Yes, there was danger. The hurt stayed a steady burning pain that took her breath.

"What de matter, you?" one of the children asked her.

"Shhh!" said Josias. "Somethin'!"

The children's eyes grew large and frightened. They pulled closer to Josias, holding tightly to their berry buckets full of warm food.

"We best get on, fast as we can," Josias said.

"No. No," said Bessie Freedom, and she began to cry.

"They be ghost here. I can feel it. Awful ghost!"

She dropped her bucket, and half of the good food Mother had made spilled on the ground. Bessie started running back. But Josias caught her before the other children panicked.

"Here," he said to Pearl, "hold on to her." For Pearl still sat on the path, holding her foot. Josias didn't realize she was hurt. He swung around just as the old Hide-behind was stepping from behind a shagbark hickory. The thing jumped back. Josias didn't see it at all, not even its movement. But he could feel it.

"We better get out o' here, so," he said. "Hurry, chil'ren!" He picked up Bessie's bucket and saved about half of its contents.

Pearl managed to get to her feet. She shoved Bessie in front of her.

"Ouch!" she said, hopping on one foot.

"What wrong with you now?" Josias said to her.

"Nothin' wrong with me!" she answered. But her voice shook. The pain was still there. It ached hard. She bit her lip, began walking, calling out inside to herself, "Ouch! Ooh, it hurts!"

Josias handed Bessie her bucket. "Now you hold on to it this time," he said. "Hold my han' now. Jes' 'member folks gone be hungry." He looked all around them. Nothing but the forest to see. But he could feel. Oh, he could feel an awful something. "Hurry!" he whispered. "To de grown folks." And they all hurried off.

Pearl brought up the rear. *"There's food for you, ole Hidebehind,"* she whispered to the spirit under her breath.

"Know you don't care much for slop spill, but you can try it." Huh! Not one de chil'ren think to wait for me. Not even Josias! *"Oh, Hide-behind! I'm gone leave you here so's you can scare these po' babies on de way back, too."*

She was in a mean mood. She hobbled along, trying to catch the others. Soon she wasn't far behind. But her foot kept up its aching pain.

I'll get Mother Pearl to rub it when I gets back, she thought.

The Hide-behind followed them across a bubbling sweetwater brook. It had taken the brook in one leap. It caused some of the children to slip on the rocks. They got their shifts soaking wet.

It followed them through a scary way of whispering pines. When the children looked over their shoulders, there was nothing scary to see. Every now and then one of the see-alls would pop up out of nowhere and disappear again. It seemed that they, too, were being upset by something, they knew not what.

By the time the straggly band of children reached Abyssinia, half of them were crying. Even Josias felt tight inside, ready to burst into tears. And he was so relieved to see the grown folks laboring as they always did.

The children hurried down the rows. Pearl hobbled along behind them.

"What it is! What happen?!" said the nearest folks on hearing the crying and seeing the tears. Folks gathered swiftly.

"Didn't see no see-all's signal," said Miz Molly, who was right there. A signal would be a wood pigeon circling low over Abyssinia with a fall leaf tied to its foot.

"Somethin' awful on de long path," Josias said. "Somethin', cain't see it, cain't hear it, but know it be there."

"Know it awful, so!" cried Bessie Freedom, trembling and crying.

"Hush! Hush now!" said Miz Molly, holding Bessie to her. "If there be somethin' ghosty, we gone let Salt take care of it." She gave a troubled glance toward the long, flatter path to Promise.

At once the field men, Ezekiel and one named Cuffee, called an African, took off running. In minutes they had climbed the height up to Promise. The children watched them disappear in the trees up there.

"So," said Miz Molly. She wiped sweat from her face and neck with a blue kerchief while patting Bessie with the other hand. "Yall not feelin' nothin' funny out here now, is you?" she asked the children.

"No'm," they said in unison. Pearl mumbled, as if agreeing.

"Then whatever they is, Salt gone take care of it. Now. Whatchall doin' out here? What be in de buckets?"

"Mother Pearl mawmaw done fixed de food," said Josias. "Say it ain't right yall do all de work an' not have no good eatin' 'fore end of dayclean."

"Did she now!" said Miz Molly. "Well. She sure somethin'!"

"Yeah!" said the others. "Sure de best mawmaw woman, true." They smiled on Pretty Pearl, patted her head. For wasn't she the child of the good mawmaw? She

[193]

grinned just like a child back at them. She tried to stand straight so no one would notice she was hurting.

The grown folks walked off toward shade trees and sat down with the buckets.

"Uuum-uuum! It a feast!" Pearl could hear them saying.

You don't know nothin'! she thought. She felt upset, mean and scared at once. She plopped down and tried to relax.

The children and Pearl were bunched together sitting in the rows between tomato plants. Absently, some of them had begun picking a few tomatoes and sucking the delicious juice. The grown folks didn't mind them. Let the children rest while they kept a protective eye on them, was what they thought. The younguns had come a long way and it was hot; been frightened by something.

"Don't you want no tomata?" Bessie asked Pearl. She sat as close to Pearl as she could get without climbing into her lap.

"Them dusty things?" Pearl said coolly.

"You can wipe off de dust. Ain't nothin'," said Bessie, but Pearl ignored her.

"Best we be goin' back, don't you think, Josias?" she asked. Just then something happened.

"Look! Look there!" softly spoke Josias. He pointed to the height off a ways, where he and Pearl had climbed.

Up there they could clearly see Black Salt, Ezekiel, the African Cuffee and, lo and behold, Dwahro dressed in work clothes, just like a young man.

The four of them were armed with plains guns.

Dwahro held his like a soldier ready to march.

Fool! thought Pearl. Where's you fancy suit? Wait I get hold of you, dumb Dwahro. Gone pull you back in, too. You just wait!

It appeared to Pretty Pearl that Dwahro had taken up with the other side.

He has to pretend he somebody's son. He want to be human so! She was mad at Dwahro. She envied him. To see him getting on so well hurt her pride. And with a gun! she thought. Just like he a warrior, be trusted at Black Salt's back.

The men up there and Dwahro moved off, skirting the brink of the height.

"They take care of it now. What it is, they take care of it for true!" said Josias.

"Yeah," answered the children, "for true, so!"

Yall don't know nothin', Pearl thought. But she was growing more anxious every minute.

"We can go now," said Josias. He trotted over to say good-bye to the grown folks and to collect the buckets, which the folks had emptied into their gourds. Always they carried the gourds around neck or waist to take care of their thirst and hunger. A few of them had been making sounds of the bobwhite quail, to call the sangers. And now some few hunters who had heard wandered in and over to the shade trees for the tasty food.

Josias trotted back with the buckets. Pearl noticed how easily he loped along. Like a harbinger of old Africa, she thought. A harbinger could run for a day and night without stopping. She was reminded of de Conquer, then.

The aching in her foot seemed to have subsided.

It was only de Hide-behind, she thought, half to herself and half to the best god. There weren't no danger.

"Each take a bucket," Josias told the children. "Sling him over de shoulder and in back of de arm. Him out o' you way like that." He distributed the buckets.

"Put one in you gunnysack, Pearl," he said. "It empty now."

Who you to tell me? she thought, but said not a word and did what she was told.

Wait we get back on de long path, you gone see somethin', she thought anxiously.

The children lined up behind Josias. And single file, they headed across Abyssinia toward the height.

What? "What yall doin'?" she asked. "Where yall goin'?"

"Goin' home," said Josias. The children waved goodbye to the grown-ups. The grown-ups were heading back to their labor. Some of them who saw waved back at the children.

"But that ain't de way," said Pearl.

" 'Tis," said Josias. "We ain't goin' near that other path 'til Salt, my daddy, an' de mens figures out what's there."

"But . . . but . . ." began Pretty Pearl. She could not finish. She was at a loss for words. Her heart sank. Out there she had left the Hide-behind. Black Salt and his men, and that Dwahro, were on their way there! Why hadn't she realized? If she had got over there, she might have pulled the Hide-behind back into the de Conquer root before Dwahro discovered it.

That ole Hide-behind! Pearl thought with anguish. That Dwahro! He gone tell Mother Pearl on me, too. I'm gone be in trouble, too!

More trouble than she knew.

CHAPTER TWELVE

By the time the children had made the difficult climb up
the height, they were thoroughly exhausted and in need
of rest. Many of them fell to their knees, once over the
top. Others simply fell flat on their stomachs and rested,
heads on their arms.

"We best get back," said Pearl anxiously. Although
she felt she would collapse herself, she had to get back.
She hoped she would run into Dwahro coming from the
long path.

"Can't force de chil'ren when they ain't got de
strength," Josias was saying. "Don't much like no path
no more," he said. "Not after de long path. But all seems

[198]

safe right here." He looked all around. "We 'most close to home and nothin' feel scary."

It was not long before he roused the children and urged them along. They would not argue with Josias; they did as they were told. For they had long since learned that their lives might depend on their unquestioning loyalty to the leader of them, son of Black Salt.

Soon they were passing among the sheds toward the cabins and Freedom Lane. It felt so good to be back, Pearl thought. The children hurried to the cabins. Just as Josias and Pearl were rounding them, Black Salt and Dwahro came up on one side of them.

"Yall back?" asked Josias.

"Yeah," answered Black Salt.

"What was it, Papa?" asked Josias.

"Couldn't say," said Black Salt. "Feel like a trick done been placed, so Cuffee tell me. Cuffee, he sometime talk about de spells of old, de Mystery, he calls 'em. But I don't know. He say he has a 'jack' o' charms, gone put it on de path. But it ain't a man, what it is out there. That I know for sure," Black Salt finished.

Josias went ahead with his father. The two see-alls who had been hidden along the long path came in now, shaking their heads. They went directly to Black Salt. Pearl was left with Dwahro.

"I know what you did, I know what you did!" Dwahro whispered. "And you better *un*did it, 'cause I'm gone tell Mother Pearl. She gone fix you, you heathen chile!"

"Don't tell her!" said Pretty Pearl. "I can fix it!"

"Well, then, go fix it. Hurry!" he said.

"Keep a god's eye on my back," Pearl whispered hurriedly. "Watch for that African, Cuffee—he still in de compound?"

Dwahro stared straight ahead, as if listening with his eyes. "He still here," he said. "Don't let him see you out there!"

"I won't," she said. "And you watch for Josias. He stickin' to me like honey and I de bee."

"Don't worry 'bout it, I said get you out there and fix it! Hurry, you bad chile!"

She thought of pulling Dwahro in and keeping him in. Telling her what to do, and calling her names. But there were old folks around. She hadn't even seen them all yet. No telling who might be looking. Besides, Dwahro had to cover her back. She ran quickly away behind a cabin, dodging from one cover to the next. Almost like a Hide-behind herself.

Dwahro had already started off, calling attention to himself by dancing a graceful step or two. And singing in a comic, whining voice:

> *"My ole massa promise me,*
> *When he die he set me free.*
> *He live so long, he head got bald.*
> *Freedom! Mercy, night be day.*
> *Massa cold dead—where my pay!"*

He dashed inside a cabin, dashed out again, wearing his fine suit of clothes. Beautiful stars and magical moons.

"Oh, I'm fine. I'm so fine," he told himself. "Salt say I de bestest tracker he seen in a long time. Tell me Josias be one side, I be de other side, Black Salt."

Dwahro took Freedom Lane in two leaps and a bound. "Now ain't I somethin'? Ain't I, yall?" he said, not loud. He pranced and agitated until he had a good number of children watching him. His feet never stopped moving. He kept a god's eye out for Cuffee and Josias. They were right there. Cuffee came up to watch with a couple more old men. Ezekiel was there, pausing a moment to watch Dwahro before he went down the height to Abyssinia to finish out the dayclean. Cuffee was older, and he had finished his chore at Abyssinia this dayclean. He might as well stay where he was.

Salt gave a glance to Dwahro. With his keen eye he watched, judging a moment. But he had to store the rifles and check the perimeter of the compound. What he had seen today on the mountain had troubled him. And he must choose his words carefully tonight to the inside folks. Now, this strangeness over on the long path was another worry. The see-alls had come in because they couldn't take the terror they felt out there. They said he, Salt, better fear.

Dwahro had hold of everybody so Pearl could do her work. Mother Pearl was over there in the oaks with a big scrubbing tub full of wet clothes. She was up to her elbows in water and lye soap. She and the children had strung up heavy twine between the oaks to make clothes-lines. And she was washing clothes and hanging them to dry in a steady rhythm. She saw Dwahro. She saw Josias.

She didn't take the time to wonder about Pretty. Chile was right sassy, but never mind that now.

Ain't nothin' but a god baby, still, thought Mother about Pretty. Ain't nothin' wrong with that.

§   §

"What I done? What I done!" Pearl whispered. She was running swiftly through the forest on the long path. She was panting, scared to death.

Somethin' not right, she thought. What I done? What I done!

All at once the Hide-behind was there. Jumping right in her path and then behind a hickory, almost before she could blink. In fact, unlike before, she wasn't sure she had seen it at all. She felt as if she had imagined she had.

"Hide-behind!" she called. "Git on in here!" She held her de Conquer root in her right hand and raised her left arm high. A moment passed. Then another. The Hide-behind darted close. It darted behind Pearl, making her spine tingle with terror. She imagined she could feel its red eyes burning holes in her. It darted back and forth and behind trees and bushes. But it would not come inside.

"Hide-behind! Hide-behind!" Pearl hollered, forgetting to be quiet.

But the Hide-behind would not come on her de Conquer command.

I know! thought Pearl. I'll get de Hodag to shoo it in. Before she could raise her arm again and say, "Come on out, Hodag!" the Hodag was there. It wagged its razor-sharp tail and sniffed around, slicing bushes in half.

"Hodag, how'd you *do* that!" Pearl cried. "I didn't let you out." But she had no time for questions. The Hodag was cutting up the woods.

"Now stop it, Hodag," she said. "Listen. Go bring de Hide-behind to me. Hear? Just shoo it over here so's I can put it away. It done cause me trouble, too."

But the Hodag wouldn't listen. He ran off, heading west. His wagging tail cut through stands of trees. Pearl could hear them crashing down like thunder.

Oh, me! What I done!

Now the Hodag was gone and the Hide-behind was way off now, trying to follow the tricky Hodag. But it had to dodge falling trees and hide behind what was left standing at the same time. And so its progress wasn't very fast.

I got to get back, thought Pearl. What am I gone do! Got to tell Mother Pearl. All they is to it. De Hodag and de Hide-behind is free! What it mean?

Pearl had turned to go back when she stopped still. She stared down, then held her de Conquer root out before her so she could look at it. The root appeared old and withered today. Was she imagining things? No, it did look old. It looked like it had dried up. Did I forget something? She couldn't tell.

Pearl had to walk back to the compound. It had been a long dayclean, and dayclean wasn't even over. She thought if she had to walk another step, she would fall down. She did fall down to rest, twice. Oh, it felt good to press her face on the grassy earth! Felt cool on her brow, and she breathed in the sweet grasses. Almost fell asleep right there on the path. But she thought she saw the Hide-behind coming as she dozed. She forced herself up and hurried on back.

By the time she got to the Lane, it was nearly five o'clock. Josias was nowhere to be seen, nor was Black Salt or that furry rat, Pearl thought meanly, Dwahro. Mother Pearl had all the washing done. Her washtub and board had been put away. The clothes hung, drying in the late-afternoon heat before the sun slipped off behind the high trees. Mother and the children had cut up vegetables on a table in one of the cabins. Now they carried them out to the great, black cooking pot at the end of Freedom Lane. The children had round baskets of quartered vegetables—potatoes, onions, carrots, mushrooms, cabbage, tomatoes, corn and squash. Mother Pearl had chunks of beef already searing in the pot in bacon fat.

"Uh-huh, uh-huh!" she murmured as she stirred the meat. The Real People had supplied them with a side of beef. Mother Pearl knew how to take from the side the round, the rump and the flank, cut them up small, stretch them with vegetables, making enough stew to feed a whole crowd. She made thick, sweet gravy from cider, water and the fried beef blood at the bottom of the pot. Oh, sprinkle seasonings, stir a little love! "Uu-um!" she said. "Throw in de veg'bles, chil'ren." And the children emptied their baskets into the pot. They shook their baskets over the stew, letting the juice from sliced tomatoes drip through the basket weave.

Pretty Pearl came up fast. But the children were too close, she could not speak out. Urgently, she signaled to Mother Pearl that there was trouble.

The next moment Mother Pearl was saying, "Now chil'ren, time yall set de coals in them holes and warm de water buckets. So's when de folks come back, de water be nice and warm for washing. Yes?"

"Yes ma'am," said the children. They ran to get coal pans and coal shovels. They came back and dug hot coals out of the fire with their shovels. When they had pans full of coals, they headed for the holes in the ground by the cabins and filled them. They got buckets of water and placed them over the holes.

"Mother Pearl, somethin' awful's happenin'," Pretty said, whimpering.

"What it is? Tell me true," said Mother, stirring and stoking the fire at the same time.

"Ole Hide-behind and Hodag done gone. Hide-behind just scarin' everybody," said Pearl.

"Who let it out?" asked Mother. She peered at Pearl. Saw her de Conquer root and sucked in her breath. "What you done done! Chile, what you done!" Mother said.

"Nothin'. Nothin'!" Pearl said, her fear rising as fast as she could speak. "Hodag just up and be out. And chop off de trees on him way west."

"I said what you been doin'!" Mother Pearl said. She threw down her stirring spoon and grabbed Pretty and shook her. "Look me in de eye, god chile!" Mother whispered.

With that command, Pearl had to look and had to tell the truth. "I was bein' angry—mean as I could be," Pretty said. "I let out de Hide-behind, just for somethin' to do. Be mad at Josias, so."

All of a sudden, Mother hugged Pretty to her. "Pretty, baby, you don' know what you done! Oh, baby chile, I so sorry!" And then she let Pearl go. And swiftly she was gone, disappeared.

Pearl found herself stirring the pot. The children were still fixing the water and the coals. They always got interested in playing around their work.

Wish I was you! she thought. Thought I was, but I ain't!

In a moment Mother Pearl was back. It was as if Pearl was moved over to the side and she didn't see how. And Mother Pearl was stirring the pot again. The pot was bubbling now. Mother took up the flour jar and poured a good bit of the flour into the stew, stirring all the time. Little pebbles of flour rose around the meat chunks. As Mother stirred, the pebbles grew smaller and the stew thickened.

"I got de Hide-behind," said Mother. "He got smart with me, but it easy to pull him in." She touched her root necklace. Her face was sad; and now she kept her eyes away from Pearl's. "But that Hodag done gone," she said. "Don't 'spect we ever see that animal agin for a while, not until John de Conquer find him sometime. He done put down a whole stan' o' trees."

Mother was acting formal now. She kept her eyes on the stew as she talked. "I'm gone tell Salt that a groun' wind musta come up sudden-like. Shoot. We use them cut-down trees to build us a cabin one time. But fo' now, we gone sleep on de groun'. You, me and Dwahro, talk lots tonight! Pretty, how could you!"

Pearl felt terrible. Mother Pearl just clamped her mouth shut and wouldn't say another word.

How could she what? Pretty wondered. How could she be mean? She'd been mean before and Mother Pearl had never acted so serious about it.

Like . . . like Mother and me be separate, so. Like never before, thought Pretty. I don't know. Somethin' awful is goin' on and I did it. Somethin' worse than terrible. It de Hide-behind. It got away from me.

Pearl stood on one foot and then, the other. Her big toe was aching her again. De Conquer! What you want with me! But there was no sure message from her brother. The aching was steady and hard enough to turn down the corners of her mouth and cause her eyes to fill with tears. Pearl slumped down to the side of the cooking pot. She was almost hidden from view by it. There she sat the whole time, as late afternoon grew to evening. The inside folks came in from their separate labors.

They ate the stew. They sang the songs. Pretty hardly touched her food. She did not have the heart to sing. Dwahro was over there with the children and Josias. When Josias had come over to sit with her, she had turned away, wouldn't talk to him.

It him fault I get myself into trouble, she thought. After a while he had gone back to the children and Dwahro.

Black Salt talked this night, the second night that he had talked. It was after the supper pot had been taken away. The fire was hot with glowing coals.

The night had come quickly to the forest place. And Salt stood before them, his face aglow, a beacon in the darkness.

"We went to de mountain," he began.

"You got a right," someone said, and was still.

"We went high as we could, climb de tree for higher," Black Salt said.

"Got a right to de tree of life!" a voice spoke, trembling. It was the African, Cuffee. Pearl knew Cuffee came from the coast of Africa, where a child was given a birth name depending on the day of the week on which it was born. Cuffee was Coo-fee, or Friday.

"And we could see what they was to see," said Black Salt. "Oh, the rivers and lakes, like tatters o' shiny, blue cloth!" His voice, stirring with emotion.

"Ain't it free, ain't it free!" spoke Swassi.

"It was free," spoke Salt. "Freely given us to use by those who held the sacred land. By Ani-yun'Wiya, the principal people, the Real People."

"Cherokee." Someone spoke the name like a sighing.

"But it ain't free no more. We see de railway comin'. It long way off yet, but it comin'. Mens, dynamitin' they way through rock, through mountain. Gone make they way to here one day. Nothin' stoppin' them," Black Salt said.

There was silence now, as all listened with rapt attention.

"But worse than them that's bought de land to build de railway is de other. De bird men. Comin' on strong."

"What?" said Ezekiel, finding his voice. "What this you talkin' 'bout, Salt? Bird men?"

"Bird men," said Black Salt. "We seen it all. They call them fowlers and they after the great nests of pigeons to sell de young, too, called squabs. Old Canoe say so. Now these fowlers can fill a game bag with one shot fired into a pigeon tree. But they ain't satisfied with fillin' one bag. They done set out nets."

"Nets!" Ezekiel said. "You sure?"

"I tell you, you can see for long ways from de mountain. And what you can't see, Old Canoe's men done run secretly near and found out for true," Black Salt assured him.

"De fowlers has staked large nets, and they taken two hundred, three hundred birds at a haul. They followin' de flocks from one roostin' place to de next. Old Canoe and his men find out fowlers trace de birds' whereabouts by somethin' called telegraph, and then they overtakin' de flock by railway.

"Well," Salt added, "it true. We has to leave here, heaven help us!"

There was a long silence. And there was crying. Moaning. Sobbing and sighing. Folks rocked and swayed. No singing now. They knew that Salt spoke true.

"Shhhhh now," he said, after a time of letting them have their emotions. "I'm gone stay with you. I'm gone lead you—what I say! And we don't have to leave just yet. We can scare de flocks off, maybe, and give us some more time. But not much. We gone have to leave here. Make up you minds 'bout that."

"But where we gone go!" asked Maw Julanna. "I is too old to be trekkin' far."

"Maw Julanna, trust me. Me and Old Canoe, me and de mens and womens here, we gone figure it all out. We ain't gone leave you behind!"

Maw Julanna was quiet then.

The inside folks stayed up late that night, talking quietly. Sometimes they would moan and cry. One would rock and hold another. The people grew closer, if that was possible. For all of them feared most losing what they all cherished above life itself: the free land.

It was well past midnight before the folks straggled off to bed. They had to wait until they were exhausted before they could fall to sleep.

"Papa says they is room in de cabins for de womens," Josias said to Mother Pearl. "He say that Dwahro, de tracker, can come in de men's cabin with us."

Dwahro grinned and made to get to his feet. Mother Pearl motioned him with one finger to stay where he was.

"That right nice of him, too, you papa," said Mother Pearl. "But we most-ways fine jes' out here under de sky. But come sometime next week, we might take some fallen trees by de long path and make us a small shed, away from de air."

"Didn't know they was trees down over there," Josias said.

"Well, it appears it jes' happen," said Mother Pearl. "They some groun' wind, I figures, knock a stand o' them big trees over."

"Must've been some wind," said Josias.

"Oh, it had to be. It had to be," Mother went on. "And lucky it wore itself out on them trees and not make it over here."

"Must've been a whirlwind," said Josias. "We see 'em sometimes, away off in de valleys."

"Had to be a whirlwind," said Mother Pearl. "I happen be over there lookin' for me some root medicine and I see de down trees. Tell Salt all about it in de marnin'."

"Yes ma'am," said Josias. "I'll tell him yall gone stay outside. Sleep you easy."

"Easy," said Mother and Dwahro. Pretty Pearl said not a word.

When the lights in the cabins had been blown out and Mother had spread her apron out over the three of them, she began talking. Dwahro never got a chance to tell about his wonderful day with Black Salt. How he had been given men clothes and men gun. How he had gone with the men to study the long path. Only it wasn't any find, it was just the Hide-behind, Pearl doing mischief. He didn't get to tell any of that, or about the time he spent with Salt and some men and Josias and the see-alls, and the pigeons. Now he'd been given the chance to spend the night in the cabin with the men, but Mother had not let him.

"Listen!" she said. "Hear it? Hear it? It singin'. It tonin' a hundred different tones. That hypocrite is somethin'."

"You sayin' de Conquer?" whispered Dwahro. "Playin' his drum?"

"I'm sayin' John de Conquer," Mother said. "Him playin' de hypocrite."

"He comin' now? He comin' here?" asked Dwahro.

"He comin' here, don't know about now," said Mother Pearl. "And why him comin'?" she went on. "Pearl done lost what de Conquer give her. Her root done dried up and died!"

Pretty Pearl commenced to cry. Her hands covered her face.

"How come I lost de root? What I done!" she cried. Her shoulders shook. She swayed, forward and backward and from side to side. Silently, she cried and cried. She felt her heart would break.

Mother Pearl never answered her. She didn't pat her. Dwahro didn't make up a song or a dance to cheer her.

"Oh, it's a bad time," whispered Mother Pearl. "It gettin' to be a godless time!

"But we wait for de Conquer," she added, softly. She did not look at Pretty. "Yea, un-hunh. See what brother him gone do with this *god*-forsaken chile!"

Mother Pearl lay awake all of the night. Dwahro stayed awake as long as he felt like being more than human. When he wanted to be the son of Black Salt, he would practice sleeping and dreaming. But even practicing or awake, he could hear the hypocrite. Both he and Mother

Pearl heard it, always sounding its many moods of sound. It was ever drumming, *ta-ta-tum*. A steady heartbeat. Coming nearer.

Pretty Pearl cried herself out. She could hear nothing more than the woods and night. Finally, she slept the fitful sleep of a troubled child.

CHAPTER THIRTEEN

Life was a toil and life was a trouble for Pretty Pearl Perry, formerly of Mount Kenya. She seemed unable to eat anything.

Don't feel much like playin' with de chil'ren, she thought. Inside herself was a sorrow feeling that made her shoulders hunch. It kept her head from lifting. Pretty had her eyes cast on the ground. She wasn't pretty anymore, and she knew it. She couldn't keep her hair combed. Her ebony bow kept falling off. The last time it fell, it broke into pieces that got smaller and smaller until they were no bigger than grains of sand.

Mother Pearl went, "Tsk, tsk, de god chile is lost. 'Tis

most strange how de world turn. Tsk, tsk."

All she could do was to keep an eye on the child, keep Pretty near her until de Conquer came.

"Can hear de drum," Mother said one day to no one in particular. She was at her boiling supper kettle, stirring a pot of hominy and seared wild boar the men had captured and slaughtered. Only Pearl was in Freedom Lane with her. Pearl not-so-pretty-now stayed there by the fire in the heat of afternoon.

"I'm cold," she said.

"You always cold now," Mother Pearl said. She knitted Pretty-once a shawl to keep her skinny neck and shoulders warm.

"Don't feel like doin' nothin'," Pearl murmured.

The children had given up trying to get her back to her old self. It had been two days now since her John de Conquer had withered and died. Mother Pearl had taken it away. She had given Pretty a simple dark root similar to the de Conquer.

"Hasn't got no strength," Mother said. "It just for show, so de chil'ren don't ask no questions you."

Pretty wore the useless root and no one was the wiser. Young Josias came around more than once to look at Pearl. He would stand off a ways and eye her tenderly, saying nothing.

"Come on here and taste de pot," Mother told him each time he came. And slowly, he would walk over. Mother would hold the spoon for him, with one hand under it to catch the dripping. "Now," she told him. "Blow on it first." He blew on the wood spoon of hominy and meat. Then he took the food in his mouth and ate it boiling hot, the way he had been taught all his life to take food.

"You next," Mother said, nodding at Pearl not-so-pretty-now. Mother thrust the spoon in her direction. Pearl leaned over slightly and took a bit of food from the spoon.

It took Josias all of one day to catch on to the fact that only when he came around did Mother Pearl find a way to get young Pearl to eat a little something. Once he understood, Josias came around as often as he could. Mother would offer him a spoon and would quite naturally offer Pearl one.

So the days passed with Pearl always cold, never playing, looking like an old, shriveled something, not a young one and not a woman, and certainly not a god child. She looked awful. Her eyes were dulled. Her shift was soiled and shabby.

"Somethin' wrong with her?" Black Salt said, stopping from his rounds to question Mother Pearl. "I seen how she don't move from de fireplace."

"She growin' " was all Mother would tell him.

"She lookin' peaked to me," Salt said.

"She growin'," Mother repeated, and worked her work and kept the cook pot full and steaming. She stopped to frantically scratch the palm of her hand for a good five minutes.

"What's-a wrong with you hand?" asked Black Salt. "You catchin' some poison oak?"

"Don't think so," said Mother Pearl. Think it a sign we

gone have us some visitor! she thought excitedly. "It jes' itchin'," she said out loud.

Black Salt looked at Mother hard. He looked at Pearl not-so-pretty-now. He had enough trouble without trying to sort out this woman and this child, didn't he?

Black Salt went away then. He would talk this night. When all the inside folks gathered around the supper kettle, Black Salt sat quietly among them. And when they had finished and it was dark, he told them what he had done.

"De mens and me, we done settled some of de flocks of pigeons a ways from here. See-alls lead us in de pigeon move. They knows how birds thinks about movin' away to a new nestin' ground. We got some of them moved. But it won't mean they will stay moved. And it won't mean they is all moved. 'Bout half of 'em fixin' to stay where they is. Which is good for us in de way of knowing who comin'. And bad for us in de way of folks stumblin' on de Promise land."

Black Salt stood there a long time without speaking. They could tell by the firelight in his eyes what was going on inside him. Oh, he didn't want to leave. He didn't want to move them. They knew that. Oh, Salt loved Promise. He had made Promise a safe way, a hiding place in the southland where there was no hiding place. He had kept them all together. He had led them, fed them and protected them.

"I keep tryin' not to say what I knows one day I has to say!" he cried. Covered his mouth with one hand, then let his arm fall to his side again. "I cain't say it yet. Not yet! I keep tryin' to hold true what is real danger and what is not. Now them fowler mens with they nets ain't made another move yet. They got enough birds for a time, I s'pect. They got to keep an eye on de market for birds. So maybe de price went down and they wait for it to go up again. So we wait awhile, too. We wait. Just hold still, yall. We wait."

That was all he said that night.

The next dayclean, the visitor came. A see-all on the far side of Abyssinia was the first to know. Couldn't believe her eyes. Couldn't believe the size of that visitor, even when she turned loose a homer pigeon to warn all in the fields and up in the cabins and on Freedom Lane.

And the visitor came crashing out of the woods almost at suppertime. He strode into the valley of Abyssinia grinning from ear to ear. He tipped his cap to every woman. He shook the hand of Cuffee, the African, bowed to him in ceremony. And shook the hands of all the men. But he was off, striding down the rows and climbing the height like it was no more than an anthill. And up there Black Salt waited with Dwahro and his son, Josias. All three of them had pistols in their belts. For even though this was a black man coming, they now had become cautious of fowlers and railways and all men who were strangers coming through. Black Salt had not forgotten the strangeness on the long path.

The visitor climbed over the height and made his way around the cabins. He held his cap over his heart when he discovered old Minnie in her chair.

"How you doin', maw woman?" he said. "Hee, hee,

hee," and did not pause for her reply. He headed for Freedom Lane, although he wouldn't have named it that if it had been him naming. "It's de street, all right," he said to no one in particular. "And it look like folks been expectin' me." Old folks stood around. Black Salt, Dwahro and Josias came quietly, respectfully forward. They had taken care of the homing pigeon. They knew that just one stranger came. But before they got very far, Mother Pearl gave out a whoop and a holler. At once, she caught herself from making so much noise. Pearl not-so-pretty-now rose slowly to her feet. She looked as if she were in a dream as she stared at the stranger.

Dwahro stopped dead still all of a sudden. At his reaction, Black Salt reached for his gun. For he had grown to like the pleasant, obedient Dwahro who followed him about just like his own son. He had learned to trust all of Dwahro's sudden moves.

"Hey, whoa there, Mr. Big. Don't be pullin' no fire iron on me. No sir," said the stranger in a heavy, rasping voice. " 'Cause I'm biggah and I'm baddah and you surely don't want to see me start up. Ho!" He gave Black Salt a huge and friendly smile. But it did not mask the warning in his eyes.

"Who are you, then?" said Black Salt. "State your name and your business. How came you by way of this hiding place here?"

"Who, me?" said the stranger. "I follows my nose. But ask that little Pearl, who me!" he said. "What gone wrong with you, little bit?" he said to her. "Don't you recognize me?"

It was then that Pearl commenced jumping up and down, the most excitement she had shown in days. For yes, indeed, she did recognize the stranger.

"Ask that pot and kettle woman, that mawmaw most fine woman, who me!" said the stranger. Mother Pearl threw back her head and laughed. She never stopped stirring her pot. For it was not John de Conquer who had come to visit.

"Ask that skinny gent'man beside you, lookin' like he ready to dance on his way to war, who me!" Dwahro clapped his hands and smacked the stranger on the shoulder. He grabbed the stranger's hand and clasped it hard, laughing softly all at once. Dwahro's heart was full, like a rain barrel after a cloudburst.

"I'm six foot twelve tall," said the stranger. "I either comes from way far or de Black River country, Miss'-sippi, hot dawg! Who knows and who's to tell wheres I come from! I weighed twenty-five pound plus eleven when I be born. I is now big like a giant. And no-body know my middle name. You may call me John." He laughed. "I got a new red suit in my git bag. I got a three-dollar hat with a red hatband. I got new shoes. I got a red neck scarf. I got de blues. I got bad ways and good times. I got a big heart and a bigger mouth!"

John laughed in a wheeze that shook his massive shoulders and made hardly a sound. Then he sang:

"*I got a gal in New Or-leans,*
And her name be Sally Ann.

She but so big and she mighty sweet,
And Big John be her man, Lawd, Lawd,
And Big John be her man.

"They calls me John Henry Roustabout," said John Henry. "Now you know my middle name. But don't you dares to call me Henry! I is the best and the baddest steel-drivin', rail-layin' fool in all de southland. What I say!" He raised his hammer high above his head and grinned at the folks standing around.

Folks were stunned at this huge John Henry and his hammer. They'd never seen a hammer that weighed fifty pounds, nor a giant. Word spread like wildfire. It was nearly the end of dayclean. The sun was on its last stroll, and folks came running from everywhere to see.

Black Salt couldn't believe his eyes. "I didn't see you had no hammer before now. Where it come from?" he asked.

"You ain't see it 'cause you not s'pose to see it 'til I say so," said John Henry pleasantly. "I hid it behind me 'cause I felt like it. I often feels like foolin' with folks. Now you know me." Again he smiled pleasantly at Black Salt and his people. But he gave a gentle touch to Pretty Pearl, who had come near him, and a nod of familiar greeting to Mother Pearl.

"I be big brother to Pretty, done fall on hard times," he said gently. "I be son of Big Mama mawmaw woman over at de cookin' pot. Ain't she somethin'? Ain't she a stone cook? And I be cousin to this here dancin', singin' one, Dwahro. Now you surely know me."

Then John Henry gathered poor, scrawny Pearl in his arms and hugged her close. "How you doin', honey?" he said. He kneeled and spoke softly in her ear. "Don't you cry no more. Big John be here to soothe you." And Pearl buried her face in his neck.

"So glad to see you, John Henry," she whispered back. "Never did remember you much. I sorry. But you gone so long. Oh, take me away with you!"

"Shhhh," he whispered in her ear. "De Conquer comin' soon and we all gone talk it out."

"I'm scared," said Pearl. "Do you know what I done?"

"What could little you done done that's so twice terrible?" Big John Henry said. "Heh, heh," he laughed. "Don't you worry 'bout it. I'm gone see 'bout fixin' it with our brother."

Black Salt quietly spoke to John Henry. "Call me Black Salt," he said and extended his hand.

John Henry rose to his full height. He towered over Salt. He was black and he was big and he kept a sure hand on his sister, Pearl.

"Black Salt be leader man," said John Henry. "Glad to knows de man can keep peoples together in these times. You a good man. I ain't good, but I is a hard worker." John Henry laughed out of one side of his mouth.

Salt smiled up at the giant. "You black for sure," he said. "And you a good talker for true. Change you wanderin' ways and all de people follow your lead."

"Never mind," said John Henry. "I'm headin' for a mountain tunnel they calls Big Bend. You ever hears of it?"

"No," said Salt. "It gone carry de railway?"

"They say it might," said John Henry.

"Railway be like de devil. We stay away from it," said Salt.

"For true, it de devil. But it catch my interest and I cain't stay away from it," John Henry said. "I's a steel-drivin' man, don't you know."

"You a railroad man, come scoutin' ahead?" asked Salt, stiffening.

"Don't get me wrong," said John Henry. "We been contestin', me and mens who work as drivers and shakers. Now I's a driver," he said, his thumb stabbing his chest. "I hammers a steel drill into rock and granite. I make holes for de explosives. Now de shaker, he hold de drill and turn it. Keep it sharp edge in de most secure position. An' now," he said, proudly, "I'ma gone drill a mountain high! For de best job and hardest be blastin' that Big Bend through de mountain. Yey-suh! An' if they's a steam drill around, like they rumor it, I'ma gone beat it back and knock it down with my hammer in my hand!"

A thrill and a murmur went through the crowd of folks standing all around.

"Sho' wish I could see that contest!" said Ezekiel for all of them.

Folks moved closer to John Henry Roustabout. "You is awful most tall," said Swassi. She reached her hand up, trying to touch John Henry's shoulder, but she could not.

"Tall enough to hang de wash clothes from de treetops!" said Mother Pearl. She came up now, wiping her hands on her big apron. Tears filled her eyes. John Henry grabbed her and they fell to hugging and sniffling, just like a son and mother who had been apart for too long.

They were truly a son and a mother when they were most human. And now their love and affection was sweet and comforting.

Mother Pearl leaned back and studied John Henry. "You sure is big!" she said, and everybody laughed.

"I ain't got my heighth jes' yet," John Henry joked. The inside folks fell to chuckling at that.

"When you git it, how tall will you be?" asked Mother Pearl. She and John Henry put on a show.

"Too tall to bend," said John Henry.

"Tree do not bend, do break," said the African, Cuffee.

They all looked around, surprised, for Cuffee rarely spoke any words they could understand.

"How long will you be when you gets you heighth?" asked Josias. He was fascinated with the giant, John Henry.

"Too long for de bed, and long enough to stay a short while" was big John's reply.

"I comes because I hear de hypocrite right in my path, like here be in my path," he whispered just for Mother. "I on my way to de Big Bend and I hear it."

"You 'member you a god?" Mother whispered quickly.

"Almost forgot, then I hear him soundin' drum!" he whispered.

They separated then, and Dwahro asked him how long he could stay.

"Hope it be a good long visit," said Ezekiel. "We may have some trouble and has to move. Railway comin', fowl hunters comin'. No good hidin' no more."

"Why yall want to hide in de first place is beyond me," said John Henry. They were moving off toward the Freedom fire.

"We de inside folks," someone thought to say.

"What that s'pose to mean?" said John Henry. He towered above all of them. He had one hand on Pearl's head. And Mother Pearl had him clasped by the wrist and pulled him along toward her cook pot.

"Hurry, yall," she said. "My food fixin' to burn up!"

They hurried. Hurried to wash up and slake their thirst with fresh, cold spring water.

"Wish I had me some whiskey to mix with de branch water," John Henry said.

No one said anything. For spirits of liquor were strictly forbidden in Promise land. Inside folks watched in awe as big John Henry removed his shirt to have Mother Pearl put it in her washtub. They had never seen so many muscles, so thick and supple. The giant's dark skin shone ebony pure. His strength was alive and rippling under his skin.

All the folks were soon seated before the pot. They had filled their bowls with food. The conversation among the folks with John Henry continued. He was to them a man with knowledge of the world.

"What it like, be a black man out there on you own?"

asked Dwahro. Mother Pearl looked at him sharply.

"And all by youself," someone else added.

John Henry ate one bowl of dinner in two swallows. Mother Pearl filled his bowl again before he spoke.

"Ummmm," he murmured, keeping his voice low. "Whatchall think!" Pearl not-so-pretty-now was right there with him, like a baby bird under the papa's wing. Under the other "wing" was his hammer. John Henry fed little Pearl tiny portions of his supper. And she ate whatever he gave her.

"Not know what to think," said Ezekiel, and others agreed.

"Well, it ain't so bad out there and it ain't too good," John Henry said. "Depend on who you run into and where."

"In other words, it chancy out in de world," said Mother Pearl.

"Oh, de world of mens and folks is chancy, for true," said John Henry. "But I loves a challenge. I gits my challenges 'most every day. I takes my hammer into a camp. De white mens is de bosses. I comes in, actin' small. I lifts my hammer and lays it down, lifts it, lets it fall. On and on. They think I just ordinary. But de black folks workin' there, they know better. For word spread throughout that John Henry bigger and better than anyone seen. So they watch and they wait. Pretty soon some red-eye fellow has to bet he can hammer me down. He sure this colored man is too big and slow and drink too much to has de strength. And de bets go down. And I win, de black folks win ever' time!"

Inside folks laughed in triumph at that.

"But then I gots to move on," John Henry said. "White mens don't want to be beat. And they cause trouble for black who beat de white."

"What I was thinkin'," said Black Salt. "Always knew that would be so." He had been quiet all this time, studying the great black man, John Henry. He found it odd that this man had stumbled onto their Promise and was related to the mawmaw and her people. He decided it was fate. What else could it be brought them together? Fate and luck.

"But I don't get it," said Miz Molly. She sat near Black Salt and she had Bessie Freedom on her lap. "You mean to say black mens and de white workin' in de same place, together?"

"Sure," said John Henry. "We is some free, after all. Don't mean to say they ain't strife, but lemme tell you. De black folks is movin' and workin' every whichaway."

"And bein' beat out, too," said Black Salt. "Bein' monkeyed with and burned up at de stake, I hears, and hung up to de poplar and lynched."

"You sayin' true, but listen," John Henry said. "I been up to Philly-New York. Did not stay long. But they be thousands black folk there. There be a black sea cap'n, name of Brooks, and he comman' a vessel manned only with colored seamen."

"No!" said Ezekiel.

" 'Tis true!" John Henry exclaimed. "And say de seaman go all de way to Africa. Then to a place they calls You-rope; and then on back to Philly-New York."

The African, Cuffee, was standing. He stared at John Henry. "Africa," he whispered. "A black ship. A black-manned ship!"

" 'Tis true!" said John Henry. "And they's lots more I knows and I has seen. I went there for de work, for they is five hundred black longshoremen. And just now they puttin' colored chil'ren in public school in Oakland, in de California town, along with de white chil'ren."

"No!" cried Miz Molly. "I cain't stand it!"

"It true," said John Henry. "The folks is movin' along in de world. Yall just holdin' back, hidin' here."

There was quiet. The African, Cuffee, still stood, swaying slightly. He looked off, far away. "Which way?" he whispered. "Which way, Philly-New York town?" He turned his body ever so slowly.

"Be north," a see-all said.

"It east, above us," John Henry said. "Clear to de coastland. Stop right there." Cuffee had turned himself to the east, and there he stopped and sat down, facing the east. He closed his eyes. Like a blind man, he held his face up to the darkening trees.

"I think we best stop de talkin' now," said Black Salt, " 'fore folks get too riled."

"Lemme say one more thang," said John Henry. "I hear by the words of a ex-slave name of Fred Rick Douglass. He de bestest leader colored man anybody hear of. And he say they is five million colored folks in these states."

"No!" folks said in unison. Black Salt was stunned by the number.

"One half million of us in de north. De rest be here in de southland, bein' whupped, bein' hung, they be burnin' out our colored schools. An' jes' above us in Kentuckplace, de Ku Kluck ride every night. They mostly soldiers of de late rebel armies. And they ride and kill black folks in every county. They slaughter de folks when they tries to vote. So. All I has to say. Ain't no use you hidin' down here," John Henry finished.

"Time," said Black Salt. It was late. Some children had fallen asleep. But Pearl not-so-pretty-now was wide awake. So was Josias. Some of the older folks got to their feet, with the help of those younger.

"Done sat too long," spoke Maw Julanna. She leaned heavily against Mother Pearl.

"Take you time," Mother Pearl said gently.

"Cain't take much," said Maw Julanna. "Ain't got much to take." And they both laughed knowingly.

Black Salt knew what he must do. If the railway and the fowlers and Old Canoe had not quite convinced him, the words of a black, giant outside man come from nowhere had. He headed for his cabin. He did not think to offer Dwahro a covered resting place this night.

Dwahro longed to follow him. But one look from Mother Pearl told him he could not.

Old Cuffee knew what he must do also. Now he got to his feet without help. He looked once to the east, fixed it in his mind, and went to bed.

CHAPTER FOURTEEN

Black Salt took no chances. At daybreak he sent six homers at half-hour intervals to Ani-yun'Wiya. He took no
chance that one or two of the pigeons trained for distance might be caught in a net somewhere. It was not
possible that all six would be caught, of that he was
certain. Each pigeon carried the same message: "Come.
We move. Bring sledges, men."

It was dawn. He had been up most of the night while
the rest slept, having had only two hours of sleep before
the first light came. Now he paced the men's cabin, not
making a sound. It was still dark in the cabin. He walked
out of doors in his soft moccasins that Ani-yun'Wiya had

fashioned of fine leather. He smelled the fresh, coming day, and it was good. Salt trod softly to the campfire where it smoldered low. Carefully, he made his way around the sleeping forms of the mawmaw woman Mother; around Dwahro; the sickly child, young Pearl; and the great giant, John Henry. He looked on them as they lay there. He wondered about them. And he was thankful for them, thankful that his people had all these various yet able kinds among them. But the child was sick. Strangely fallen weak, as though one of old Cuffee's charms had tricked her. He had grown fond of the child, as had his son, Josias. But he had no time to help heal her now. Leave it to her own people. He must.

Black Salt never knew that only the child slept the sleep of humans. He trudged on to one of the outbuildings. It was a coop where the best homing pigeons were kept, away from the broods in the trees.

Then was the moment that Mother Pearl, Dwahro and John Henry had another chance to talk in private.

"Man take his task most serious," John Henry said about Black Salt, in a voice just loud enough to be heard by Mother and Dwahro. Pearl not-so-pretty-now heard nothing.

In the hours that Black Salt had slept, they had talked of nothing but young Pearl's trouble. And the coming of John de Conquer.

"She just a babe," John Henry had said, flexing his muscles there in the dark. He had his arms propped behind his head. "Why come he gone be so hard and take away de root necklace he given to her?"

"You know," said Mother Pearl then. "De Conquer tell her, never use it 'gainst no chil'ren."

"Well. It was a small mistake."

"Not so, not accordin' to de Conquer, it ain't."

"Well," John had said again. "We see when he come."

They listened now. The singing drum had stopped once, twice. Now it stopped and started at steady intervals.

"What that s'pose to mean?" Dwahro wanted to know.

"Mean he sendin' message to us," said John Henry.

"Meanin' he ain't far by," said Mother Pearl. "De Conquer got a lot to say to me 'bout what he seen and done and when he comin'."

"What he say! What he say!" spoke Dwahro excitedly.

"Shhhh!" said Mother Pearl.

"Calm you nerves," Big John told him. "De Conquer be along by 'n' by."

They were quiet. It was then they saw as plain as day that Cuffee had awakened and was quietly gathering all he owned into a bundle. He rolled the bundle inside his sleeping pallet. He put inside a small sack of burlap full of dried meat, apples, carrots and a whole cabbage. He had another sack full of his roots and medicines, charms and separate "hands" for "laying de trick." He tied his pallet tightly with twine and lifted it over his shoulder. Dressed, he snuck out of the cabin and headed away from Freedom Lane to the east. He faded within the forest that he called a sacred place.

They watched him go, seeing him as though it were

day. They made no comment, did not try to interfere with him.

"You the cause of that," said Mother Pearl, when Cuffee was out of hearing.

"Uuum-huum," John Henry murmured. "I sure did do that. That ain't bad, so."

"Ain't good, so, neither," Mother said. "That old African got no business walkin' out by hisself. No protection to de back, him. No safe way up ahead."

"Shoot," said Dwahro. "De African out of de old time. Him would not leave lest him know he make it. Long way," Dwahro went on, feeling out toward the African. "Him de owner of medicine. Root doctor, him, he can heal, he can foretell, he can change a thing into another thing. He has spirit, him, not unlike de spirit Dwahro. One difference. De spirit him not too powerful. It will die with him."

"Him only still a old human with power," said Mother. "He think in he head he stronger than he be."

John Henry chuckled at that and closed his eyes, resting.

Later, when it was light, Black Salt had finished his task with the pigeons. There was left the preparation of the camp for their departure. He told himself to say nothing in so many words. Let all of the inside folks gather what would happen little by little, was his plan. That way, the blow would come slowly and would be cushioned by his care. He figured it would take some time to depart without a trace.

Salt came back to the men's cabin. The men were awakening, stretching, reaching for their rough work clothes. At once Salt noticed that the hard, three-plank platform where Cuffee had slept these many years was empty of the African's pallet of striped cotton ticking.

"*Ma-foo-bey!*" Salt whispered, stunned. How often had he and the men heard old Cuffee say the same thing in shocked surprise. "Cuffee run. Run, African. Selah! Good luck!" Black Salt murmured.

"We can go fetch him, if we lope," said Ezekiel. "You want us to brang him back home?"

"No. Oh, no! " said Salt. "He on *his* way home. Let him go. He will make it, with all his 'tricks.' "

Salt left them then. "Get up, quick now," he told them, as he ducked out of the door. "We got hard work." And they knew. They said not a word, but hurried into their clothes. Each had a job, but this day they would be given new jobs. Some to gather the ripe food, and near ripe, and green that would ripen. Some to dig up the root food, pack up the cellars and leave full gunnysacks of potatoes, apples, carrots ready to be loaded when the time came.

In the days to come, they would strike the camp. They would take with them all they could carry. They would pile the logs neatly, and perhaps Old Canoe and his men might find a use for them. They would kill what few animals they had and they would salt the meat. They would dry some of it. They would cure as many hides as they could in the time they had. They would bundle woven cloth, twine, thread, yarn. They would take their spinning wheels and hand looms, but they would leave all but a few of their rain barrels. They would roll pallets and carry them on their backs. They would take their dipper gourds, their buckets and bowls, the butter churns, their axes and hoes and sang hoes, their beet leaves and ginseng roots and beef tallow and horseradish leaves. Garlic and wild ginger and all such herbs and roots, packed in neat bundles. They would take their shovels and pokers, their black powder, their pistols and long guns and knives and hammers. Their coverlets, their lamps and candles, their lye soaps.

They would take all their clothing and towels, rags, scarves, mirrors and few personal belongings. They would leave their springhouse, their cellars, their huge, iron cook pot, for it would be too heavy for the sledges. They would take their washtubs. And much much more.

They would leave the forest, the springs, the sunlight dappled, the shade of a summer's day. They would leave the quiet, the pigeons—all but their best homers. Leave their graves, for there were the dead, a few, buried in the burying ground. They called the graveyard "de field yon-dro." It was not far, back across Abyssinia, among the sang areas. There were the graves marked by strange curving and straight sculptures made from tree limbs. These were stripped of their bark and carved in the shapes of birds and animals, faces of the dead. Odd they were, these memorials done by Cuffee to honor those who were gone for good. They would leave these because they had to. They would leave the land of Promise.

"You leavin' de bad memories?" asked John Henry,

coming up beside Black Salt on this morning of his knowing what he must do. Most of the inside folks were
around Mother Pearl's cooking kettle, having their corn
mush breakfast, with sweet cream and honey. Salt was off
in the oak trees by himself, eating his breakfast with his
back to a strong tree trunk. John Henry joined him, sat
down and ate with him.

"I'm leavin' good memories, too," Salt said finally.
"But I 'spect wherever we go, we find us a freedom road
one time—how you know we fixin' to go?"

"Because that African already go," John Henry told
him. "He was smart, and you ain't dumb. Besides, that's
what de folks whisperin' about. Sayin, 'Have to go, my
Lawd, have to go.' Some of them cryin' even."

Salt lifted his spoon to his lips, then let it fall into the
bowl. He couldn't swallow. "I'm sorry for they tears," he
said gruffly.

John Henry looked in his eyes. Saw no tears there. Salt
looked into John Henry's eyes and saw what he could not
name. "Who you?" he murmured. "Who is you, really,
John Henry?"

John Henry was startled. Then he grinned from ear to
ear, showing a black tooth, masking what he could. "I is
a great god," he said. "Come from Mount Kenya. Come
out of Africa, like old Cuffee."

Black Salt stared at him, carefully sat his bowl down.
"I almost believe you, too," he said. "I almost wants
to."

"Jes' let outchu mind what you know to be," John

Henry said, "and let *all most believe* in all de way. Believe in de god John Henry, and I'll have you out o' here in less than any time."

"Hunh!" exclaimed Salt. "You somethin', playin' with folks every other minute. You comin' with us, you and you people?"

John Henry relaxed. "Uuum," he said, finishing his breakfast. "I'ma gone stick with you until you done started de peoples and got everythang organized. Talk to Mother, too, see what she want from me. I don't abandons my people."

"Good," said Salt. "We all feels more secure havin' you around. But listen. I have sent messages to our friends, the Cherokee. They be comin' with men and horses. They already promise to lead us out of here when de time come, if it ever was comin'. Now, here it is." He sighed deeply. This time tears did fill Black Salt's eyes.

"Nothin' to it, Mr. Big," John Henry said kindly. "You tells me what you wants done, and I do it. Just think, me, John Henry, has left more places more times than you can name. And I made out all right."

"You didn't have a hundred fifty souls to account for, though," Black Salt said.

" 'Tis de truth," John Henry answered. "That why you got me here now, to pull you on out of de molasses."

Salt grunted, eyeing the big man. "You got a humor twist for anythin'."

"Think I might," said John Henry. "What you want me to do now?"

"We pack what we can," said Salt. "Mostly we wait for Cherokee. We keep watch and wait."

That was so. There were long gunnysacks to pack at a central place among the live oaks. All day the women and the men brought goods from everywhere in the compound and stacked them among the oaks. There they filled the gunnysacks.

"Where are we goin', Salt?" quietly, one of the men thought to ask.

"I reckon across de Jordan," Salt told him. "I ain't thought beyond that."

"Don't you go through Kentuck-place," John Henry said. He was always at Black Salt's side now, doing the heavy work for all of them. John Henry never seemed to tire. And he kept his hammer close by him every moment.

"Kentucky is directly north," said Black Salt. "It is the shortest route."

"You listen to me," John Henry said. "I ain't boastin' now. I been everywhere. I seen everythang. You follow me toward de Big Bend and then cut on north. They's a place called Huntington. You crosses there, you hear?"

"I hear you," Black Salt said. He looked up at the great, tall black man. Who wouldn't believe in a man who could grow so high! "You mind if I takes a second opinion?"

"From who?" asked John Henry. "De African done gone, and 'spect he's de only one who know what out there. Yall ain't been no place for some time."

"Not Cuffee," said Salt. "But de old one, Old Canoe of de Cherokee."

"I hear tell Cherokee done be smart-talkin', readin' and writin'."

"They's more and less, too," said Salt. "They have helped us all de way, since we come here. Help us hide. Bring us supplies."

"You pay 'em?" asked John Henry. "Don't never trust nobody you pays."

"Wrong," Black Salt said, as the men and women listened. "When first we settled here, we had nothing, no tools, little food, sick people. Nothing. And Ani-yun'-Wiya provided for us without seeking payment. They gave what we needed. They brought medicines for de sick. Taught de women weaving, and so forth."

"So then," John Henry said, "whatchu call 'em?—soundin' true."

"Ani-yun'Wiya, de name they calls themselves. And they is true," said Black Salt.

Later, when he had John Henry with him on a promontory in the woods, east of the camp, Black Salt asked more questions. They surveyed the hills and mountains for a distance. They saw no unusual movement.

"They comin' from that direction?" asked John Henry. He had been working all day. He had been everywhere in the land of Promise, helping everyone. And now he stood steady at Black Salt's back.

"You ain't even breathin' hard," Black Salt observed proudly, before he answered Big John. He laughed and continued, "Ani-yun'Wiya come any which way it safe. I reckon they will come in small numbers, separate. De sledge men and two warriors. De packhorse men on they horses, armed. And Old Canoe and some of his warriors. Don't know who or what he bring. But you can figure. One Cherokee is equal to five or ten white men, dependin' on his age and clan."

"Interestin'," John Henry said. "Wonder maybe sometime I might contest with de likes of them!"

"You big and you strong," said Black Salt, chuckling, "but I wouldn't advise you tangle with those who can take on de cavalry. Warrior ride up to de enemy and tap him shoulder and ride away. He prove bullets can't touch him."

John Henry laughed silently, his massive shoulders shaking, hands on his hips. "Not my color, him," he said, "but sure sound like my kind!"

Old Canoe's men slipped into camp separately, just as Black Salt knew they would. When the first men, the packhorse men, came in quietly, casually, he breathed easily for the first time. "My birds got through," he murmured to himself. "Praise be!" His homers could cruise at forty miles an hour.

All the inside folks were in the camp. It was the late afternoon following the day Salt had let loose his homing pigeons. At once Ani-yun'Wiya rested, watered and fed their pack animals and their horses with the help of Salt's people. All this done with quiet efficiency. An hour later the sledge men arrived. These were men on horseback.

Attached to their horses by long shafts were travois or sledges made of platforms dragged along the ground on two poles. These worked quite well on the paths of Ani-yun'Wiya, and along the easier trails of most American Indians of the plains and the east. Ani-yun'Wiya knew hundreds and hundreds of trails through the great forest, along mountain passes.

It was suppertime by the time Old Canoe himself, and his ten best warriors, entered the camp. They came noiselessly, each leading a fine pony. After their animals were tended to, they ate with the inside folks around the fire. They made up quite a crowd themselves. There were about six of them for every twenty-five of the inside folks. Quite a good number, given the fierceness of their abilities at war and their skill at hiding and traveling in secret.

It was not long before Black Salt stood before his people and Ani-yun'Wiya.

"Praise be!" he exclaimed. There was a low murmuring of exclamation from the inside folks. "We been given a row, and it been green and full aplenty."

"For true!" came the reply in hushed voices.

"I been talkin' a lot."

"Yay-suh, you got a right."

"I been thinkin' a lot."

"Know you dippin' in de well. Still water run deep," someone said.

"Now come de time for to tell de last time," said Black Salt.

"Oh, no. Oh, no, but you got a right!" This came from Ezekiel.

"We had nothing when we came here. Nothing in our hands," Salt said.

"Poor fugitives!" Swassi nearly sang, swaying from side to side. Her eyes were closed. Her face glistened in the firelight.

Black Salt looked on her fondly for a long moment before he spoke again.

"But our hearts were full of hope, sweet with freedom's promise."

"Hush! Hush! Look over Jordan!" sang Miz Molly. She held both Bessie Freedom and Poor Tree. Their faces were upturned to her.

"A little at a time," spoke Black Salt, his voice rising slightly on a minor note. "A little at a time. We gone."

"A little at a time," they murmured. There were gasps, as their hearts tightened and they felt the cold squeeze of the wanderer's touch.

"But we got our friends," Black Salt said, "Ani-yun'-Wiya." Swiftly, Old Canoe's men rose. They stood two abreast, facing Black Salt, standing sideways to the inside folks.

"We got our giant to be with us on de long course," Black Salt said.

John Henry had been sitting at Black Salt's feet, with little Pearl not-so-pretty-now on his lap. Now he sat her down with Dwahro and he stood beside Ani-yun'Wiya. They did not even glance at him, but cast their eyes to the ground. They knew full well what it was they saw, knew the inside folks had a powerful spirit in the form of a black giant.

John Henry had been quiet, eyes on Salt and the exotic-looking Indian men. He had seen Indians before, but never this kind. Never warriors.

Can tell it how they stand, he thought. But they respect a John Henry, me. 'Cause I a stone warrior of de Mount.

"Praise be, big John Henry," piped up a child. It was Poor Tree. Everybody had to laugh; then they, too, sang it out: "Praise be, big John Henry!"

"I comes from de big Black River country where de sun never shine," boasted John Henry. "I be John Henry Roustabout, and don't dare to call me Henry!"

"Whoo-ee, listen!" someone whispered.

"I got a itch on my feet and a worrisome wander on my weary mind," he said. "I chases git to gone, and you best be ready and willin' with me when I leave."

"Where we gone go, John Henry?" the inside folks wanted to know.

Black Salt raised his hand for silence. Ani-yun'Wiya waited for John Henry to sit. When he had, and had young, sad Pearl back on his lap, they sat quietly down themselves.

"We gone go a little at a time across de Jordan." Black Salt spoke gently.

"We gone wade in de water?" asked Ezekiel.

"We gone see what is there when we gits there," Black Salt said. "Old Canoe," he said, "you got anything to say about what ways and how? Do de folks need to know much or little?"

Old Canoe slowly rose again. He faced the inside folks, his head slightly bowed, eyes away from those whose spirits he felt most strongly.

"I have sat my horse high on the banks of the great, muddy water," he said. "There are steamboats and small boats. There are boats and guides to be had if you pay. But that is not the hard part, crossing the water. It is the long way there that must be considered. The path takes you through the roughest of mountains, through three states, Tennessee, Virginia, West Virginia, where you will cross.

"We know the paths," he said, "the deep and empty places, hard for the whites. We will lead. We will take much of the supplies ahead to points where you will stop to camp along the way. We divide up—small groups move best. It would be good if we could traverse twenty miles a day. Best to make the trip in twenty days. Still good if it takes thirty, even thirty-five. For the mountain highs grow cooler now. Let it come to pass." Finished, Old Canoe sat down.

"And so it will come to pass," said Black Salt. "No more questions this night. Everyone have all things you carry ready anytime. Have de chil'ren always ready. We gone, a little at a time."

And so it was that the inside folks must make their move through the outside. Swassi, Ezekiel, the children, many of the others and Mother Pearl wiped their eyes.

A shame! A cryin' shame! Mother Pearl cried out inside.

But the inside folks had grown tough and finely controlled within. Had not their old ones come the long way, the deathly way from Africa? The Africans had survived the slavers and their ships, and the long middle passage across a great ocean. And the inside folks, themselves, grandsons and granddaughters of Africa—had they not endured the field, the breaking back, the whip?

Not one of them cried again this night, or the next and next. They might cry again if ever they were safe again. But for now they turned hard as trees that must bend with the wind. The corewood was unyielding.

Their hearts beat strong.

CHAPTER FIFTEEN

They left, a few at a time. Since all were ready, it did not matter who left when, and next. They left in small groups, with at least one man chosen among the folks themselves, plus one of Old Canoe's armed warriors. The inside folks decided which of them would travel together. They volunteered who would go when and next.

"I wants to have Bessie and Poor Tree with me," said Miz Molly one day. "They keeps my old bones warm, huggin' me so when they sleeps."

So Miz Molly had her way. She would ride one of the sledges, packed with their belongings and some supplies, when it was her time to leave. And one day her time came.

"Feel like movin'," she said, to no one in particular. "Feel like I wants to take a stroll."

There was to be no ceremony of parting at Freedom Lane. Black Salt was there. Those who were around looked on silently. And silence was the key. Holding on was the test. Miz Molly smiled primly before the corners of her mouth turned down. Yet, bravely, she waved at those who glanced around, waving, and then turned quickly away. Miz Molly settled herself on the sledge amidst raccoon and rabbit pelts and other belongings of the folks.

Ani-yun'Wiya guide instructed her to relax herself, but to hold on to the sides of the travois. Then he strapped her in with rope around the middle of the sledge. Bessie and Poor Tree were told to walk alongside the sledge. One younger woman, Mary Pleasant, and the inside man Lucas Adams would go with them. So it was that the two orphaned children, the younger man and woman and Miz Molly became something of a family. Even Ani-yun'-Wiya, who said his name was Thomas Groundhog, became part of the family in his own way. With his bow and arrow he would bring them prizes of wild game, turkey and rabbit. He was a good provider all along the long way. He never once had to shoot his gun.

Those who walked carried their pallets, leather pouches of water and dried foodstuffs. Lucas had on a long shirt. Under it he had concealed a pistol through his belt.

It took a full week before it was noticeable that the numbers of inside folks had grown smaller in the Promise land. And in the middle of that week the last visitor appeared.

Deep in the dark, when a midnight rain fell on the coals of the cook fire, the singing drum came near. The rain fell on the four who lay still by the fire. Came down on them in beats of rhythm and sound not unlike that from a hypocrite drum.

"What it is!" Big John Henry spoke softly, and he sat up. He studied the compound. The Real People who were in the camp, ready to carry off more of the inside folks at dayclean, were asleep. Some of the folks rested fitfully. John nudged Mother Pearl. "You hear it?" he said about the hypocrite drumming.

"Hear it," she said, and she too sat up. "Inside folks," she whispered, "sleep you long, until I say to waken." She shook her fingers at them. It was a light spell she put on them. They would sleep soundly through the night.

"Carry de chile," Mother Pearl told John Henry. "Dwahro?" she said.

"Ma'am?" said Dwahro. He'd listened to the drum for a long time. He knew it was out there. He didn't know whether to be happy or sad about that.

"Come on," said Mother. They got up then. John Henry Roustabout wrapped the child in the shawl Mother had made her. Then he picked up sleeping Pearl.

"She don't weigh a hen feather," he whispered. "She pinin' her heart away."

"Come!" said Mother Pearl urgently.

They strode down the length of Freedom Lane. They were the dark, the rain, they were like the trees, full and complete in the night. They walked with John Henry in the lead, holding Pearl not-so-pretty-now high in his arms. The rain fell full in her eyes. It woke her. John Henry covered her mouth before she could scream with the surprise of riding so high.

"We takin' us a stroll," Big John told her.

"Don't carry me to de Big Bend," young Pearl whimpered.

"Who said that?" John Henry said. "I ain't said that. Mother Pearl here with us. Dwahro here."

"Is 'em?" said Pearl. "Thought you carryin' me off to tunnel me."

"You a sleepy baby," John Henry told her. She snuggled closer.

"Where we goin' to?" she wanted to know. But John wouldn't say. For to say would admit that the hypocrite was beating strong and that she couldn't hear it.

Let him handle it, thought John Henry. Let him tell her all they is. Gone tell him I on her side. John de Conquer!

They could see the light ahead. They were deep in the forest now. The see-alls who were left, who spent the night in the woods, did not see this. Mother Pearl had charmed them. "Whoever here," she had mumbled, flicking her fingers this way and that, "sleep you easy *now*!"

The light was not the light of day. It was not starlight.

"What it is!" whispered Pearl. This light she was made to see.

"Don't you know it?" said John Henry, before he thought. For Pearl had forgotten the light of de Conquer.

It was not sunlight, or lamplight, or twilight. It had a fruity scent and a taste of tropical flowers. It was not too bright, blue or glaring.

It was bring-to light. It was come-to light. It was show-the-way light. It was see the light. It was light up and throw light on. It was stand-in-the-light. It was the shining light.

De Conquerlight.

"So be it," sighed Mother Pearl, clasping her hands and pressing them on her lips.

"Oh, me!" sighed Dwahro. He held his fist against his chest. What's to become of me! he thought.

Pearl not-so-pretty-now looked on the light with dread. She covered her eyes and sobbed into her hands.

"Don't do that. Don't, li'l sis. Please, don't cry so," John Henry said soothingly. "We almost there now."

"No! No!" cried Pearl and squirmed this way and that, as if she were having the worst nightmare.

John Henry held on to her. "Scarin' a baby so ain't right," he said in his deep bass voice.

"Who you to say!" hissed Mother Pearl.

"I is de oldest," said John Henry. "He don't scare me."

"He de rightest," Mother Pearl said. "You best remember that."

"We all got a right," John Henry said, and would say no more.

Then de Conquerlight covered them. It massed over them and around them and under them, like a shell. They stood there, unable to think or move.

"Sit down," said a familiar voice. There was a shade tree full in the light. The light faded somewhat. And they sat down in the shade of a dayclean that de Conquerlight gave to them alone.

He was there. John de Conquer, the great, good bringer of hope and help. The earth below the forest mast opened and de Conquer rose out of it seated in a chair made from the trunk of an African baobab tree.

His ebony crown shone black, shiny and pure. His long robe of spun gold and black African cotton was perfect in its gleam and glow. The slippers he wore looked comfortable. They were gold and black and well worn, shaped to his feet tenderly.

"Ain't it nice, meetin' like this in de great forest?" he said. "John Henry, why don't you sit down, rest yourself?"

"I prefers to stand so you can see my size," John Henry said. He kept his eye on his brother. The looks between them never wavered. Big John put Pearl down into Mother Pearl's lap. Young Pearl held Mother as tight as she could.

"You always was a big one," said John de Conquer. "I do believe you done grown bigger."

"And still growin'," John Henry said. "But I see you

not growed atall. You still lookin' like a short stick wrapped in a long ribbon."

De Conquer laughed. "That's a good one, John," he said. "You been gone a long time, but you not lost de humor."

"*I* should have been John de Conquer!" John Henry cried out suddenly in anguish. "*I* is oldest, tallest, blackest and de best cotton-rollin', steel-drivin' roustabout in this whole country. Who make you de head god! Why I left!"

"I knew why you left." John de Conquer spoke gently. "That's why I let you go. But nobody *makes* de head god. De head god just *is.*"

"Hunh! It don't seem right. I just is, too. I tells everybody I was born, but I don't know that. I don't remember that," John Henry said.

"You and me and Mother Pearl and Pretty be born of a mountain. And what you has to complain about, you go tell it on de mountain, Mount Highness."

"Mount Kenya," whispered Mother Pearl. For it was the mountain de Conquer spoke of. "Wish to see that lovely sight! All de lesser gods and de chil'ren—how's they doin', de Conquer?"

"They doin' just about as much business as ever," de Conquer answered.

"And de snow and glaciers, they still there on de Mount?" she asked.

"Was, last time I looked," de Conquer told her, "almost right on that ole equator, too."

"And de grassland, and de Indian Ocean coast! I re-

member it all agin! And they Kikuyu. They Embu people! Mercy!'' cried Mother Pearl.

"Nothin' changed 'bout that whole place much,'' he
said.

"Well, I don't miss it. I left,'' John Henry spoke up,
"and I glad I left. Rather be in de new world of men. But
let's get on with it, de Conquer. We know you come for
a reason. You done called us. So let's get to it.''

John de Conquer's dark face appeared to darken. "Sit
down, John Henry,'' he commanded. John Henry could
not resist him. And quickly he sat down.

De Conquer smiled. "My neck was gettin' stiff strainin'
to see you up so high.''

But John Henry looked glum, his big hands spread on
his knees.

There was silence. De Conquer looked at each one of
them. Pearl not-so-pretty-now had dried her tears. But
her face was still streaked with dirt. He looked at young
Pearl with deep caring in his eyes. He studied her, pulling her to him with his will. Then he let her go and she
relaxed against Mother again.

He not so scary, she thought. Not yet, he not.

"Well,'' said de Conquer, finally. "I am awful glad to
see each one of you. Glad to see you make out so well,
Dwahro. After a slow start, that is.'' He smiled, and
Dwahro bowed his head. "I seen you tried to get away
from Pretty Pearl. But then, you help her all you can, you
help with de thieves. You de best one for makin' a song
and a dance. I seen you with de chil'ren.''

Dwahro looked at de Conquer. Saw his eyes. Fearfully,

[253]

he pleaded with those eyes. But de Conquer said no more to him. He went on to Mother Pearl.

"You done all right," he said to her. Mother Pearl sighed and breathed deeply, wiping her eyes. "You a comfort to all de black inside folks there. You help de chil'ren and Black Salt leader. You comfort de old and teach de young. Feed all de strengthenin' food. You a good woman. You done fine, Mother Pearl."

"Thank you, best one," she said simply.

"John Henry." De Conquer's voice changed, deepened. It was a voice of authority and command. It sounded as if it would not be trifled with. "You done good and you done bad," de Conquer said. "Wherever you go, de peoples rally 'round you. You gives 'em so much courage and hope, jes' like I do. You shows them de strength you has and how to face a challenge and meet it. But you unfaithful and harsh with de good women. You drink and tarry too much. You fightin' all de time. What kind of way is that for a giant, black god to be!"

"I was jes' bein' human," John Henry said. "I was jes' livin', de way all de folks be livin'. I ain't ask for nothin' extra. I don't use de power but for to ketch a fool gone trick me from behind. I ain't ask you for nothin', I don't want nothin' from you, too. I work myself in de groun' for little pay. But I always works hard and no complaint." John Henry spoke these words with the seriousness of a man who knew a hard bargain when he saw one.

For de Conquer was weighing their lives among humans on a scale of Mount Highness gods. He put each

[254]

one of them on one side of the scale and their deeds on the other. The one who did not balance the scale with the proper deeds would have to answer for it.

John Henry knew this. Mother Pearl and Dwahro knew it, too.

Big John held little Pearl's hand tightly. "She ain't but a baby still!" John Henry said, reminded of her terrible trouble.

The look on de Conquer's face grew darker. His eyes were luminous coals. "Not so," said de Conquer. "Sis Pearl a god chile! *A god chile!*" De Conquer's voice rose on the de Conquerlight. "She has grown like we all grown for years beyond measure," his voice boomed. The hypocrite he always carried was suddenly in his hands. Now he beat on it, in a steady, slow rhythm full of sorrow. "She has lived knowin' right from wrong. She has gone out into de world to help the peoples because she wanted to! That be de god test—her, here! And I gave her fair warnin'!"

Pearl cringed against Mother Pearl. John Henry took her up in his great, strong arms and held her tightly.

"Don't look at him eyes," John Henry whispered. "Don't look at him."

"LOOK AT ME!" de Conquer cried out in the voice of the god he was. "SIS PEARL!"

Slowly Pearl turned her eyes. She looked into the face of de Conquer. She climbed out of the great, strong arms of John Henry. She was greater than a spirit, Dwahro. And greater was her trouble. For she *had* been god child, once.

What de Conquer spoke to her he wished to keep between them. He spoke softly, the way a god is supposed to speak to a god child. He spoke soothingly, patting her head, touching her arms as he spoke.

"It all right, Sis Pearl," he told her. "I can make you pretty again. I can make you eat again, and feel strong again. Come on, sit up here by de Conquer."

"John. John, bro," she moaned, settling in beside him, almost under his drum, she had become that skinny and shrunken. "I missed you so much!" she whimpered.

He took her hands in his. "I saw that," he said. "I know you did miss me. Some of it my fault; I got to weigh that, too. I thought you was ready for you own self before you were, prob'ly."

"I thought I was ready, too," she said, her voice trembling. "Didn't I do some good, didn't I?"

"Let's see, now," de Conquer said. "You de one wants to start out, helps de folks."

"Yes," said Pearl.

"You and I play de card game, Mount Highness Five-Card Deal You Down, and you hoped to beat me. It was a wrong try, Sis Pearl. For you can't beat de best god brother, you bein' just a god chile."

Pearl's lips trembled and her eyes filled with tears.

"You makin' her cry!" John Henry rose up to his full height and towered over his brother and Pearl and the drum in the baobab chair. "What you sayin', makin' a baby cry!"

"John Henry, if you don't set down, I'm gone place

you so far down, you be down under!" de Conquer said, and he meant it.

"Go ahead," John Henry said. "I ain't scared of anythin' you can do, and I knows what you can do, too. I wants to hear what you sayin' to my baby sister."

De Conquer sighed. "Well, to keep de peace, 'cause I sure don't wants to hurt you, John Henry. You my big brother, after all."

"Hunh!" John Henry said.

"God blood be thicker than water," Mother Pearl said, with hope in her heart.

"Now," said John de Conquer, "we be weighin' de deeds." Testin' de test! he thought.

"Do we has to?" asked Pearl not-so-pretty-now.

"I said so." De Conquer spoke kindly but firmly.

"You showed patience," he said, patting young Pearl's shoulder. "You made de right move on Hunger, too, but I has to finish it. Yet you kept close watch over de black folks when they first set out to live in de forest.

"I gave you my power of John de Conquer root," de Conquer continued. "You remember de rules I give you about it?"

Pearl not-so-pretty-now thought hard. "No sir," she said. "I mean, I 'member some. But so much happen . . ."

"A god chile must always think first," said de Conquer, "and I gave you fair warning," said de Conquer. "I told you to wear de necklace and promise it to *nobody*. I said you could flake some of it off for folks, but never take it

[257]

off. Never hurt no humans with it unless they 'bout to hurt you first. And never ever hurt no human chil'ren out of spite or anger.''

Great tears rolled down young Pearl's face. John Henry, standing by his brother's throne, leaned over and brushed the tears away. Mother Pearl and Dwahro came near the throne then. They looked sadly on poor Pearl not-so-pretty-now. Mother Pearl clasped one of her hands, and Dwahro the other.

"Well, you didn't promise de necklace," de Conquer told Pearl. "You only took it off for Mother Pearl 'cause it dried up, useless. But I tole you *never* take it off, and you did take it off.''

There was silence while they pondered this. Then de Conquer spoke again.

"You felt like hurtin' and scarin' chil'ren on de long path," he said. "You was tired and cranky; you didn't like young Josias havin' so much power over de chil'ren. You wanted to show what you can do. You was bein' mean, and so you did it. And they never done nothin' bad to you. Never hurt you. They always lookin' up to you, Sis Pearl, and you had to go be so mean to them."

De Conquer didn't stop there; he went on, "You lost control over de spirits I give to you like they you very own. You even fool with Dwahro, bein' just mean. He start it, but he only spirited. You lost control of Hodag. I got him back, though, called him to de drum. And now I got Hodag caged in de drum 'til him learn de lesson.

"You ever wonder what happen to that woodpecker,

that Fool-la-fafa I give you, when you de Conquer root wither up and die?" de Conquer asked.

"Ohhhh . . . !" Young Pearl sucked in her breath.

"I know," said de Conquer. "You so busy tryin' to fix things and save you own hide, you forgot about de spirit, Fool-la-fafa." De Conquer took something from the pocket of his gown. It was an ordinary bird, a woodpecker of normal size. He flung it up in the air and it flew away into the de Conquerlight.

"There go de Fool-la-fafa," he said. "It got squeezed when him de Conquer root wither. Never be no six-foot bird agin! Be ever just a ordinary woodpecker."

Young Pearl bowed her head in shame. She didn't know how she could have forgotten the outlandish Fool-la-fafa, but she had.

"You let out de Hide-behind deliberately to scare de chil'ren," de Conquer continued after a pause. "That was bad, Sis Pearl. But worst was you anger turned on Josias and little Bessie, and all de others. You hatefulness turn on them. Usin' him de Conquer root for that. A god chile won't be hateful to they friends! You be brought into this world knowin' that."

"I forgot," Pearl sobbed into her hands. "I was just . . . livin' like a free chile, an' I forgets all about de god chile. I just forgot everythin'!"

"I warn you to watch out, not be feelin' human, so. Tole you, once you on you own, de knowledge to fit de power already there. But you ain't listen to me.

"So," he finished. "De wrong deeds outweigh de righteous ones. Come. Stand before me." He lifted young Pearl down.

"Don't spank me, please, bro," she pleaded.

"Have I ever spank you?" de Conquer asked.

"Why, de idea!" Mother Pearl said.

De Conquer placed his hand on young Pearl's head.

All at once she felt a sharp pain at her temple. Then it was gone as swiftly as it had come.

Suddenly Pearl was not skinny and scrawny anymore. Her hair wasn't a tangled mess. Instead of an ebony bow, a calico ribbon held her smooth, combed hair in place. Slowly, carefully, Pearl touched her face. It felt nice. Its freshness went all the way down inside her. De Conquer held a mirror so she could see. And she saw she had become quite pretty again.

In a blink of de Conquer's eye, Pearl not-so-pretty-now had become Pretty Pearl. And yet no longer was she Pretty Pearl of the Mountain. But this she had not come to realize.

"Oh, John, bro, thank you much! Oh, I thought . . ." She didn't know what she thought her god brother was going to do to her. "Thank you so much!" she said.

Mother Pearl blew her nose in her handkerchief. She was crying, but not from happiness. She seemed overcome with sorrow.

"It be all right, now," Pearl told her. "See, I'm Pretty again, so why you keep on cryin'?"

Mother Pearl shook her head. Just once she hugged Pearl tightly to her. She whispered, "My sweet, los' god chile!"

"What?" said Pretty Pearl. Mother Pearl wouldn't say it again. But Mother thought, Best you be forgettin' what you was.

And right then John de Conquer commenced working through Mother Pearl to start Pretty Pearl forgetting.

Mother Pearl sat down and Pretty sat down beside her.

Dwahro found himself standing alone before de Conquer's throne. John Henry had moved off, looking sullen. It struck Dwahro that they were having turns before the best god. And now it was his turn again. Dwahro looked at Mother and he looked at Pretty Pearl. Then he turned to face de Conquer.

"I . . . I don't get what be happenin' here," Dwahro said. "I ain't much, jes' a spirit. I don't understand . . ."

De Conquer smiled at him. He placed his hand on Dwahro's shoulder. "You may have started out as *jes'* one of de spirits," he said, "but Dwahro, you has done distinguished youself, for true! You turn out best of all! Couldn't be more proud of you. De way you give to de peoples without no selfishness, just like Mother Pearl. Most proud of you, Dwahro. You actin' de best way a human is to act. No one can fault you for wantin' to be so human. You spirited! Take what you wants."

De Conquer lifted his hand, dismissing Dwahro, before Dwahro could tell him he might like to have a long, silken robe like de Conquer's. Dwahro was awfully shaken. For a flash of a moment there had been a stabbing pain where de Conquer's hand had rested on his shoulder. Now it was gone. Dwahro could hardly believe that the great god, de

Conquer, had praised him in front of Mother Pearl and Pretty and John Henry. And he just a spirit!

He did not yet know he had become far more than a spirit.

"Thank . . . thank you!" he murmured. "Tries always to do my best." He continued to stand before the throne, for he needed courage to say what he wanted to say to John de Conquer.

But de Conquer had his mind on someone else. Had his eye on someone else, too. He was looking at his brother, John Henry. John Henry was looking right back at him. The looks between them were so powerful, Dwahro was forced to his knees beside Mother and Pretty.

"What happenin'?" he whispered to Mother.

"Shhhh!" she warned. And he kept still, his mind racing, fearing.

"John Henry Roustabout," said John de Conquer.

"That my name," said John Henry. "I can outhammer anyone with my spike drill, outroust de cotton bale man and outlabor any man born to die."

"But you is a god of Mount Kenya," said de Conquer, "like I is *him* best god of de Mountain-high. You ain't s'pose to die like a man."

"Hunh!" said John Henry. "I s'pose to do what I does and what I wants to do!"

"And you wants to go to de Big Bend and contest with de new steam drill. You and you black mens gone lay down de bets and make some money!" de Conquer said. "That all you think about, is winnin' some money?"

"I got a right!" cried John Henry.

"You got a right, and you got a responsibility!" de Conquer told him. "John Henry, you de one of us lookin' most human. You de tallest and de blackest. All de peoples everywhere lookin' up to you. You can go to de Big Bend and contest with that new steam drill. You can beat it one time with you spike drill and you hammer in you hand. But you gone pay de price, too."

"I'ma gone beat it down to de groun'!" John Henry said.

"*One* time!" said de Conquer in his god-command voice. "Jes' one time, you can beat de machine. 'Cause you gone break you back doin' it, you gone break you *heart* doin' it. And if you must be actin' and feelin' like a man, you must know that a man can't live with a broken back and a broken heart, both."

"I thought I was a god," mused John Henry.

"That de point!" said de Conquer. "You can't have it both ways! You can't be a god when you livin' like a gamblin' man. And even a great, big man like you can beat de machine but one time. 'Cause they always be *another* machine, and another and another. But there won't be another one like John Henry Roustabout. For he will already die with his hammer in his hand. He will done paid de price."

John Henry listened. He could find no words to say.

"What a man wants to do with a machine," said de Conquer, "be to work with it for decent pay, if he can. Organize, for it gone throw a heap o' men out of work. Help de peoples. Stay alive! 'Cause a man ain't nothin' but a *man*. And if John Henry gone beat de machine one time, he be only a *man*. And he gone die. Now I is finished."

De Conquer rose, and his baobab throne sank beneath the mast of forest ground. His hypocrite, with its long, beaten-gold strap over his shoulder, hung at his side. His delicate fingers tapped on the hypocrite. The drum began to sing. *Ta-ta-tum*. Sang a song of freedom. *Ta-ta-tum*. Of hard times but better days.

The light that was not sunlight or lamplight, or even twilight, began to fade. The fruity scent and the taste of tropical flowers stayed a moment longer.

De Conquer's loving look lingered on Pretty Pearl, Dwahro and big John Henry.

"I loves you all!" de Conquer whispered. "You who can't remember, know me by my de Conquer root. Good luck!"

He was gone. A small, neat, good luck de Conquer bush sprang from the ground where de Conquer and his throne had been.

The bring-to, come-to, show-the-way, shining light was gone. They stood there in the dark of night. There was no moon. There were distant stars.

"Time we best get back," Mother Pearl said, "but first . . ." She bent down in front of the neat de Conquer bush. She took parts of the roots and gave them to Pretty and Dwahro and John Henry. "Y'all keep these," she said. "Brang you most good kind o' luck, jes' like de Conquer say."

John Henry put his de Conquer root in his pocket. So

did Dwahro. Pearl threw away the useless root she'd worn since her other de Conquer root had withered. Mother Pearl tied the new de Conquer root tightly to her hair chain.

"There," Pretty said. She couldn't see it in the dark. But she could touch it. "It feelin' almost like new. I got me a de Conquer agin!"

"For good luck's sake," Mother Pearl said, sighing a sorrowful sound.

"Yesum," Pretty answered happily. "Nothin' be sad about that."

They made their way back to the compound, unobserved.

"You think we'll see de Conquer again soon?" Pearl asked her big brother.

"Hunh!" grunted John Henry Roustabout. "Soon ain't long enough for me. Don't you worry, hon. We on our way now."

Mother Pearl could see her way ever so well through the dark. And the giant, John Henry, carrying Pretty Pearl high in his arms, and Dwahro, were obliged to follow her lead.

CHAPTER SIXTEEN

The great forest was. Once it had been all of Georgia.
Now it was much, much less and it would become ever
less. And yet the forest was, still, and it moaned and
echoed with nature's whisperings. Light was a mist filtering down in muted colors where once there had been a
Freedom Lane cleared from the forest.

The light played odd patterns on pine limbs and oak
bark where once there had been a land of Promise, where
there had been cabins and smoke from a cook fire. Once
there had been paths, bared ground, buckets over coal
holes for heating water; clotheslines in the trees, hides

tanning, meat and fruit drying; there had been sheds full of harvested food, and outhouses, and old folks and young folks. The great forest was where there had been human life, once; there would be human life there again someday. Leaves of gold and red were falling.

But now there was not even a human echo. The inside folks were all gone. All that was worthwhile taking had gone with them. They had left the boards from their houses, and these still remained crisply stacked. Silent. Dead wood. Dead leaves made a colorful blanket there where there was no one.

Under the forest mast, seeds were preparing to grow trees for the next season where the paths of the folks had been and where their Freedom Lane had been. Farther away and down from the height, the valley of Abyssinia was without a hoe to chop the weeds. A growing veil spread over the gardens. The ginseng still grew in secret, wild places, although the planted ginseng fields were becoming overgrown with wild plants and bushes.

In the weeks that the inside folks had quit farming, there had been rains and plenty of sun and growth. Drenching downpours. And long days of scorching heat. The inside folks had started on their long way. And all that they had once claimed as theirs now was turning back to nature.

No one could own the forest. They knew that, for Ani-yun'Wiya had taught that what was nature's was to hold, not to keep. They, the people, were along the hard trail upward, northward. They would keep to the ridges above rivers, where only the most fit could travel, hidden in the most secret trees. They would keep to the Warriors' Path.

"When they tell your grandchildren," said Old Canoe, not without humor, "that Daniel Boone cut his Wilderness Trail first, say that our ancient Warriors' Path was already well worn.

"Now you know the true meaning of being 'on the warpath,'" said Old Canoe, smiling his wan smile. "Our ancients walked the Appalachians, the Allegheny and the Blue Ridge long before Boone helped to barter away two million acres of Cherokee lands."

The inside folks would cross three states to get to the river they called their Jordan. They would make certain they took everything they needed before they left the land of Promise for the final time. The party to leave ahead of Black Salt and Old Canoe would be a half day out before Salt and his party would silently take to the trail.

Salt, John Henry, Josias, Swassi, Pretty Pearl, Mother Pearl and Dwahro were the party, plus the best guide and the wisest on horseback, Old Canoe. They had two travois, attached to ponies to be guided by John Henry and Black Salt. Swassi would ride one pony and Mother Pearl might ride the other whenever she wished. Old Canoe would ride his horse. He was ever cautious of those who were more than human. He would not look at them, out of respect. Soon, he must find the time to think about them.

Anyone who was tired could ride with Old Canoe, or

ride on top of the supplies and possessions lashed to the travois. Pretty Pearl and Josias would walk along behind John Henry, bringing up the rear. All the men were armed. Everyone carried pallets and personal bundles of items they could not bear to leave behind.

They had made ready to start out, and John Henry commenced fooling with Swassi. She was a pretty woman, shy and sweet, small of bone and with dark eyes.

"You wants to travel with John Henry?" John Henry asked her. "Take you to de Big Bend and dress you finer than all de womens when I wins de contest." He was about to take Swassi's hand when, suddenly, Black Salt had him by the wrist and flung his arm away from Swassi.

"Oh-oh!" said John Henry, laughing his big sound. "So that how it be!" He looked at Swassi and he looked at Black Salt.

Swassi's eyes grew wide as she stared from John Henry to Salt. Shyly, she lowered her head, but Black Salt wouldn't look away.

"It how things might be." Salt spoke softly to John Henry. He kept his gentle look on Swassi. "I weren't knowin' 'til right now that de way it might be was in my mind, wantin' it to be."

"Ho!" said John Henry. "You hear that, Miz Swassi? De head man done stake his claim!"

"I am declarin' myself," said Salt. Again, he spoke softly, simply. "I have no claim. That be up to Swassi."

Swassi looked up at Salt, beaming. Ever so slightly, she nodded at him, and again, shyly, held her eyes away. It was then that Salt lifted her onto the pony he would lead.

From that moment on, she and Black Salt were never far apart.

"Well, since that how it be," said John Henry. He cleared his throat. "No hard feelin's, Big Man," he said to Salt. "I has always got to test and contest, don't you know."

"I knows that," said Black Salt. "I don't hold that against no John Henry."

"We friends, then?" John Henry asked, grinning. Slowly, he extended one mighty hand.

"Always," said Black Salt, and he meant it. They shook hands and slapped one another's shoulders a moment.

All was well between them, the biggest man and the leader of men. And these two put themselves and those they cared about in the hands of an old man belonging to an ancient people and another race. An old one they would trust with their lives, for he was the best and the wisest of all the men they knew. He had planned the route of the inside folks. There could be no other outcome than a sucessful journey. And even Salt did not know the plan in great detail. But it would take them along the route the others had taken.

Old Canoe spoke about it occasionally as they went along. "We take the route of least resistance," he said. "My men know if their path is crossed by strangers, then they must change the path. Never worry. It is a long trail."

Along the way he taught them how to close off their minds from the monotony, from fatigue. He even taught them how to rest on their feet, blanking their minds so that they felt less weariness, then letting their thoughts slide easily into long wishes and daydreams.

They headed out of Georgia, traveling from a point above the rolling Piedmont Plateau through the rugged Appalachian Highlands west of the Blue Ridge. During their first evening of rest two of Old Canoe's men appeared out of nowhere.

"They have come for the travois," he told the inside folks. "They must take the sledges on a straighter path."

"Where did they come from?" Black Salt asked. "They been with us all de time?"

"They have guarded our backs," said Old Canoe.

"What he think gone jump up on us?" John Henry asked Salt when they had started out again.

"Who knows? Bear, perhaps, panthers. Maybe white men."

"I can wrassle a panther as well as a man," John Henry said.

"Know you can," Black Salt said, "but we let de Cherokee do it his way."

Without the travois, Black Salt's party traveled at a steady pace but with heavier loads.

They traveled a hundred miles or more in all to set themselves free of the state of Georgia. And took a trail through gently rolling valleys among folded mountains. They headed into the Cumberland Plateau in the extreme northwestern corner of the state. There they found a narrow valley between two broad, flat-topped ranges. The ranges were Lookout Mountain and Sand Mountain.

"Now we leave this state," said Old Canoe one day toward evening. "Take a good look behind you, and then don't look back again."

They did as he told them. Pretty Pearl held Josias' hand on one side and Mother Pearl's on the other. "Does it make you sad to leave?" she asked Josias.

He shook his head. He was unable to speak about it, and Pretty knew he was sad.

"Hush! Hush! Couldn't hear nobody pray!" Mother Pearl murmured. She looked out over the vast land and she seemed to see beyond it.

Well, I'm not sad, thought Pretty. I feels just fine since I seen my brother John de Conquer. He made me be myself again. And he wasn't too awful mad with me for bein' mean and all. Least I can't tell that he was.

Pretty had been in a fine mood since they'd left three or four days ago. She'd lost all track of time. But she did not really mind that they trekked the whole dayclean, slept for five hours at evening and started out again after midnight. Ani-yun'Wiya taught them how to care for their sore and aching feet. Every few hours they used medicines from forest herb plants Old Canoe had given them. This stopped their toes from blistering.

Pretty had thought about using power to rid herself of tiredness and sore muscles. She had the new de Conquer root to help her. But she wasn't sure she should use it, not unless she talked to Mother Pearl about it first.

But I never gets de chance talk to her alone, Pearl thought.

They all slept in a group each night, deep in the

woods, hidden. They lay in a circle around a low, smoldering fire. And Pearl never got a chance to talk.

By the middle of the fifth day they walked far into the Valley of East Tennessee, up on the ancient Warriors' Path along the ridges. The rugged paths. They could look down on the Valley that was almost fifty miles wide.

"When I get to here, I am home," Old Canoe told Black Salt. "For this was land of three of the Five Civilized Tribes—Cherokee, Creek, Chickasaw. The Choctaw and Seminole lived farther south, but they made up the five tribes."

"When was that?" Black Salt asked.

"Before they moved us out," Old Canoe said, and said no more about it.

The way was long. They traveled by day and for half of the night. They ate game hunted with bow and arrow by Old Canoe, Black Salt at his side. They drank from fresh lakes and streams. They grew lean, toughened from the hard walk. Old Canoe gave them strong herbs to drink, which made them stronger. And they made their own ginseng tea, which gave them strength of mind. They never complained. They were mostly quiet, silent, hoarding their wills.

Mother Pearl never rode on the ponies, although Josias and Pretty Pearl did, and Swassi did, with Black Salt. Sometimes Pearl rode on John Henry's shoulders. John Henry would laugh and pick up both Josias and Pretty and sling them up over his shoulders as if they were the little homing pigeons that flew in the trees, following them to the new place. They would ride high and handsome, ducking branches as best they could.

John Henry always had a humorous word and a boast or song for them.

>*"I's a railway man, a railway man,"*

sang John Henry, never raising his voice too loud,

>*"A clickety-clack, up and back.*
>*Just singin' my song.*
>*I's here today, but tomorrow I's gone.*
>*Oh, I's a railway man, jes' singin' my song."*

One day they passed far west of a great valley that Old Canoe described to them. But they would not see it. They took to the Cumberland Mountains, and as the sun was going down, they crossed a gap in the great mountains. It looked like a gorge, 500 feet deep. They looked down on that Cumberland Gap from a great height. The view was breathtaking. And they felt their own strength tremble at the sight of the strong land.

Old Canoe made a sign with his hand. One of his warriors appeared where there had been only trees. He rode a spotted pony. He came up to Old Canoe, and the two of them sat a moment. There were settlers down below them.

"They black folks out there too?" Salt wanted to know.

"Not many that are masters of themselves," Old Canoe said. "You have there Kentucky, and there Virginia, and everywhere you have those who would re-enslave your kind and mine."

Carefully, Old Canoe and his warrior led Black Salt and his party along the high ridge of the ancient Warriors' Path. As they went slowly, picking their way, Old Canoe sang softly a sacred song. It enveloped them in its profoundly ancient sound.

It had been a long trek, but they were in the state of Virginia. They slept in caves that Ani-yun'Wiya knew. They avoided hunters and trappers by taking the most difficult routes. Now Swassi rode as much as she could. Mother Pearl rode sometimes, just to keep folks from wondering at her strength, and she older than all of them except Old Canoe.

Days and days passed. At night they dropped from exhaustion.

"How long we been goin'?" Pretty Pearl asked John Henry one day when she and Josias and big John were out collecting wood for the fire.

"I counts ten, twelve days, maybe then some," said John Henry.

"Twelve days?" asked Josias.

"A week and plus," John said. "Long days."

"And are we far?" Pretty asked. "How far to de river Jordan?"

"We hit West Virginny soon," said John Henry.

"How soon?" Pretty wanted to know. "Do we go by de Big Bend where you be workin'?"

"No'm," said John Henry. "Big Bend be east of where you goin'."

"What you mean?" Pretty Pearl looked alarmed. "You comin' with us too."

"Sure I am," he said. "I'm comin' with you as fer as de big Jordan. But then I gots to go."

"Oh, John!" said Pearl. She looked about ready to cry.

"Well, you know I got to go sometime." John Henry hugged Pearl, and whispered, "I even tole de Conquer I had to go.

"Here, Josias," he said. "Take this here bundlewood on to you pappy."

"You comin', Pretty?" Josias asked. He took the bundle and headed away.

"Comin' directly," she called to his back. But Pretty paused a moment. "Do you think I might use my power?" she said to John Henry when they were alone. "I got me a de Conquer root again. Ain't had one chance to ask Mother Pearl nothin' about my power. What you think about that, John Henry?"

John Henry stared at her. "Sis Pretty, weren't you listenin' what de Conquer say?"

"What?" she said. "Back then, at Promise? In de trees and all that light! I heard my heart rushin' in my ears! He scare me so at first. Tremble me so! Thought he gone beat me, too."

"Oh, my!" said John Henry. "Oh, my little Pretty!" He kneeled down next to Pearl. Even with that, he was as tall as an ordinary man, and Pearl had to strain to look up at him.

"What you mean, oh my?" she asked him. "And why you lookin' so sorrow at me?"

"Pretty, honey," John Henry said, "didn't you hear de Conquer say, if I beats de stream drill, I will pay de price? And de price be to die."

"So? He didn't mean it, too," Pretty said. "Make you die, John Henry? Why, you a god."

"That be true," John Henry said, gently, "but I be actin' like a man, long time. And I will die with my hammer in my han' if I beats that steam drill."

"Oh, John," Pretty said, laughing. "Then just don't you beat him drill, that's all."

"But don't you see de god trick?" he said. Big John wasn't laughing at all. "That's my punishment for actin' up, sportin' around, bein' *bad*. I *has* to beat that steam drill. Old brother best, de Conquer, he knew I would."

John Henry's face was resigned and sad. He ran his fingers through his sister's long, dark hair. He kissed her cheek tenderly, as if he thought it was the last kiss he had to give.

All of a sudden it felt like a cold wind blew in Pretty's heart. All the words she had paid little heed to that de Conquer had spoken now came to her in a rush.

"No!" she whispered, her eyes wide. She looked terrified. "Oh, no, he didn't mean that!"

John Henry folded his tiny sister close. "It not so bad," he said. "To be human is about worth de whole world, to my mind. And to Dwahro. Old de Conquer done give Dwahro his most favorite wish." John Henry threw back his head and laughed. His mood had changed that quick. "And Dwahro ain't even found out yet—hee, hee! He so busy walkin' around like a man, he don't know he become one. Don't tell him! Don't tell him! Let that old one-time spirit of a god find out hisself—heh, heh . . . heh, heh, heh. . . ."

Pretty Pearl was rigid, holding herself in. She started trembling. She couldn't form the question she had to ask. And it was as if John Henry knew what it was. He got up. He was so tall, she couldn't take her eyes off him. She wanted to fly high up into his arms where she would be safe. . . .

Pretty touched the de Conquer root Mother Pearl had given her. But she didn't fly. Nothing at all happened when she touched the root.

"It don't have de power," she said.

"No," John Henry said. His voice was stern. "It never did have as much as you." He stared down at her. "It bring you luck now." He waited.

Then Josias came up. He walked on past Pearl to gather another load of wood. Pearl had dropped some that he took up.

"Here, let me do that," said big John, taking the wood.

"Papa say one more load be more than enough," Josias said.

"All right then," John Henry said. He turned and headed back with the load.

Josias waited for Pearl. He smiled at her, but sobered when he saw the dark look on her face.

"What de matter you, Pretty?" he asked.

"Don't know," she said.

"You don't feel good no more, be trekkin' over de whole country to a new land?"

"I don't know!" she exclaimed. "I don't know how I should be feelin'. I has to go find Mother Pearl!"

"Well, find her, she right back there." Josias said. "She ain't moved from de cook fire, she ain't goin' no place."

"I don't know that!" cried Pretty, and she ran back to Black Salt's camp as fast as she could.

CHAPTER SEVENTEEN

Mother Pearl stayed by the fire through the suppertime. She wouldn't take a walk with Pretty or talk much. Mother Pearl seemed happiest when Swassi was near her, and Swassi was always there.

"I'll go for a walk with you, Pretty," Swassi said. "We can go a little ways, pick some flowers." But they all could see that she was worn out.

Pretty didn't say anything. She came up and sat close to Mother Pearl, peering into her face often. But Mother kept her eyes on the fire and the cook pot full of supper.

"Um-um!" she said. "Smell him wild rabbit, too? Ain't nothin' like rabbit stew with de onion and taters."

"Mother Pearl, I has to talk with you!" Pretty whispered once, when she got the chance.

"I know you do," said Mother back. "We gone talk, too, soon as folks be asleep. I know you do."

And that evening folks went to sleep as soon as the sun was far down and the forest trees held the night. Pretty lay still in the crook of John Henry's arm. Mother Pearl was right beside her. And Pretty lay there, wide awake, waiting. But then she didn't know whether she had fallen asleep and awakened again. She might have been half asleep and half awake. She was comfortable, warm, in the crook of her brother's arm. She could feel Mother Pearl at her back, and it seemed to her that Mother was talking to her. Talking quietly, in that low voice she had that made Pretty feel most safe. Everybody else was asleep. Even Dwahro. That Dwahro, who would pretend so to sleep, really was asleep now. Don't he know yet? Pearl was thinking. And she still didn't know whether she was awake or not.

Mother Pearl's voice went on, soothingly. She was telling Pretty everything. Pretty talked, too. What Mother Pearl told her made her feel almost sad, but not quite. She also felt good inside. It was as if Mother Pearl was giving her many, many lifetimes of talking and storytelling.

Late in the night they were awakened by old Canoe. They gathered their bundles and rolled up their pallets. Mother Pearl had spread her apron over herself, Pretty and Dwahro, on the far side of Mother. So that when Pretty Pearl awakened, she had in her mind the shape of that great old she poplar that Dwahro had painted on Mother's apron. It filled her up inside like a legend.

There was no talking there, in the faint light of the fire. Old Canoe and Salt carefully put it out. Then they traveled by starlight, slowly, with Old Canoe in the lead. With Salt and Swassi bringing up the rear. Old Canoe's warrior had disappeared again.

They traveled through the night and through a false dawn. Later they watched the eastern sky light up. There were clouds. There was a morning rain that hardly touched them as they moved under the heavy trees.

"And de light come down,"

sang Swassi, softly, softly.

"And de light come down."

Surprised, Salt turned to look at her. She walked there, a step in front of him. Rarely had any of them heard her sing. She was always so quiet. Now her sweet voice stirred them. Salt touched her gently on the shoulder.

There, on his lead horse, Old Canoe listened. He listened with astonishment as the giant one of the inside folks began to hum. Here were "other" beings who could become human, or so he had thought. Old Canoe no longer knew if this was so. Maybe he had been mistaken. Perhaps he was just getting old. Seeing things. Old Canoe sighed. He let it go.

Pretty stayed close to Mother Pearl or John Henry throughout the day.

"We can run off de path," Josias said to her. "We can sneak up on de warrior out there, hidin', and scare him some."

"No such," she said, although she was interested. "How you 'spect to sneak up on him warrior, and him already out of sight?"

"He ain't far, him, I bet. You wants to try?" asked Josias.

"No such," she said. "I got to stay close."

"Go on, chile, go play, if you wants to," said Mother Pearl. But Pretty wouldn't go.

She felt she ought to be thinking—she didn't know what about. It was as if part of her mind had left her. She kept trying to remember something she had forgotten. But she couldn't recall what it was she must remember. She and John Henry had talked while picking up firewood. She remembered that, but she had forgotten what they talked about. She planned to ask John Henry about that, too. But then she forgot all about asking. Way deep in her mind, she thought she had had a dream. She could feel the shape of it in the safe sound of Mother Pearl's voice deep in the night. But it made her head dizzy in the heat to think so much.

They were up high. The air would be hot one moment and cool the next. Then they were passing out of the state of Virginia and into that called West Virginia, so John Henry told Pretty and Josias.

"How you know which is which?" Josias asked John Henry.

" 'Cause I hear Black Salt and de old Indian talkin'," John Henry said. "Say this here be de Indians' hunting lands, be West Virginny only a little while. Once be all Virginny, but no more. It be a new state. West Virginny!

"Yes sir, this West Virginny," John Henry went on. "I been here, but not this fer west. We is west. See? Look down there."

"You mean at de river?" asked Pretty.

"That's it," said John Henry. "Over on de left. Them say it called Tug Fork River. It divide us from them hills over in Kentuck-place."

"He been here, but where he goin'?" Josias asked Pretty.

"Don't know," she said. "I cain't seem to remember much no more."

John Henry smiled on them, listening. "Too much happenin'," he said quickly. "I tole you. I'ma go to de Big Bend."

"And where is it?" Pretty asked. "I wish to see it. Can I go with you, John Henry?"

John Henry shook his head. "Oh, baby sis," Big John began, "you don't wants to see that place. They say they keep a thousand men a-laborin' there."

"A thousand men!" Josias exclaimed.

"Uh-huh," John said, "near Talcott, Summers County, West Virginny. You see, they got this river there, Greenbrier, make a big bend makin' its way around de end of a way-high mountain. And then it join de New River. And de mountain called Big Bend Mountain from that ten-mile bend in de Greenbrier River. Most natural, they namin' de tunnel same name."

Pretty Pearl stumbled on the path. John Henry reached down and swung her up onto his shoulder. "You wants to come up here, too?" he asked Josias. Eagerly, Josias nodded, and John Henry swung him up high on his left shoulder.

"Ooooh! We up high and high!" Pretty exclaimed.

"We not too heavy?" asked Josias.

" 'Bout as heavy as two sacks o' cloud." John Henry laughed.

"Tell us some more 'bout de Big Bend," Josias asked.

"Yeah, tell us some more," Pretty said. She did not like to remind herself that one day soon, John Henry would leave. But she did like hearing about the Big Bend.

"Well, they likes to call de Big Bend de Great Bend Tunnel sometimes. Him tunnel gone become some one mile and quarter long through de mountain. When him finish, we gone see daylight clean through."

"Daylight!" Josias cried in wonderment.

"It be a red shale mountain," John Henry said. "See, that's how I'ma gone win de contest with that ole steam drill."

"How?" Pretty asked. "How, 'cause it a red shale mountain?"

"Absolutely," John Henry said. "That shale be loose rock, gone choke up de steam drill, but it ain't gone choke John Henry and his hammer!"

"Tell it!" said Josias.

"Well, it like this," said John Henry. "This ain't no social at de Big Bend. De laborers, mostly formerly slave men, live in wooden shanties. Tunnel sickness be a killer, 'cause of heat and bad air in de tunnel. And killer be when they blow de rock out with dy-na-mite. Oh, that be rough blowing sky high! And fallin' rock be a killer for true—watch out! Say ordinary mens dyin' like flies. Sayin' company buryin' de dead without no markers, put 'em in one big grave for all. Fear de mens gone run away 'cause of so much death."

"Oh, no," said Pretty. Suddenly she began to cry.

They were still walking the high path. Mother Pearl, ahead of John Henry, stopped when she heard Pretty. "What the matter her?" she asked.

"I was tellin' 'bout de Big Bend," John Henry explained. "Think I talk too much."

Mother Pearl gave him a smack on his ribs. It was about as high as she could reach. "The idea!" she said. "Ain't you got no better sense?" she asked in a whisper.

John Henry reached up, patted Pretty's cheek. "Don't you worry about me, sweet one," he told her. "No killer heat, nor blow-up, nor rock gone ketch John Henry, no sir! An' I'ma gone hammer with *two* hammers, one in each hand, too. An' ain't nothin' gone ketch me, too."

"Where *is* your hammer now?" asked Josias, suddenly. "I ain't seen it in a long time."

"Heh, heh," said John Henry.

"He done lay it on de sledge the Indian mens taken away," said Mother Pearl quickly.

John Henry breathed a sigh of relief.

"Oh," said Josias. "Then how you get it back? Them sledges be gone."

"Get it back where we meet later on," John Henry said, and that was all.

On and on they went, where numerous streams cut the plateau into a series of rounded hills. They kept to the highest hills and they followed the Big Sandy River north along the Kentucky border. After four more days they came to a point that Old Canoe said was right by Huntington but to the east.

"There," he said. Straight ahead of them they saw, lying broad and beautiful in the sun, an enormous river.

"Oh!" said Swassi.

No one else could say a word. They looked a moment. "Come," said Old Canoe. "For us, it is gathering time."

He led them where the woods were deepest. Where the cover was good. Where all was still, and yet, as they came near, they saw forms there. It was sundown. And all the people were gathered, stretching over a mile. They did not see every one of the inside folks, but they were gathered there. Swassi and Mother Pearl walked among them. Crying, hugging Simmie, Jabbho, Maw Julanna. There were no words. And then John Henry and Salt and Dwahro went through.

That Dwahro. All at once he was struck dumb. Tears sprang in his eyes. Off by himself by a young sycamore tree. He turned his head away and carefully lifted his hand to one eye. And felt the tears there. His fingers were wet with real tears. He knew! He sighed deeply. *Thank you, de Conquer!* And breathed like a man. Then he understood that he had been breathing, sleeping and *not* pretending for a good long while.

Dwahro was overcome. Standing there, he was thankful, and he bowed his head humbly. At that moment he felt a flood of human emotions. Yet he was able to take hold and stop his crying. He spoke to no one about what was in his heart. He did not sing or dance. Dwahro wouldn't put on a show this day, or the next one, either.

Fare you well, O best one, John de Conquer!

Spirit, Dwahro was no more. He was the young man Dwahro, and he was proud and humbly thankful.

That evening Old Canoe talked quietly. Not all the inside folks were able to hear, being spread over a distance as they were. But Old Canoe talked conversationally. After a sentence or two, a chattering would begin. Someone would jump up and move quietly away, telling up and down the line what had been said. And those who were told would pass the word on. It sounded as though a great many leaves were rustling in the woods.

"You may sleep through the night this night," said old Canoe. "Tomorrow some of you will drift into town and collect supplies. A few at a time, all week, collecting the supplies. And all week we will cross just west of the place of Huntington. It would not do to have a whole place watch us barter for boats and watch us go. There are some boats that will be provided by our friends to the north, the Shawnee. I have sent word. And the first boat will be here in the morning. You decide who will go first."

"But where we goin'?" someone asked.

"We have promised to get you across the river. After that, you will decide yourselves where to go. In the morning," said Old Canoe, "your leader, Black Salt, will speak to the Shawnee men who will be waiting. There is a big town west of here. Not far. They call it Ironton. They say, go north of the town and then, go west. They say there are many good places farther north and west. Small settlements where you will not be harmed or bothered."

Old Canoe sat down and Black Salt stood, taking command. "We here cannot thank de Real People enough for all they has done for us," Black Salt began. "All we have are words. We got nothin' much more. They don't want nothin' from us, de Real People don't. What they did for us can't be bought or sold. To say thanks a thousand times would never pay for what they done for us." Black Salt reached out. "All this way! And not because they has to, but 'cause it the right thing to do. That's all, it that simple." He dropped his arms. "And so, Old Canoe and you warriors. Praise be! We will try to live up to you, is all we can do.

"Marnin' I will talk to de Shawnee people. Don't know them," Salt said, "but if Ani-yun'Wiya say they be true men, then I will listen. I listen to Ani-yun'Wiya and he be true. So I listen to Shawnee people. But never you worry. We gone keep on doin' a little at a time. When I give a command, inside folks, you do as I say. We all gone go to de same place, wherever it be. We never be more than a half a day's walk from one another. I swear that to you."

Black Salt finished. All the people were exhausted and they lay down. Old Canoe and his men went off, and they counseled with a small party of Shawnee.

And all that night, at the camp of Black Salt, the inside folks slept deeply. Mother Pearl stayed awake. She made sure the fire did burn with hot coals that warmed the folks near it. And with her power, she allowed those same coals to fan their heat outward so that all the folks were warmed. For the night air had turned fall crisp. She listened to the snores and coughs of the tired and worn folks. She smiled there in the dark, summoning warm feelings she had for these people.

The nicest, bravest folks any place could want, she thought. Oh, they fine folks, makin' their way. They been good. Let life be good to them. Let luck go with them. She scraped her de Conquer root and let de Conquer flakes catch on the breeze and blow over them. And the de Conquer flakes did fall on the folks sleeping. Wherever they went, they would carry de Conquer. And de Conquer would fall to earth and grow, and the folks would know to pick the root and cherish it.

How they gone know? thought Mother Pearl. De chile is how.

Mother Pearl got up stiffly, rubbing her right hip. This human stuff ain't all it cut out to be, she thought. They can keep they joint misery, shoot.

Favoring her right leg, she hobbled around until she was there by Dwahro, John Henry and Pretty Pearl. Mother Pearl had to be careful now. She knew what she must do. And ever so quietly, she knelt down.

Took off her apron, spread it over Pretty and Dwahro. It was then she looked closely at John Henry, and saw his eyes were open. She put her finger to her lips to keep him quiet. John Henry blinked and watched, but he would not say anything. He knew that whatever Mother Pearl must do, she had the right. And it would be done in the name of the best god of Mount Highness, John de Conquer.

Mother Pearl waved her hand over Pretty Pearl's face. Pretty Pearl sat up, dreaming. In her dreaming, she could hear Mother Pearl's voice as she had before. It was warm and soft, making her feel most safe. This time, she knew exactly what Mother Pearl had to say.

"One long time," Mother Pearl began, "there was a god, John de Conquer. You remember, I told you that before."

"Yes," Pretty said. Her eyes were open. Her lips moved, but she was sleeping, dreaming.

"John de Conquer help de poor folks and de good folks," said Mother Pearl. "He help de black folks and keep them safe. He play on his hypocrite and all de peoples know when him comin'. All de peoples did laugh and sing to see de Conquer fool de bad folks. Yes, they did."

"Tell about how he became a bird," said Pretty. She forgot about herself. She had forgotten the real part she had played.

"De Conquer make him de albatross. He fly high up in de slaver sails. He come all de way to Savannah. He lie down in southern soil. He predict de War. He rise out of southern soil ever' time de people need him. He got messengers all over de land. Yes, he has."

Mother Pearl told. Pretty listened, questioned, until she understood the changed tale. Then Mother Pearl laid her down again next to Dwahro. She touched Pretty's face one last time.

"Good-bye, my Pretty," she said. "Oh, yes, this be de saddest thing I do. For I must go home. De Conquer say so. You won't need the god-woman part to fit, not now. But you be all right after while. Now. You and Dwahro. An' all de inside folks!"

Mother Pearl lifted her arms outward to the people. "Take care of this orphan chile with she brothers, Dwahro and John Henry. Pret' near time John Henry got to go his way. But Dwahro go with Pretty. An' you, good inside folks, watch out for these poor orphans. Oh, I know you will."

Painfully, Mother Pearl got to her feet. She gazed around her. "Swassi, Black Salt, all de inside folks, I is ready!"

Heard in the darkness was a fluttering of wings, as though a great bird had landed. It was surrounded in de Conquerlight. It was de Conquer Albatross.

"Black Salt, I give you a name!" spoke Mother Pearl. She gave to him his last name. "All de inside folks, I is gone!" Where Mother Pearl had been, a bird, albatross, flew into the air. De Conquer and Mother Pearl Albatrosses were both in the air.

"Where you goin' like that?" said John Henry Roustabout. He'd been watching everything. Had his arms comfortably behind his head. He could see the two birds as though it were daylight.

"How you doin', John Henry?" said de Conquer Albatross.

"Doin' all right," said John Henry. "But where you two headin' dressed up in feathers?"

"De ship with him black cap'n be sailin'," said Mother Pearl.

"Him got de black crew! You mean de ship ole Cuffee lookin' to find," said John Henry.

"That de one," said de Conquer. "It headed for that Africa of mine. Me and Mother Pearl wants to see that Mount Highness as soon as we can."

"I see," said John Henry.

The two albatrosses came to sit perched on John Henry's knees. "Listen, bro," said John de Conquer. "I can't go away like this and not tell you somethin'."

"What's that?" asked John Henry.

"You can come back with us now on de ship if you wants to. I ain't gone take you pride away and you god power, if you comes back home now. But if you do come home, you has to stay home. No more roamin'."

John Henry laughed. "Hee, hee, hee. Ho, ho! Hee! I is John Henry and I was born to roam. I'ma gone make me two hammers out of my one hammer. I'ma gone make 'em twenty-an'-pound hammers. And I'ma gone go to de Big Bend and hammer *down*! *Yea, man*, I is John Henry. Hammer *down*!"

So let it be! De Conquer Albatross flapped his wings and flew straight up. So did Mother Pearl Albatross. Then de

Conquer swooped down and hovered above Pretty Pearl and Dwahro.

"Good-bye, Sis Pretty," he said in her ear. "You'll keep de Conquer close, you hear? I is takin' Mother Pearl with me. The time you two split him de Conquer root, she be but a moment of you future. But she come with me and she be a god mother forever. Now you take de human and de life part and live happy.

"You too, Dwahro," de Conquer whispered in Dwahro's ear. "Now. We gone."

The birds, albatrosses, flapped and flew high up and away.

John Henry lay there, as calm as he could be, taking in the night air.

"Huh!" he said to himself. "I forgots to ask if that old Cuffee make it or not." But then it came to him. Those birds were flying. And through de Conquer's eyes, John Henry saw the ship.

There he saw the old African. Cuffee was as forward as he could get on the ship. The ocean sprayed him, drenched him as the ship's huge prow plunged under the waves and up again. He never took his eyes away from the ocean. For out there lay his Africa. It waited for him. It knew old Cuffee was coming home.

CHAPTER EIGHTEEN

They were a large crowd. They looked like a small army, or a village, themselves, scattered as they were over one mile. But they were well hidden with all their supplies. They remained very still among the shadows of the great forest trees. And they knew well that they must not stay long in one place.

"Odds are nothin' gone harm us here," Black Salt told them. "But we is black and a good bunch of us, too. Best to move as quick as we can. Break up and move out and across, a few at a time."

Those few who had gone with Black Salt to meet the

Shawnee party straggled back with tales of the Jordan from its bank. Ezekiel was one of them. "They calls it Ohio, but I knows better. It de River Jordan, all right," he said excitedly. "Oh, it big! Oh, I don't know about some boat!" Then he grinned. Although he was frightened to cross water in a narrow boat, he was also eager, as were the others. "And them Shawnee," he said. "They don't look anythin' like de Real People. Uh-unh! They looks almost like white folks, skin is so light."

The inside folks were eager and frightened. Most did not want to cross the water in daylight, and all were afraid to cross it at night. Those who could be persuaded to go across a few at a time, every few hours, did so. Twenty went across that first day, starting at six in the morning. That night fifty made it across. By the morning of the third day, all were across except for Black Salt and his party. They were ready.

John Henry was saying good-bye. He had his arm around Pretty and she held on to his fingers. They stood there with Dwahro talking to Salt. Swassi was close by. She had combed Pretty's hair as she always did, she thought.

"I'ma gone find my tunnel now," John Henry Roustabout was saying.

"Well if you got to go, good luck to you," Black Salt said. He shook John Henry's hand.

"I always gets de better of luck," John Henry said. "I's de black giant. My better comes best and my luck be luckiest."

Black Salt laughed. "Don't you worry 'bout you sister

and cousin," he told John Henry. Salt looked fondly on Pearl and Dwahro. "Most de chil'ren is orphaned. I will make these two part of my house, wherever it be."

"Black Salt, I do thank you for that, for all you kindness to them. I'll send along some money as soon as I kin." John Henry hid away the sadness he felt. For he knew he would die with his hammers in his hand.

"Don't worry none about it. Me and Dwahro, here, and my Josias, we gone set us out a farm," Salt explained. "I been savin' long time to buy lands. All de inside folks gone get a piece of land. All who want it. De ginseng still be a good crop, too."

Josias was there next to Salt. He looked proudly up at his father, then he grinned at Pretty and Dwahro. They grinned back. Pretty had been feeling like an orphan ever since that morning three days ago when she found a big apron covering her and her cousin, Dwahro. She fingered the great tree painted on the apron. She knew Dwahro had painted the picture sometime, when she was little. John Henry had told her so. And she knew the apron had belonged to her mother. But she didn't remember her mother. "All that beginning be far long," John Henry had told her. "But you 'member de stories she told," John Henry had said. "You never can forget de stories." And indeed, Pretty found that when she wanted to, she could remember them. She had a shawl said to be made by her mother; she wore it now.

Dwahro remembered little. He did not remember spirits or anything. He knew he could paint fine paintings. He knew he could dance and sing. That made him happy.

"So then," said John Henry, "be makin' my way, me and my hammers."

There in his left hand were two hammers; he slung them over his shoulder.

"Where they come from?" Josias asked. "Thought you only has one hammer."

"Be my hammers, is all," said John Henry. "They be ridin' all de way on de sledges." He grinned. "Had 'em here, all de time we be talkin'. Course, you ain't notice, 'cause I's such a good-lookin' giant."

Dwahro laughed.

"You sure somethin', for true," Black Salt said.

"Good-bye, Miz Swassi," John Henry said, going over to her and taking her hand. He kissed her hand. That caused a commotion among Dwahro, Josias and Pretty. Pretty covered her mouth, giggling. "If I hates anything, Miz Swassi," Big John told her for all of them to hear, "I hates leavin' you behind!"

With that Black Salt folded his arms. Resignedly, he waited patiently for John Henry to be on his way. "You got food enough?" he asked.

"I can ketch all de food I needs," John Henry said. "Well." He ruffled Pretty's hair and folded her close. "Be seein' you, little one," he said, bending down and kissing her cheek. She clung to his neck, crying, "No! No!"

Swassi came to comfort her. Took her in her arms. That was how John Henry left them, with Pretty sobbing, and all of them sober and saddened.

" 'Bye, cousin," Dwahro called.

"See you, son," John Henry called, softly, and he was gone among the shade trees, hurrying through the forest. When he was out of their sight, he leaped a hill at a time eastward toward the Big Bend. And when he saw the Greenbrier River shining in the sun, he leaped across it, too. He was laughing and shouting when he strode into camp. Right then the boss man kept his eye on him.

The black laborers jumped up at the sight of him. "Whoo-ee, you big and big!" they said, and they slapped their bets down.

"I's John Henry Roustabout," John Henry told them. "Tie a tiger to my wrist and a panther 'round my throat. Be my bracelet and my necklace, 'cause I is tough, don't you know! I come here to find me a steam drill."

"It here!" the men told him. "Whatchu gone do with it?"

"Gone test it and whump it and use it for my toothpick," he boasted.

They laughed and laughed at John Henry. That night they played some cards with him in one of the shanties. These were tough, wrestling and fighting, hard-drinking men. But that didn't do them much good with John Henry. He beat them at cards anyway.

"Gone have to wait for you next payday for sure to test that steam drill," he told them. " 'Cause you all is badly bent this week."

And late that night, sleeping on his pallet, John Henry thought about the inside folks, Pretty and Dwahro. He closed his eyes on his sorrow and heavy heart at leaving those he loved. He knew that the time he had said good-bye to them would be the last they ever saw of him. For he could feel that Big Bend over him.

Remember me, he thought to Pretty in his dream of winning. *'Member John Henry Roustabout. Say I wasn't good and I wasn't bad. Tell 'em a man ain't nothin' but a man. Say I beat that steam drill down one time, and that I died with my hammers in my hand.*

§ §

Black Salt and his party crossed the Jordan one early evening. They had said good-bye to their constant friends, the Cherokees.

Ani-yun'Wiya watched from a shielded place high on a bluff on the West Virginia side of the river. When the flatboat oared by two Shawnee men and Black Salt was across, Old Canoe turned his horse. Without ceremony he and all his men disappeared into the forest.

Black Salt and his party traveled four days to a place called Amestown. It was a small settlement in southwestern Ohio and one of the places the Shawnee men had told Salt how to get to. Black Salt had then drawn maps of four or five places.

Amestown was ninety miles from the Jordan/Ohio. It was twelve or so miles from the National Pike, the great roadway that ran from Cumberland, Maryland, through Columbus and Springfield, Ohio, to Vandalia, Illinois. Salt knew the National Pike was the road to carry his farm produce and the produce of the other inside folks east and west to the cities and towns.

All of the inside folks settled down in the area. Besides

Amestown, some settled at Boldtown and Pitchout and the black town of Paintersfork. They were never far from one another. They bartered with one another for what they needed. There was much moving about from one homestead to another in the beginning, especially among the orphan children. It turned out that Bessie Freedom and Miz Molly and Ezekiel came to live on the land with Salt's party, which was smaller now. All together there were eight people to start a homestead. They were Black Salt, Swassi, Pretty Pearl, Josias, Dwahro, Bessie, Miz Molly and Ezekiel.

They built a log cabin. Slowly, over time, they built barns, sheds and outhouses. All of the inside folks helped build one another's buildings.

One day Black Salt called the people of his homestead together. It was the day they were moving into the log cabin. The cabin had two large rooms that would be divided into four smaller rooms. They would cook outside as they always had, and they would eat around the cook fire. It would be a long time before they would give up that custom of washing up, gathering, talking and taking their meals outside. For it was a tradition handed down from the slave street of slavery times. It had been a comfort to slave people who had one street that they cherished for themselves.

Black Salt stood before them with his arm around Swassi. "We gettin' married," he said simply.

Everybody grinned, but stayed quiet. "They's the Baptist folk over in de place call it Yellow Creek. Say we can marry there. We will, this very Sunday.

"I want everybody know me and us by de last name I has taken. And that be name of Perry. Don't know where it come from, but it be in my head all de time. Call me Mister Selah Black S. Perry. After Sunday, Swassi be my wife, Miz Swassi Perry. This be the land of Salt Perry and his party. Each one of you has a right to Perry if you wants it." And then Salt sang the words that he was most fond of singing to them:

> "You got a right, I got a right,
>   We all got a right to de tree of life."

It was a song and a feeling that went to the heart of them.

So it was that Black S. Perry's party became the Perry people. Pretty Pearl Perry, Bessie Freedom Perry, Miz Molly Perry, Dwahro Perry, Josias Perry, and Ezekiel Perry. All took the name of Selah Black Salt Perry, the first, and they were most proud of it. But no one called the leader Mister Perry or Selah. All who knew him well, those being the inside folks, called him Salt or Black Salt. And those who did not know him well, who sold him and his people land and supplies, called him Mister Black Salt.

So it was that Salt and all his people settled down. Pretty Pearl Perry grew and was most happy being one of the family of Salt and Swassi, just like Josias. She and Josias were very close and would always remain so. Josias was turning into a leader just like his father. And Pretty became the best sang hunter that any of the people had ever seen. "Know exactly where to find it," she told Josias.

Often she and Salt and Josias traveled miles and miles in the hills, and she would lead them straight to a large sang patch. The community of inside folks at Amestown and the other villages became well known for their fine sang. They sold and shipped it all over along the National Pike, even outside of the country to China, as they had done before. They did prosper. And no one tried to rob them of what they had.

Pretty got the most satisfaction from riding off on horseback and hunting the dark sang areas by herself. Sometimes she did this, going off when no one could notice. Traveling deep in the forest that was left, as high up as she could go. She loved the silent, damp sang places. She found them and she walked in them as though walking inside a sacred place. She felt most close to nature here. She felt her de Conquer root most strongly here.

"John de Conquer," she would whisper to the deep shade—she didn't know why she had to whisper—"de Con-*care*!" And she would feel—she didn't know quite how to describe it. She would feel most high, which really didn't make good sense. And looking, soon she would find the John de Conquer root. It had spread far and wide.

All the people now carried John de Conquer root. They did not often wear it. Only Pretty still wore it. It was held on a mighty strong hair string around her neck. She had covered it in an old silver sachet bag she had found among her belongings. Pretty Pearl could find the John de Conquer plant in its hidden growing places even faster than she could find sang.

"What it is?" Black Salt asked her one day as they entered a deep cove and Pearl pointed her hand. Right where she pointed was John de Conquer growing quite well.

"It's de Conquer," she told him.

"I knows that," Salt said, "but it has to have a common name like ginseng or hound's tooth. What is it? What it name?"

"Oh," said Pearl. "Well." And she told the name, whispering it so only Salt and Josias could hear. "It de most secret of all plant life. No one tell him name, ever. It John de Conquer for true, so secret we don't call its other name. It ours in hard times and good times. It be our luck."

And so it was that the John de Conquer root became the most secret luck of black people, and none would tell its common name, not ever.

And the luck the inside folks had was good. Every Sunday after church, lots of them gathered at Salt's place. They'd ride up in their buckboards and wagons, on horseback or strolling on foot. The children who were growing up often liked to walk the long miles through the trees. And once at Salt's compound, they would gather under the great shade trees in front of the cabin. Long tables were set out. Folks often brought cakes and pies. Swassi and Salt and their children served ham and baked corn. Miz Molly and Ezekiel made homemade cold drinks that everybody loved, that caused folks to giggle. Made them in a huge tub using cold branch water to modify strong dandelion wine. Folks would talk about the old times, the hard times in the forest. Over and over again they relived the long journey. They called it The Trail Home.

And as always happened on a visit, someone said, "Come on now, Pretty."

Others took up the cry. "Yeah, Pretty! Come on, come on!"

Swassi had bought flowered material. Salt had traveled to the distant town of Chardon to get it for her. And now Pretty wore the nicest sun dress of flowers, and white stockings and shoes on her feet. On one side of her sat Josias, as usual, and Dwahro Perry on the other. Dwahro had on the nicest suit. It was not linen. But it was the palest cream and he was careful not to sit on the grass. He sat on a clean burlap sack. Patiently, he waited. For after Pretty Pearl always came his turn.

"She gettin' ready," Salt said, humor in his eyes.

"Oh. Oh, she gettin' ready!" Others picked it up.

They were there. All the folks she loved, Pretty thought. Sometimes her heart was just too full with all she felt for them. Particularly for Salt. Now she beamed at him.

"Now! Now! Here it come!" he said. And folks shouted and clapped their hands. They whooped and hollered with delight, the way they never could do in that land of Promise that was no more. Promise had become now, had become success.

Pretty stood. She was tall, grown very tall for her age. There was something about her that made all the inside folks look at her solemnly, respectfully. She held herself most proud. But she held herself inward, and they were never sure just what would come out of her, how she would begin.

She walked serenely back and forth in front of them. The sun broke through the shade branches. Dappled light sparked her bright dress, illuminating flowers. She did not look at them—she was seeing inward. She turned, facing them, and lifted her hands.

"One long time," she began, "de god came down from on high. Came down from Mount Kenya on a clear day."

"Oh, de god is back, de god is back!" whispered Salt. He had heard this story before, but he never knew exactly what Pearl would do with it.

"All right, Mr. Know-it-all Salt," Pretty said, and everybody laughed. "You tell me who be de god."

"That easy," Salt said. "Be John de Con-*care* of de Conquer root, too."

"That right as far as it go," Pearl said sweetly.

"It don't go far enough?" asked Miz Molly.

"Not necessarily," said Pearl. " 'Cause in that one long time, de Con-*care* weren't de only god come down."

"No?" said Josias. "Who be de others?"

"If yall be still, I'm fixin' to tell you. Best start over." She cleared her throat. "Ahem. One long time, Pretty Pearl came down from on high. . . ."

"Whoo-ee!" folks broke in. "You hear that? And she a Perry."

"Not a Perry then," she said smugly, trying to keep a straight face. She didn't know how she could make up such tales. But she could and they made her laugh inside. "Be a god chile, then."

"Ooh, a god chile!" said Miz Molly. "That so nice!" And the folks laughed.

"And I weren't de only one," Pearl continued. "That be Mount Kenya I'm comin' down, and with me is John de Con-*care* and John Henry Roustabout . . ."

"John Henry a *big* god!" Ezekiel shouted, and slapped his side.

"Yeah, he be," said Pretty. "And last but not least, cousin Dwahro come down. . . ."

"Oh, my! I cain't stand it!" said Maw Julanna. She was seated in a rocking chair. Old and as comfortable as she could be. The land of Promise lived in her mind most of the time. But Pretty's stories could bring her back.

"God, Dwahro," Salt said. "I suspected somebody could dance and sing like that has to be somethin' right high up." Folks giggled and shook, laughing.

"No suh," said Pearl. "He be spirit, Dwahro. Spirit of de gods."

"De spirit sure can move, too!" said Swassi. "You wait, spirit gone move Dwahro any minute now."

Pretty made up a good story about John Henry. It was sad, but it was good. She told how he had to beat the steam drill. "Had to," she said. "And then he become a man. And he die with two hammers in his hands."

"Don't, Pretty," Salt said, gently. "You make youself upset."

"Be all right," Pretty said after a moment. She took a deep breath. "I know John Henry do exactly what he want." They had not heard from John Henry since the time he had left them on the far side of the great river.

Pearl told a fine tale that day about John de Conquer, too. The folks loved to hear how de Conquer could live on the plantations, using just the name of John, and how he fooled the ones who owned the slaves, how he tricked them into setting him free.

"All John has to do," Pretty said, "is get de boss to see he trustworthy on de first of February. And he be runnin' free by end of March."

"Take him that long, did it?" said Salt, teasing Pretty. "They taken me on a Tuesday. I be free on Sat'day."

" 'Cause they knock you in de head on Wednesday and you ain't come to 'til Friday year!" said Pretty. "Hee!"

Everybody laughed at their good-natured play. Then some one of the children asked Dwahro to sing and dance. Pretty agreed. She was getting hoarse and needed a rest.

The folks sang and danced. Dwahro led them. He could dance the best of anyone. He could sing higher and sweeter than any man they knew.

"Dwahro, when you comin' to church with me?" asked Miz Molly as he whirled her around.

"Comin' next Sunday, now I got me this fine suit." He was dancing up a storm.

"Best you take it off, then, you dancin' so high-steppin'," she said. "You mess it all up 'fore sundown."

"*Sundown! Sundown! Now, ain't I fine like sundown!*" sang

out Dwahro, high-stepping and prancing. *"I's de twenty-one, I's de twenty-one!"*

"What you talkin' 'bout, crazy?" said Miz Molly.

"Twenty-one gen'mens settin' in de wood," Dwahro sang.
"Nineteen is sickly and twenty no good.
But I's de twenty-one and I as fine as sundown!"

"You sure somethin'," Miz Molly said, laughing, and they all agreed. Dwahro had spirit that kept them feeling good when they were down. At the end of the day he lifted *their* spirits and let them sleep easy.

But they loved best when Pretty turned serious about de Conquer. When they were all tired and panting from singing and dancing with Dwahro, Pretty told the tale in her stirring voice:

"John de Con-*care* live in de southern soil. Him albatross, him manlike and him best god of Mount Kenya. Anytime we need him hard, he hit that hypocrite. *Ta-ta-tum.* It singin' freedom. *Ta-ta-tum.* Teachin', 'Know him by de Conquer, secret root.' *Ta-ta-tum.* Him comin' home to us, hold us safe. *John de Conquer!*"

"Yea, Lawd," the folks murmured, and sat there, satisfied, enjoying themselves.

So it was that Pretty Pearl came down from on high. Yes, she did. Say it was one long time ago.

ABOUT THE AUTHOR

Virginia Hamilton is the youngest child in a large family that has lived in the sweeping landscape of southern Ohio ever since her Grandfather Perry settled there after escaping from slavery in the South. And it was the echoes of her Ohio upbringing—her relatives who became known for telling tall tales, her mother always telling her to "go take a look" at something or someone, her learning to think and to manage childhood feelings in terms of stories—that later jelled into the proper combination of drama and emotional wisdom that makes her one of the finest storytellers of today.

Ever since her first book, ZEELY, was published in 1967, Virginia Hamilton has gained a devoted following among young readers, and has won every major award or honor accorded to American authors of children's books. Her novel M.C. HIGGINS, THE GREAT won the 1975 Newbery Medal, the National Book Award, the *Boston Globe/Horn Book* Award, and the Lewis Carroll Shelf Award; SWEET WHISPERS, BROTHER RUSH was a 1983 Newbery Honor book; THE PLANET OF JUNIOR BROWN was a 1972 Newbery Honor book; and eight of her books have appeared on ALA Notable Books lists. As Betsy Hearne writes in *Twentieth-Century Children's Writers*, "Virginia Hamilton has heightened the standards for children's literature as few other authors have."

Ms. Hamilton is married to the distinguished poet and anthologist Arnold Adoff. They live with their two children in Ohio.